THE TERRANOVAS

THE TERRANOVAS

A War Family

A NOVEL

by

Valentine Cardinale

iUniverse, Inc.

New York Lincoln Shanghai

The Terranovas
A War Family

Copyright © 2005 by Valentine Cardinale

iUniverse books may be ordered through booksellers or by contacting:

iUniverse
2021 Pine Lake Road, Suite 100
Lincoln, NE 68512
www.iuniverse.com
1-800-Authors (1-800-288-4677)

ISBN: 0-595-33888-7

Printed in the United States of America

For Gracie and all the other
casualties on the home front
and
for Brian Valentine

CONTENTS

▼

1944

1951

1968

1944

CHAPTER 1

▼

The signs were everywhere. After reading the newspapers, or listening to the radio, or watching those searing Movietone images of soldiers slugging it out on the beaches and rubble of bombarded islands and towns, anyone could see that the war was entering a bloodier, more decisive stage. For the first time, Americans on the home front sensed that the tide of battle was turning in favor of the Allies. By June, the Red Army had liberated Leningrad, recaptured the Crimean peninsula, and attacked Finland along a broad front. After slogging its way up the Italian peninsula, the U.S. Fifth Army entered Rome in the early morning of June 4. Two days later, an armada of more than 6,000 ships carrying more than 185,000 men and 20,000 vehicles began landing on the beaches of Normandy in the largest seaborne invasion the world had ever seen. By June 10, the Allied invasion force in France had swelled to more than 326,000 troops. One week later, in the most ambitious amphibious assault in the Pacific theater of the war, 127,000 American soldiers and marines in 535 fighting ships and transports stormed the Marianas. The fighting was fierce all over. On D-Day alone, June 6, there were more than 10,000 Allied casualties, and thousands more were killed or wounded in the weeks that followed. Although Christina Terranova was only five years old and living in New York City, she should have been listed among them. In retrospect, she was a casualty of war. Only, no one knew it at the time. Least of all, her family.

Of all the Terranova children, eight-year-old Michael had more than a passing or play-time interest in the war. He knew the combatants and the major battles, he was quick to pull down the window shades during air raid tests, and he was faithful about collecting foil from empty packs of cigarettes for the war effort. When he wasn't doing his homework or reading Batman comics or listening to "The Lone Ranger," he loved drawing pictures of war planes, especially Spitfires, his favorite weapon of war.

This night, Michael was sitting at the dinner table, working on a composition entitled "The Lessons of War." After taking off his glasses with the clear, plastic frames, he rubbed his tired, deep brown eyes and sighed. He was hungry, but he was not quite ready to plunge into his soup—mama's wonderful minestrone, his favorite. There was another page to go before the composition was finished. Around the table, there was no chatter, only the sound of spoons tapping bowls and long, exaggerated slurps from five-year-old Christopher, which prompted an admonition from mama. "Please, no make so much noise when you eat. It is not so nice to hear." Christopher giggled, thrust out a facetious pinky, and took a spoonful without making a sound. Twelve-year-old Camille shook her head at her little brother. She often found his antics annoying, mainly because many were targeted at her.

Across the table, Christina—Christopher's twin—pushed the bowl of soup away without touching a drop and rose awkwardly from the table. Michael was surprised. She was always such a good eater, a faithful follower of mama's Eleventh Commandment: "Remember those poor, starving people in Europe. Eat everything on your plate." If anyone needed more motivation, she would add this reminder, "Just because papa has the grocery store, he is no Rockefeller."

Christina coughed and stumbled slightly before groping her way into the first bedroom, which she shared with her older sister Camille. Mama sprang up and followed her. Close behind were Michael and Camille. Only Christopher kept eating. Mama didn't need a thermometer to tell that her daughter was running a fever. After feeling her head, she helped the little girl unbuckle her shoes and slip under the sheet. There was no need for blankets this early June evening.

Almost in a whisper, Christina asked for her small, wooden bank in the shape of a log cabin. It contained some coins, pennies mostly, that Christina was saving for a trip to Coney Island in the summer. The bank was a souvenir-gift Camille brought back two summers ago from a two-week stay with a family in East Dorset, Vermont. The trip was arranged through the city of New York and a West Side settlement house as part of a summer fresh-air program for needy city kids. Christina took the bank and pulled it close to her under the sheet.

Mama sat at the end of the bed and waited until Christina drifted off, then returned to the dining room.

"What's wrong with her?" asked Christopher.

"Her—your sister—is sick."

"Can I have her minestrone?"

"Go ahead, I have more. Then go wash and brush your teeth. Get ready for bed."

Michael noticed the worried look on mama's face, but he kept working on his final composition of the school year. He expected her to ask if she could help, but he knew that his immigrant mother had trouble with the language.

"Can I help you make the…how do you say?" she asked.

"The composition. It's okay, mama, I'm almost finished, thanks. Why don't you finish your soup?" said Michael, brushing a mop of light brown hair away from his glasses.

"I eat later with papa." She gathered up the dishes and brought them into the kitchen.

Michael knew the routine. By 9:30 or 10 o'clock, sometimes later, papa would be home from the store, another meal would be served, and mama and papa would talk about their day. Tonight, mama would have to tell him about Christina, and Michael knew that papa didn't handle sickness very well, especially when it was one of the kids who was sick. He remembered how worried and nervous papa was when he, Michael, came down with ringworm.

Her kitchen duties done, Anna Terranova went to work on Camille's graduation dress at the Singer. There was little time to lose. Mama knew how anxious her daughter was about having the garment finished on time. Donning a pair of glasses she used for close work, she began sewing. Gently pressing the treadle, she guided the light pink fabric under the needle.

How far she had come since her arrival in America! Anna was a thin, nervous woman when she landed on Ellis Island off New York City after a long, turbulent ocean voyage, but now, some 20 years later, she was a robust, confident presence whose life revolved around her husband Arturo and her four children. She had lively, dark eyes, a gently sloping nose, and small but full lips. Framing her fine, classical face was thick, black hair, usually worn in a bun. Although she prized her times alone and liked to keep busy doing a variety of things, she loved people, talking and laughing, just being together with family and friends. One of her favorite pastimes was playing cards, and she loved to win.

Over the years, Anna acquired an impressive array of skills, which gave her the assurance she needed as she tried to build a life for herself in America. She made store-quality clothes, curtains, and other personal and household items, thanks to her training with a master clothes maker in Italy and her experience as a seamstress in a dress and accessories factory in downtown New York City. She had an incurable green thumb, which she put to good use creating a compact tomato and basil victory garden on her fire escape. She was an excellent cook, especially when it came to things Italian, which, in her case, encompassed a broad range of treats, from *pasta e ragu* to *pizza dolce.* One needed to become accustomed to her American dishes, however. It took some time for the kids to realize that pancakes were not made in olive oil, in the size of frying pans.

This was her favorite time of day, after dinner. It was time to relax, perhaps have a sip of vermouth, and get ready for tomorrow and the future. With the current school year almost finished, she was thinking about the fall and where she should send her children to school. There was so much to be done. It had been only three months since the Terranovas moved into their new apartment on West Fiftieth Street in Manhattan.

Like any good new-apartment dwellers, their efforts at first were focused on making the place as livable as possible, which meant removing the grime and garbage left by the former tenants. They scrubbed floors, washed walls, cleaned windows. It was dirty, sweaty work needing many hands, so early on, except to go to school, the Terranova children stayed close to the hearth (or the coal stove in their case). Later, as the household shifted into a decorating mode, they painted, hung curtains, and arranged holy pictures. Gradually, they began to venture into the streets, meeting friends and learning the ways of a new neighborhood in a city where nuances of customs, attitudes, and speech often differed from block to block, even building to building. To papa was left the seemingly impossible task of keeping the family grocery business afloat in a wartime America choked by shortages of such basic grocery goods as butter, coffee, and sugar.

Only six blocks separated the old four-room flat from the new six-room apartment, but, as the family soon discovered, what a world of difference between the two! Moving from Fifty-sixth Street to Fiftieth Street was a major change for Anna and Arturo Terranova and their four children, and not merely because it brought the family into new, more expansive physical quarters. It was also an emotional experience that in some ways was as exciting, and as liberating, as traveling from the Old World to the new.

After grandma Terranova died last year, it was as if the shadow of a powerful, and sometimes domineering, spirit had been lifted from this traditional Italian household. Within the family, an emphasis on old rules and customs began crumbling and giving way to more flexibility and freedom that seemed to coincide with the move to Fiftieth Street. No one was more thrilled about the move than Anna, but even Arturo, ever respectful of his mother's memory, secretly saw a chance for his family to start anew.

Conveniently situated around the corner from the Terranova grocery store, the new apartment fell into a real estate configuration commonly known as "railroad rooms." Six rooms—a kitchen (including bath tub and small, private toilet), dining/family room, three bedrooms, and a living room or front room—were all in a line as straight as a railroad track. Although the ceilings were cracked and the walls uneven and begging for new paint, the apartment was a few steps up from the one on Fifty-sixth Street. Papa used to call the old apartment *Casa Scuzzi* because the children, mainly his oldest, Camille, were embarrassed to call it home. Strange dogs roamed the hallways, a gypsy family beckoned passers-by and told fortunes from a ground-floor apartment, and in the building next door was a dark, dank junk shop where the kids exchanged empty gallon wine bottles for two pennies apiece.

Mama and papa used to laugh about the whole thing, even when with embarrassment they recalled what Camille did one day on her way home from school. Walking and talking with a girl friend, she suddenly found herself outside her front door on Fifty-sixth Street. Her face turning scarlet, Camille walked right past her house, without acknowledging that this was where she lived. "She would never do that now," Arturo later proudly told Anna in their new apartment. How many families today could boast of having a dumbwaiter in their home (even if it seldom worked)?

Anna smiled when she remembered that remark, but her joy faded when her thoughts turned back to Christina. *Why is this little girl burning up?*

After ironing a blouse for school, Camille sat down on a stool next to mama and watched and waited. Would it ever be finished in time? Her dark, flowing hair and worried, hazel eyes glowed under the rude ceiling light. She was a beautiful girl, but she didn't seem to be aware of her emerging loveliness yet. She seemed quite serious about everything. As her eyes followed mama's quick hands, Camille nervously twirled the plastic ID disc that hung around her neck. The thin, ivory object, distributed to each of the students at school, was meant to identify a child in case of an enemy air raid or invasion. Such catastrophic events seemed more like something one saw in the movies than in real life. Of course, there was always a lurking fear an attack could take place—but the war always felt so far away, over there.

"Lower, mama, lower. The hem's too high," whined Camille. She was not one to hide her feelings, which were quick to rise to the surface.

"Shoosh, for Pete sake," said mama in her own special English. "No be afraid. You have nice legs."

"No I don't. I have fat legs, like pianos," Camille insisted, unmasking a self-image that did not measure up to reality.

Nearby, Christopher, who was chasing some German tin soldiers across the linoleum, laughed. "Piano legs! Piano legs!" he roared as he gunned down a squad of enemy soldiers, his light brown eyes blazing in victory. Amazing what one American can do! His military maneuvers complete for now, Christopher got up and turned on the radio. The Voice, Frank Sinatra singing "All or Nothing at All," came swooning out of the box.

"Oh, leave that on, Christopher," Camille pleaded.

"No, I don't like it." He snapped off the radio and formed up the soldiers for a new battle.

Camille locked eyes with mama. "Did you see that? What a brat! I'm going to tell papa on him when he comes home."

"Go ahead," Christopher fired back. "I'll tell papa on you."

"I didn't do anything, brat!"

"Piano legs!"

Enough! It was time for mama to enter the fray. "I tell you before, Christopher. Get ready for bed."

"I am getting ready, mama. Just one more war."

Michael stopped writing. "Come on, Christopher! Don't be such a brat."

Christopher's lips started quivering. Hearing it from someone he looked up to and admired was a bit much, and he began sobbing. "I am not a brat!"

Mama pressed a finger to her lips. "*Sta zitto!* Shoosh, all of you!"

Christina was moaning. When mama got up to check, she found the little girl soaking with perspiration. Camille, always mama's helper, reached in the drawer for a new pair of pajamas without being told.

Michael shrugged at the futility of the continuing feud between his older sister and brother and began writing again.

> *Above all, the lesson of war is that this is a time of unity. We must trust our leaders. We must do what they want us to do. Most of all, we must win this war.*

There, it was finished. Michael reread the composition. He liked it. He hoped Sister Medina would, too.

For as long as he could remember, Michael had been fascinated by the use of words, especially if they were ones he had never heard before. Whenever he came across a new word, he wrote it down and promised to look it up when he got home. Most of the time, he did, but there was always a word in his pocket awaiting a definition. As his vocabulary grew, he felt more American and less Italian, which was alright with him, because it made him feel he belonged. Michael read the composition one more time. He wondered how he could interject a word like the one he had heard Jimmy Rice use in a composition the other day. *Integument! Wonder what it means. Someday I will use words like that in my work.*

Later that evening, Michael lay in bed, wide awake, when the air raid sirens started wailing. He remembered how frightened he was the first time he heard them go off. He didn't feel that way anymore. Perhaps the sirens had become a common occurrence, and he had gotten used to them, as did all of the Terranova kids. Mama padded past him, her well-worn slippers slapping against her calloused heels. Michael got up out of bed and followed her. Everyone else was asleep. Papa was not home yet.

In the front room, Anna pulled down the shade of one window, while Michael reached for the other shade. She seemed surprised to see him in the darkened room.

"I'll help you, mama," he whispered.

"You should be asleep. You have school," she reminded him.

The shades, which were black on the outside and green on the inside, were supposed to be drawn, in compliance with Uncle Sam's requests, to prevent possible enemy planes from spotting any light on the ground and, therefore, pinpointing targets in the city. Made civic sense to Michael, but he sometimes wondered how any plane could ever miss anything in this city.

They both peeked out of the sides of the shades. Michael was amazed at how the lights of so many apartments could be seen, and the All Clear had not been given. Below, Mr. Clarke, the air raid warden, wobbled down the street, barely visible under the low-lit street lamps. He was drunk again, but he didn't shirk his duties. "Lights out!" he shouted again and again. Michael turned to mama. Both of them tried to muffle a laugh. Above the buildings, floodlights shot beams into a moody sky in mock searches for squadrons of planes. The reminders were there, but war seemed so distant.

The front room faced Fiftieth Street between Ninth and Tenth Avenues in a beat-up, working class section of the West Side known as Hell's Kitchen. Residents preferred to call it merely "the neighborhood." Some also alluded to it as "the avenue," referring to the wide, bustling road known as Tenth Avenue that ran parallel to that other wide thoroughfare, Ninth Avenue, and literally cut, with its trolley tracks in the old days, through this forgotten wedge by the Hudson River.

Like most streets on the West Side, Fiftieth Street was lined on both sides by rows of interlocking buildings. Except for an office structure, which housed the New York Telephone Company, the buildings were dull red-brick, four- or five-story tenements. Typically, a concrete stoop with rusty railings sometimes painted black led to a large, weathered door that opened up into a dimly lit hall-way. The hallway usually guided tenants and visitors to five levels of railroad flats, counting the ground floor. A few tenements also had rooms in the basement rented off the books to vagrants or porters.

On the street level of some buildings were small shops, including a laundry and a couple of restaurants. The corners on each block were prime locations for retail establishments, including a bakery operated by the Cushman's chain, a gro-cery store, and two saloons, one on Ninth and one on Tenth. One corner also boasted a shoe-shine stand.

Michael and mama sat on the sofa, which was draped in a white sheet that served notice that this was the "good furniture," for special occasions only. It was a treat for them to sit for a moment in the front room, even enveloped as they were in darkness. Camille was beginning to bring girlfriends up to the house, and they danced in bare feet to records in the front room, but most of the family's activities were centered around the dining room and kitchen. Michael wondered why sometimes. Perhaps it was because the rooms got progressively colder as they chugged, in a straight line, from the kitchen to the front room. More likely, it was because the front room was considered the best room in the house, to be reserved for company, birthdays, holidays, and, God forbid, wakes.

Near each window was an armchair, also in white sheets. Standing guard by another wall was a tall redwood chest containing Camille's winter wardrobe and some odds and ends. Anna's eyes fell on a pile of battered cardboard boxes in a corner of the room—the last remnants of the move from Fifty-sixth Street. She shook her head in bewilderment. She still had not decided where their con-tents—a blend of linen, knick-knacks, Christmas decorations, love letters, and grandma Terranova's old clothes—would go.

"What are you going to do with all that stuff, mama?" Michael asked.

"I wish I know." She started to laugh, and stopped. "Maybe I throw every-thing out the window." Michael loved hearing his mother laugh, even briefly.

"Can I help you?" he asked with a smile. "We'll have to watch out for Mr. Clarke." With both of them envisioning the air raid warden buried in grandma's clothes, they both collapsed in their chairs and began laughing. It took them awhile to gain control again.

So many decisions. What to do with the contents of the boxes paled in comparison to other issues. Where should the children go to school? Should Christopher and Christina go to Sacred Heart, which is closer to home, when they start school in September? Or should they follow Camille and Michael and go to Saint Paul the Apostle, a good school but a bit farther away? Should Michael be pulled out of St. Paul's, where his friends are, and moved to Sacred Heart? Public grammar school was out of the question for her.

Then there was Camille. How will she do when she starts high school? Will she make nice friends, or take up with a bad crowd? Will she meet a good boy? Will she drink too much at one of those high school parties, or worse? God forbid!

Anna leaned over and looked down through the rooms into the kitchen. "Ah, is this not so much better than Fifty-six Street?" she asked without expecting an answer.

Michael nodded.

"No fortune-tellers come here," she continued. "The dogs, they don't bite you in the hallway. No junk shop next door." Michael could sense her pride. "We have dining room now, and kitchen with bathroom and bathtub, too. Even dumbwaiter."

Michael rested his head in his mother's fleshy arms. "You think Christina will be alright, mama?" he whispered.

She didn't answer him right away, but then she said, "I say a prayer her fever stop by morning. After All Clear, I check her again. Not to worry, *figlio mio*."

CHAPTER 2

▼

Next to his family, Arturo Terranova's great pride was his grocery store. It was his baby, and he nurtured it with all the care and concern of a loving parent. Arturo, who paid $20 for all of the fixtures when he bought the store, was proud of everything about it, and he had ambitious plans for the expansion of the four-year-old establishment.

With his natural merchandising skills, the sky was the limit. Only the war was holding him back, but he would be patient, and he would continue to work hard. For Arturo, running the store was a marathon of sweat and love every day of the week except for Sunday when all work came to an abrupt halt so that he could partake of the traditional family repast that began precisely at 2 P.M., after Mass.

Tonight, Artie's, as West Siders called the store, was hardly noticeable in the blacked-out city, but in the daytime it was a neighborhood fixture, as was the short, round man with the white apron who owned it. In the light of day, the store formed the centerpiece of a row of small shops on a block of tenements on Tenth Avenue. From across a wide boulevard usually teeming with belching buses, choking cars, and acrid garbage trucks, one could see a sign in the store window boasting, in huge, firehouse-red letters, "Sandwiches 10 cents." In small, black type underneath—hardly noticeable a few feet away—were the words "and up."

On the sidewalk directly in front of the store, bushels of spinach, string beans, and potatoes competed for attention with crates of oranges and apples, adding a bit of fresh farm life to the sour smells of the city. When the sun got too bright or it rained, a moss-green canvas awning was rolled out above the stand.

Inside the store, customers were treated to a brief tour of southern Italy. It started with the pungent cylinders of tightly bound provolone that hung over the large round or twisted loaves of crusty bread in the window. Along one side of the narrow store were neatly stacked slopes of tomatoes and lettuce, along with peppers and plums so shiny they looked unreal. On the other side, a glass and white porcelain freezer showed off a colorful collection of cold cuts—ham, salami, provolone, spiced ham, bologna, Swiss cheese, and yellow American cheese—along with beckoning trays of sausage and fresh mozzarella. Sawdust covered the floor and crunched underfoot as if it were snow.

The main business was conducted at the wooden counter, a jumble of olives, candy, pickles, figs, and small pies at one end and a slicer and a scale at the other. Behind the counter, drawers with glass panels displayed varieties of dried beans. They were below shelves holding packages of pasta, corn starch, cereal, and a few canned goods. Off to the side, a black cash register rang and shot out a drawer with a turn of its handle. On a crossbeam near the back of the store, a saint in a black robe blessed all transactions.

A small room in the back of the store served as stockroom, business office, family room, kitchen, and nursery. Burlap bags of sawdust were piled in one corner, next to cases of soda and a couple of hidden cans of precious olive oil saved for the best customers and for the cooking. A short, stubby table anchored the magical sausage-making machine. Nearby was an old, wooden door that led to a spare, dark toilet with a gray slate floor. On the other side of the room, a combination coal and gas stove on four, skinny legs cooked up meatballs and sausages for sandwiches.

To the Terranovas, the store was more than a place. It was a living, breathing part of their lives. Over the years, it figured importantly in family matters, and when it came in conflict with a birthday, vacation, holiday, school visit, or some other key event, it almost always took precedence. To Arturo, business always came first. He knew the family was not always happy about that, but he had worked hard to get where he was, and the older the children got the better they would appreciate his credo, or so he thought.

Now, after 21 years in the country, Arturo thought his young business was finally taking hold, thanks to a growing lunch trade from the commercial laundry down the block. Only recently had he installed a telephone in the back room. More important, he heard radio commentators say that the war's end was now in sight. He could wait. He had already come a long way from the struggles of his first years in America when he sold vegetables, fruit, and fish door to door to a small group of *paisani*.

In those days, he used to lug bushels of fresh foods from the marketplaces downtown to his midtown customers. One snowy winter morning, carrying a bushel of fish, he was refused a seat on the bus—not once or twice, but three times—by the drivers. Cold but determined, he made his way uptown on foot, stopping from time to time on the slippery sidewalks to warm his hands in his pockets. When Arturo reached his first customer, Mrs. Fucito, she felt so sorry for him she made him come into her apartment, which occupied the entire ground floor of a building she owned on Forty-ninth Street.

"Look at you, Arturo. You're freezing and shaking," she said, sitting him down in a chair by the coal stove. Arturo always liked Mrs. Fucito; she was a tough but kind-hearted woman who came over as a child in an earlier immigration wave and spoke English fluently. A handsome woman who always looked neat and dressed for business, she owned a small coal and oil company that she inherited when her husband died. She ran it with the efficiency that would have made him proud. "What happened?" she asked Arturo.

"They would no let me on bus," he said, picking the ice out of his hair and eyebrows. "I am so sorry; I make a mess of your home."

"Don't worry, it's only water," she said. "Why would they not let you get on the bus?"

"They say the fish in my bushel stink, smell up the whole bus."

"Oh, that's terrible, Arturo."

"Is all fresh fish, the best," he continued.

"I know, I know," she said consolingly. "I buy your fish all the time. In fact, this time I will buy the entire bushel of fish. I like it so much."

"Oh, no. I cannot let you do that for me."

"Yes, you can, and I will do it," Mrs. Fucito insisted. "Now let me get you a glass of anisette. It will warm your insides. And, later, I will call the bus company and complain. You'll see. This will not happen again."

There were tears, not snow or ice, in his eyes now. "You watch. Someday I will have my own place, and I will not need the bus, and I will be treated with respect," he added. As she had predicted, the anisette warmed his insides.

From that moment, Arturo became good friends with Mrs. Fucito, often stopping by to chat with her on his rounds.

Like many immigrants, Arturo came to America to make a better life for himself and his family. When he arrived on Ellis Island, that family consisted of one person, namely his mother Gabriella, a proud, rather impatient woman with some strong, sometimes overpowering, Old World views of life and family.

Later, that family was expanded to include his wife Anna and his children, each of whom received a lukewarm welcome from grandma Terranova on their arrival into the fold. Nevertheless, Arturo tried to keep all the parties happy, whatever it took—a little flattery, feigned cheeriness, good food and wine on the table. After several years, however, Arturo's dark brown eyes were starting to show the strain.

Then, last year grandma Terranova died, and, on top of that, there was the move to the new apartment on Fiftieth Street. It was as if a blast of cool, fresh air had blown into the window on a scorching hot summer day. Though he mourned the loss of his mother, Arturo could feel a sense of relief among the family members, and he welcomed the new opportunity for them to come together as a family.

Now, here it was June 1944, and he was the owner of a young, up-and-coming grocery business in a country engaged in world war. Like most Americans, he supported the government, its leaders, and the war because the cause was good and it was the right thing to do. But, more than that, he had come to love his adopted land. Despite early hardships, it had been very good to him since he had arrived as a young adult from a nation that was now one of its enemies.

The father of four children born in the U.S.A., he proudly participated in the national war effort. Yet, with all of his patriotic fervor, papa Terranova never stopped trying to make a better life for himself and his family.

Taking advantage of the slowdown in customer traffic caused by the blackout, Arturo went to the back of the store and began reviewing, under a small lamp, tomorrow's shipment of goods from the wholesaler. If only he could get some more canned goods, as well as the flour, coffee, butter, and sugar he ordered—and it would be a miracle if the olive oil he wanted arrived. How can anyone run a business like this?

Everything was recorded in a single, thick notebook framed in a cardboard cover with a zig-zagging black-and-white design. The school kids called them composition books. Arturo used a stubby, knife-sharpened pencil to make some calculations. When he was finished, he put the pencil back in the front of his cap, closed the book, and turned on the radio.

On one station, a tired Mayor LaGuardia was urging everyone not to let up in the war effort. *Now more than ever, the citizens of our great city need to suck it in and ration.* He urged adults and children to continue collecting scrap metal. *Roll those silver balls, and bring in your grease cans.* Arturo thought about the sign in Jack the butcher's window: "Bring your fat cans here!" On another station, a sportscaster was reviewing the new baseball season and the afternoon game between the Yankees and Senators. The Yanks had won. The war news was more favorable than it had been, but the conflict was far from over. Arturo was encouraged by the Allies' advance, but he was also saddened by the devastation in Europe, particularly in the beautiful land of his birth.

Like many Italian-Americans, Arturo was conflicted by the war, and he openly shared his views with anyone who would listen, especially on weekends after a few glasses of wine. Early on, he had high praise for Mussolini for cleaning up crime and corruption in Italy, building the country's highways and train system, and boosting Italian pride once again. Later, however, he was soured and shamed when the Italian dictator took a more expansionist turn, forming an alliance with Hitler and declaring war on an already defeated France. There was never any doubt where Arturo stood when the United States entered the war against the Axis. If he weren't so old—he recently turned forty—he would have enlisted in the U.S. Army in the fight against totalitarianism. He settled on a classical music station on the radio.

The bells on the front door, left over from Christmas, jingled, signaling that a customer was entering the store. It was Mrs. Clooney, the bartender's wife who lived in one of the apartments upstairs.

"Hello, Artie, I need three pounds of potatoes, and do you have any butter at all?

"No, Mrs. Clooney, sorry. Tomorrow, I hope so."

"Oh, this war is hell, isn't it? Everything's scarce—food, gas, clothes, shoes, even people, like teachers and doctors and nurses. Well, you know. Don't know how you can run a business, Artie."

"I wait, Mrs. Clooney. Patience, what else can we do? It will be over soon."

"From your lips to God's ears, Artie. Well, I'll take a half pound of bologna, too. His lordship will be comin' home soon. He loves fried bologna."

Arturo nodded. *Strange things, some people eat.* This, from someone who enjoyed such edible treasures as squid, eel, and, on special occasions, calf's head.

After Mrs. Clooney left, the All-Clear sounded. Arturo closed his notebook, locked up, and started home. It was nearly ten o'clock.

When Arturo reached the third floor landing, he took a deep breath and pulled his keys out of the pocket of his baggy gray pants. The door opened before he could put a key in it, and he immediately caught a whiff of Vicks VapoRub in the air. Anna stood in the doorway.

"Ciao, Arturo."

"Ciao, Anna." They kissed quickly. *"Come stai?"*

"Bene, grazie, e tu?"

"Eh, okay," he replied, indicating his fatigue. *"E il figli? Sta bene?"*

For a moment, she thought about hiding Christina's condition. *"Si…ah, no. Chistina sono male."*

"Sono male? Que cosa?"

She shook her head. *"Non sapere. La tosse. La febbre"* She tried to explain further, only in English, "She has the high fever, sweating, cough. I give her the aspirin. She sleeps now."

Arturo was about to pay Christina a visit, when suddenly Camille jumped out of bed and ran towards him. Quickly, she began filling him in on the day's activities. "Hello, papa. Ben Stern—you know, the landlord's son—came by to see if I wanted to go to the movies with him on Saturday. I think he likes me. I told him No. Mom did a little more work on my graduation dress. She says I have nice legs. What's the matter with Christina? She keeps coughing and shaking. Do you think I should go sleep on the sofa in the front room?"

"Yes, yes," said Arturo, motioning her to go, but gingerly.

"I get the blanket for you," said mama.

"I don't need a blanket. It's hot tonight."

"I get you the blanket anyway. It's cold in the front room."

One more night visitor suddenly entered the dining room. "I can't sleep," said Christopher, rubbing his eyes. "I hear voices."

Camille became agitated when she saw her brother. "You have to do something about him, papa," she fumed, pointing at her younger nemesis. "He says mean things to me all the time. He's nothing but a spoiled brat."

"No, you're the brat! And you hog the bathroom! And you have piano legs!" he shouted. Then, as if he were revealing a deep, dark secret, he added, "She uses rouge, too!"

Camille reached out to grab her brother, but papa stopped her before she could make contact. "I hate you," she screamed.

"I hate you, too," Christopher screamed back.

"Some talk, both of you!" said papa. "How many time I tell you? We are family. We help each other. We take care one another. Fighting is for dogs and cats." Papa reached down and tapped Christopher in the back of the head, sending him running into his bedroom.

"You go to bed, too!" he told Camille.

She stormed into the front room. Tears in her eyes, she shouted. "I hate him! I hate him!"

"Come, Arturo, I get you something to eat," said Anna.

"Not now. I go see Christina first."

In the bedroom shared by Michael and Christopher, Michael tried to console his brother, but Christopher shook him off.. "Leave me alone," he sobbed. "No one likes me."

Michael reached over and patted him on the arm. "*I* like you, Christopher."

"You do not. You called me a brat."

"But I still like you, Christopher. You're my brother."

Papa noticed that Christina was still sleeping in spite of all the shouting. He reached over and felt her head. She was burning up and sweating. "Son of bitch," he whispered, his face a mixture of fear and anger. In the next bedroom, Michael repeated papa's words. "Son of bitch." Not once, but twice. For a moment, Christopher stopped crying, surprised by his brother's unexpected use of a curse word.

CHAPTER 3

▼

If the dining room was the hub of activity in the evening, the kitchen was where the action was in the morning, and mama was its commander. The kitchen was where the Terranovas washed their face and hands, bathed, brushed their teeth, combed their hair, applied lipstick and rouge, cooked, ate breakfast, and passed through on their way to the toilet.

On one side of the compact, narrow room were a dumbwaiter that worked when it felt like it, an icebox, a small metal table with flaps turned down on each side, and a private toilet that also served as a place to hang stockings and other personals to dry. On the other side of the room were a built-in dish closet encrusted with decades of paint; a bathtub; a sink and medicine chest; and a workhorse of a stove. The tub was topped by a long, white porcelain cover and ringed by a white linen skirt mama made. It was always a conversation piece to anyone new to the neighborhood. "A tub in the kitchen? Can you believe that?" said an insurance salesman one day. At the far end of the kitchen was an old window that stubbornly opened up to a fire escape and a tangled mess of yards, fences, and renegade trees where backyard salesmen sold vegetables or offered to put up your clothes line. Their booming sales pitches lingered long after they were gone. "Ripe tomatoes!" "Line up!"

Anna was more tired than usual when she came into the kitchen the next morning. For a long time before going to bed, she had sat up in a chair by Christina's bed, helping her sip water.

Twice more during the night she changed Christina from head to foot because of the perspiration and rubbed her down with alcohol. She finally dozed off at the end of the girl's bed. Arturo also paid a couple of visits during the night before getting up for good at four o'clock. By the time daylight had broken, he was long gone, buoyed by the fact that Christina's fever seemed to have subsided. This was to be a big day at the store for him: His deliveries were due.

Anna turned up the heat under a pot of water and waited for it to boil. *Thank God! The fever is gone, I think. Maybe she will have some farina now. I wash her down later, she will feel better.* One by one, the children came into the kitchen.

First, Michael. He loved school, or at least fourth grade, and he was usually talkative and excited in the morning, but not today. After a shortened, fitful night, he shuffled into the kitchen on sock-covered feet and sat down at the table.

"How's Christina?" he asked, straightening his glasses.

"Better," said mama. "I think the fever is gone, almost."

"She should eat something then. What do they say? Feed a cold, starve a fever."

"Yes, yes, in a little while."

Michael snapped two pieces of bread in the toaster and got up to get some hot water from the teapot.

Mama continued turning the farina. "Sit down, I make you the tea."

Next came Christopher, a huge bag of crayons in one hand and a coloring book in the other. Without saying anything, he sat down at the kitchen table and started coloring. Mama placed a glass of milk and two homemade biscotti in front of him. Mama tried to start his day off on a cheerful note. "Morning, Christopher." He mumbled back something that sounded like a greeting and picked up a biscotti and dunked it in the milk.

Last in was Camille, already dressed and ready to go. She went to the sink for a final check in the medicine chest mirror.

"Oh, oh, she's going to break the mirror," said Christopher, ever the commentator, a devilish grin creeping across his face.

Camille spun around. "Shut up, Christopher. You don't have papa stopping me from killing you now. Once a brat, always a brat."

"And you are…ugly."

"Hey, hey, you…no, she is not ugly," mama jumped in. "She is beautiful. *Abbasta!* Enough now! Have something to eat, Camille."

"I can't, mama. I'm late. I'm going to meet Dottie and Harry Slovich."

Anna knew Dottie Wood, an old friend, and Camille was out the door before mama could ask who Harry Slovich was. She would make some inquiries later. Apparently, he was someone Camille met recently.

Mama was delighted when Christina ate some farina and, later, half an American cheese sandwich and a cup of tea for lunch. But that afternoon, Christina threw up everything, and by the time papa got home that night the fever was back in its raging fury. As the family braced for another restless night, Anna was assured Arturo would call the doctor in the morning. Definitely.

But who? The Terranovas were not people who saw physicians often. All of the children were born at home with the help of midwives, and mama relied on some time-tested home remedies for a variety of minor afflictions. The last time anyone in the family paid a visit to a doctor's office was two years ago when Camille needed a checkup for her trip to Vermont. After that, Michael took sick with a bad head and chest cold and required a house visit to the apartment on Fifty-sixth Street. The family's doctor in both cases was Doctor Amonte, a bright, likeable young man who had since been commissioned to do military duty overseas, apparently in anticipation of the Allied invasion.

Left without a family doctor in their new apartment on Fiftieth Street, Anna and Arturo casually began making inquiries among friends and neighbors, several of whom mentioned Doctor Cotton, a trusted, long-time practitioner who just happened to be Italian. The only problem, it seemed, was that with the war and the shortage of medical personnel he was usually overloaded with patients and difficult to see. So be it. Desperate for help now, Arturo and Anna came to the conclusion that they had no choice. They would just have to take their chances with Doctor Cotton.

It was 9:30 the following morning, and Dr. Cotton was already behind schedule. The waiting room was overflowing with a broad cross section of West Siders, coughing and sniffling and blowing, the air thick with cigarette smoke from a longshoreman who was leaning against the wall reading the *Daily News*. Miss Francis, receptionist-secretary-phone operator, looked around and wondered whether she'd ever get home for bingo that evening.

Dr. Cotton used to pride himself on seeing everyone who wanted to see him, but lately his patient load had grown so much he was finding it difficult to live up to his personal goals. If he wasn't late in making house calls, he was referring patients, particularly newer patients, to other physicians in and around the neighborhood. It was not that he was the best doctor in the city. (In fact, he was a dedicated, competent general practitioner.) It was just that military duty was sapping the country of many physicians, leaving other, sometimes more senior members of the medical profession to take care of the health-care needs of the home front. Besides, as a long-time practitioner on the West Side, Dr. Cotton had earned the trust and respect of a wide circle of neighborhood residents, especially the elderly.

Most of his patients knew him only as Dr. Cotton, but a few were more familiar with the man behind the doctor. Born Vincenzo Cottone in Naples, he arrived in America with his parents at the age of six in an earlier immigration wave. His father's success in the restaurant business enabled the family to send young Vincenzo to medical school, where he pursued an interest in internal medicine. After completing his medical studies and training, he set up a practice on the West Side under the shingle "Vincent Cotton, M.D." He thought it best to downplay his roots in the heavily Irish and German neighborhood. Though there was a trace of an accent when he spoke, rarely did he resort to his native tongue—and only to people he knew or who knew him.

The phone in the doctor's office rang. After Miss Francis managed to offer a friendly greeting, she told the caller that the doctor was seeing a patient and couldn't talk to anyone now. When Arturo Terranova insisted on speaking with the doctor, she reluctantly put him through. Dr. Cotton was cordial, but obviously pressed for time. "Mr. Terranova, what can I do for you today?" When Arturo told him about Christina, the doctor promised to come by the house later that day.

"Oh, thank you so much, *dottore,*" said Arturo from the phone in the store, obviously relieved, hopeful, and confident Dr. Cotton would make everything better.

Nine o'clock that evening, Dr. Cotton arrived at the apartment building where the Terranovas lived. The tall, hunched man stomped out his cigarette on the sidewalk and started the climb up the three flights of stairs. When he reached the third floor, he took out a handkerchief and wiped his furrowed brow and neck. His large, bulging brown eyes struggled to read the numbers on the side-by-side doors. When he found the right apartment, he knocked.

Dr. Cotton could hear the family mobilize for the visit. Anna called out for Camille to lower the phonograph in the front room, where she was playing a Glenn Miller record.

There was something very special about a house call from a physician. For a family racked with anxiety and fear over a loved one who was sick, it was a most welcome event. When the doctor came, it was as if the whole household was tranquilized and relieved of its stress and worry. As long as the doctor was there, no harm could come to anyone, and there was a sense of pride and power that you had someone important and revered in your midst. The doctor was king, or queen, and could say and do no wrong, and the doctor's jokes were always funny. If you were lucky, the doctor might stay longer and have a cup of coffee or tea, maybe even a piece of cake, with the family, and that was a privilege that one could boast about again and again. Most of the time, however, doctors came and went—too quickly—and the peace and tranquility of the visit were replaced by a feeling of regret and emptiness and the reawakening of old fears.

When he saw Anna, Dr. Cotton tipped his hat, then took it off. *"Bono sera, Mrs. Terranova. Coma stai?"*

"Bene, dottore, grazie, e tu?" Anna took his hat and hung it up on a door hook.

"Bene, and how's…Christina, is it?"

"Come see."

"So sorry I'm late," the doctor continued, gripping his big, black bag. "So many patients to see, not enough doctors to go around. The war and everything, you know." Then, spotting Michael and Christopher, he said, "Well, who do we have here?"

"My name's Michael."

"And I'm Christopher. My mother let me stay up after my bath to see you. Are you a real doctor?"

"Sure am. I think I met you boys before, in my office." Christopher shook his head in disagreement. "Well, maybe not," the doctor corrected himself.

Christina was asleep when he entered the bedroom. The doctor turned on the overhead light, and she started stirring. When she saw the tall man with the gray face and the bulging, brown eyes, Christina screamed, but it wasn't a long, loud scream. It was a scream that wouldn't come out completely.

"S'alright, *cara mia,* it is just the doctor," said mama. "He look at you, so you feel better."

The doctor smiled broadly, but it didn't help. Christina turned away and started sobbing.

"Now, now, Christina," he pleaded. "Let's have a look at you."

It was one of those catch-as-catch-can examinations, but the doctor managed to check the vital signs. When he was finished, Dr. Cotton took Anna aside in the kitchen. Lighting up another cigarette, he said, "She has some congestion, and she has a fever. It looks like the flu."

Anna looked into his bulging brown eyes. He looked so weary. "Sit, *dottore,* I make you a cup of coffee."

"No, *grazie,* I have a couple of more patients to see tonight. Don't have a minute these days. Lousy war! Well, what are you going to do? We do the best we can, right? As for your child, keep doing what you're doing: Rub her with alcohol, give her plenty of water, and get some soup into her. I'll give you some medicine for the congestion."

Tears in her eyes, Anna reached out for the doctor's hand in gratitude. "Don't worry. She should be fine in a couple of days."

Two days later, when Arturo called the doctor's office to report no change in Christina's condition—in fact, she seemed to be getting worse—Miss Francis was determined not to put him through. "I'll have him call you, Mr. Terranova," she promised. She shook her head in disbelief, as if to say, "What's wrong with these people? Don't they understand how busy doctors are today?"

When Dr. Cotton called back, Arturo was just about to close the store. The doctor said he'd be by to see Christina the next day, and he did—early the next evening. He added a possible new diagnosis, kidney infection, and prescribed new, stronger medicine.

Over the next 24 hours, Christina's condition worsened. In addition to the fever and chills, she was breathing rapidly, and she had pains in her chest. Arturo could stand it no longer. He decided to take the child to the hospital without consulting the doctor. He wasn't even going to call an ambulance. In the middle of the night, with Anna looking on anxiously, he bundled the little girl up and carried her down the stairs. When he got outside, he looked for a cab, didn't see one, then ran as fast as he could to the hospital several blocks away.

Even at that hour of the night, the emergency room was filled with all sorts of suffering humanity. It took several hours before Christina was placed in a semi-private room, where she continued to have difficulty breathing. The next day, she was placed in an oxygen tent, through which Michael and Camille could barely see their sister when they paid a visit after school. By the time Doctor Fairchild, a first-year resident, determined that Christina had bacterial pneumonia the following day, she lapsed into a coma and died.

In an odd twist of fate, selected hospitals around the country, including a group in New York City, were just beginning to receive limited shipments of penicillin, the new wonder drug, for use by the civilian population. Up to that point, penicillin was largely limited in its use to military personnel as part of the war effort. In hindsight, the drug might have made a difference if administered in Christina's treatment.

CHAPTER 4

▼

Arturo was in the store with the children when Doctor Fairchild at the hospital phoned him and told him the news. Though overwhelmed with sadness, he just couldn't say anything to the kids. "Go pick up your mother," he gently directed Michael and Camille. "Christopher, you stay here." Camille looked at Michael. If they thought it odd that mama was coming home so early today from the hospital, they didn't say anything.

"Maybe Christina's off the critical list," Michael surmised with a jubilant hop as he reached Ninth Avenue.

"Yeah, and maybe they're sending mama home to get some rest," Camille added.

They would learn the truth when they arrived at the hospital and saw a nurse quietly consoling mama in the lobby.

Arturo continued working, doing his best to hide his grief. Mrs. Clooney thought he had a cold when she came into the store and saw him wiping his dark eyes with his white apron. When he told her what happened, she let out a scream of deep grief and threw her arms around him.. Then, remembering how the twins used to play together outside the store, she cried and hugged Christopher, who seemed both bewildered and frightened by the sudden show of emotion. "Oh, I'm so sorry! I'm so sorry!" she murmured.

One by one, others came into the store to pay their respects—the electrician-recluse a couple of doors away, the iceman who always had the smell of hard liquor on his breath, the hardware man across the street, and friends and customers, including Mrs. Clooney's husband, Clarence the bartender, and Mr. and Mrs. Zamora from around the corner. Jack the butcher came by with three pounds of chopped meat for the family, and the liquor store owner sent over a gallon of Gallo Burgundy.

It didn't take long for West Siders to learn about the death of one of their own. News like that spread like a gas-line leak. Everyone wanted to do something, no matter that the Terranovas were recent arrivals. It was a deeply rooted neighborhood tenet: Reach out and help one another, especially in times of trouble.

By the way they spoke and walked and went about their lives, Hell's Kitchen residents in the early forties were a special, colorful breed—both tough and big-hearted, poor but rich with dreams, and cocky, to be sure, yet quietly confident in their potential. They were also proud of where they were from, while they yearned for a better way of life beyond the neighborhood. Always, they labored zealously in pursuit of their dreams. When they weren't shaping the docks, West Siders were working the nearby rail yards and stockyards. They waited on customers, made beds, or washed dishes in the shops, hotels, and restaurants in and around the area. Others plied trades in dilapidated factories, shipping firms, rag businesses, and sweatshops, while increasing numbers took secretarial and clerical jobs at insurance firms, publishing houses, and other service companies. They were cops, firemen, and sanitation workers. They served as ticket takers, ushers, and janitors in the nearby theaters and movie houses. They managed households, raised families, or went to school. A few, like Arturo Terranova, owned their own businesses.

At the same time, West Siders were actively involved in the war effort. If they weren't buying war bonds, or collecting scrap metal, or using their ration books in strict accordance to the rules, they were sending their children to fight in battlefields around the world. Too many proudly displayed gold stars in their windows for the kids who never returned.

Arturo was finally able to lock up the store. With Christopher in one hand and the gallon of wine in the other, he walked home. A sign in the store window alerted everyone who hadn't heard: "Closed for death in my family."

Almost as quickly as they became aware of her passing, the neighbors learned that the Terranova girl was going to be waked at home. Although home wakes were a fairly common occurrence then, this one promised to be a painful new experience for the Terranovas, especially the children. And so Arturo braced himself for the ordeal that lay ahead.

By the time Michael was allowed to enter the front room the following afternoon, everything was in place. Anything that didn't belong was taken away.

Gone were the moving boxes, the redwood chest, everything except the sofa and matching armchairs. Rented folding chairs were placed neatly around the room. Floral arrangements lined the wall where the windows faced the street. A tall torch lamp stood devoutly nearby, casting a gentle light on the beautiful child in the small, white casket, which was symmetrically arranged between the two windows.

With his natural curiosity, Michael watched the process of grief unfold. To think he had been sitting in the darkness in this room with his mother during the air raid test just a few days ago! How everything had changed since then! And what was this deep, aching feeling in his heart that hounded him all day long? He watched, memorized every move, as each member of the family mourned the little girl in Communion white.

Mama hardly ever left the front room, trying to stay as close to the child in death as she was to her in life. Beyond being mother and daughter, they were good companions who enjoyed each other's company. They went everywhere together. Routinely, after dropping off Christopher with papa at the store, mama would take Christina shopping with her, whether it was to buy shoes or sheets or chicken parts. And on Sunday, when she went to Mass (which wasn't often because someone had to prepare the afternoon meal), mama was accompanied by Christina, who followed her Sunday missal with the reverence of someone who knew what she was reading.

Only Anna's older sister from Queens, Loretta, who came to stay for a while, managed to draw her away from the front room for something to eat or a change of clothes. Although the word for sister in Italian is *sorella*, Loretta preferred to use the more affectionate term of the dialect. "Come on, *Sor-sor*," she pleaded, "eat something. You need your strength to take care of your family. Okay?"

Anna loved her sister. So did Anna's children, who called her Aunt Loretta-Loretta (a play on her name Loretta DiLoretta). After some persuasion, Anna surrendered to her sister's plea. "Okay, I have a cup of tea."

Loretta pressed her luck. "And maybe a sandwich, too. There is plenty of food out there. Your neighbors are too generous." She spoke with slightly better command of the English language than Anna. She had been in the country longer.

For long periods, Anna was quiet and calm, under control. It was as if her daughter were merely sleeping. When she did break down, it was only when someone she had not seen in a while came into the room such as her brothers Pietro and Rafaello and their wives, who lived out of town. Anna had not seen them in more than two years. They didn't stay long, only for a couple of hours, and, with so many people crowding into the front room, it was difficult for Anna to carry on a conversation with her brothers, but she was glad they there. Before they left, they promised, in Italian, to stay in touch.

To avoid any emotionally drenching outbursts, calmer heads like Uncle Tony, Loretta's husband, kept their eye on the back door to see who was coming in next. Once, two middle-aged women all dressed in black came in and started crying and screaming, almost throwing themselves across the casket. In the neighborhood, the two women were known as "the Wailers." They earned their reputation by going from wake to wake for a good cry and, some conjectured, for something to eat. Actually, the women never knew Christina or the rest of the family. They probably had seen the white bouquet of flowers (white for a child) hanging on the front door of the building and decided to pay a surprise visit. Uncle Tony, who was quick to catch on, calmly escorted them out the back door and down the stairs.

Papa sat in one of the armchairs staring at the child in the casket. As he was greeted by each of the mourners, there were a few, awkward, but comforting, words and a warm handshake. Sometimes visitors would give him an envelope with money to help defray the cost of the funeral, and he would fill up, stick the envelope in the side pocket of his jacket, and thank them. Then he would sit silently again, alone in his thoughts. Occasionally, Christopher would come running in from the other rooms and leap on his father's lap. When he did, Arturo would start sobbing, and Christopher would run back into the other rooms. It was not that Arturo wore his emotions on his sleeve, but he was not afraid to cry in view of everyone. He damn well had good reason. Only, he didn't like anyone to ask him to explain what he was feeling.

Occasionally, Arturo exchanged glances with Anna, and the pain on their faces was obvious, so they avoided each other. Sometimes, Arturo just had to get away, especially when the front room became so crowded it was difficult to breathe, and then he would go into the kitchen or dining room and talk quietly with friends and relatives. "Eat something, Arturo," they urged him. "You'll feel better."

Arturo was a man used to working, seven days a week. As he sat crushed in the chair, he sometimes thought about his little store on Tenth Avenue. Once, early one morning, he went down to the place to check on everything. After throwing out some fruit and vegetables that had become rotten, he came back home.

Camille found it difficult to stay in the front room. When she did go in, she sat next to mama on the sofa and rested her head on her shoulder. Together with Aunt Loretta-Loretta, she helped mama find something to wear in the morning and get undressed at night. She also kept an eye on Christopher, making sure he ate and didn't annoy anyone. She felt sorry for him because he had lost his twin sister. But once, when she tried to hug him, he pulled away and ran into the hall-way and down the stairs. She ran after him. "Christopher, come here, where're you going?"

"Away, far away, I'm going to live in California."

"Oh, come on back," she pleaded.

"No, I don't like it here anymore. Everybody's crying."

She didn't know how to respond.

Michael came out into the hallway. Looking down the stairs, he asked, "Where's he going?"

"To California, to live," Camille replied, straight-faced.

"Without a suitcase?"

"I don't need any clothes there," Christopher explained

Michael offered his hand. "Come on, Christopher, I'll help you pack...and maybe we can play some checkers before you go."

Christopher weighed the offer. "Only if you don't yell at me if I do the wrong move."

"Sure, no yelling," Michael assured him.

"I'll be black."

Camille shook her head, then heaved a sigh of relief. Crisis resolved.

Friends brought some relief during the wake. One by one, and sometimes two or three at a time, classmates came to pay their respects. Some friends, including Dottie Wood and Harry Slovich, were there for hours every day.

Dottie and Camille went back a long way together—to kindergarten at St. Paul's—and Camille just knew Dottie would be her friend for life. Dottie was a thin, frail girl who looked sad and frightened most of the time but had a nice smile. She was the middle child in a family of seven children. She lived over a liquor store on Ninth Avenue that her father regularly frequented. He had a job with a steady gang on the docks that enabled him to send his kids to parochial school, but he could be verbally abusive when he drank. Dottie liked to visit Camille whenever she could, especially when Dottie's dad was home. The Terra-novas seemed like what a family should be, and Camille's parents didn't fight like hers. Besides, Mrs. Terranova cooked so many wonderful things.

Harry was a more recent addition to Camille's circle of friends. She met him when she was taking in the fruit and vegetable stand for her father one evening.

Harry was walking his dog, a dark brown mongrel with droopy eyes that looked like it was on its last legs.

"You looking for a hernia?" he asked.

The stranger's comment caught Camille off guard. "What?"

"I mean those bushels look heavy," he explained.

"They *are* heavy. You have a better way?"

Harry tied the dog's leash to a metal rail. "Here, let me help you."

Arturo, who was reexamining an order sheet behind the counter, shot a glance at Harry over his reading glasses as he came into the store, a bushel of eggplants in his hands. Harry put the bushel down and reached out to shake Arturo's hand. "Hi, I'm Harry Slovich, your new stand boy. I work cheap—some scraps for my dog Cocoa, maybe an occasional hero. Nice to meet you." Arturo, serious by nature, couldn't help but smile. Camille loved to see her father smiling. From that point on, she and Harry became good friends.

Harry had this way about him. A tall string bean of a kid who talked with rapid-fire earnestness from the side of his mouth, he made those around him laugh when he told a story, his bright blue eyes wide open and a dead serious expression on his face. He seemed to enjoy making people laugh. Not too much was known about his home life except that he lived with his mother, a sullen woman, and his dog in a neglected tenement near Eleventh Avenue. His father bolted the household when Harry was a baby—a circumstance Harry was quick to dismiss with a short explanation: "He just took off like a scared rabbit one day. That's all I know."

At Christina's wake, Camille also discovered that Harry was something of a dreamer. He said that he and his friend Maxie Myers planned to open a pet store someday when they finished school. Both loved animals as well as the outdoors. Their idea of fun was to go fishing for goldfish or crawfish in Central Park or walk across the George Washington Bridge and explore the cliffs over in New Jersey.

Another visitor to the wake was Ben Stern, the landlord's son. He came twice, once with his parents, once on his own. He wasn't telling anyone, but he was very fond of Camille. On the visit without his parents, he brought a box of chocolates.

"*Shalom!*" said Ben, extending his offering.

"*Sha…lom?*" Camille smiled.

"Yes, it means peace," he explained.

"Oh…that's very nice of you. And *Shalom* to you, as well, Ben."

He grinned, bearing large front teeth. "I was going to bring my Benny Goodman records, but I didn't know if it was appropriate."

"Oh, it's okay. We could've gone into the kitchen."

"Maybe next time."

Ben was a bright, serious-minded boy who followed the events of the war with an adult's interest.

"The invasion is going well, don't you think?"

"Oh, yes," Camille replied.

"It won't be long, we'll be in Paris," he ventured.

Camille made a noise in her throat like she agreed.

"Then, Germany."

"Would you like a sandwich or something?" Camille inquired. "We have plenty of food. The neighbors, they brought us everything. Even Mrs. Kozlowski made pirogies."

"You mean the old woman who lives next door?

"Yes, the old woman who's always slamming the door."

They both smiled. "I think I could eat something," said Ben.

Michael felt lost and uneasy as the crowds grew, particularly at night, when neighbors and relatives found time after work to come by and pay their respects. At the same time, he was strangely comforted by the presence of so many people. As long as they kept coming—and milling around and talking and eating— Michael felt less fearful, safer. He even managed to smile when someone tried to draw him into conversation.

"Well, I'll be a monkey's uncle. Is that you, Michael?" exclaimed Sadie Spazzo, a friend of the family, almost knocking his glasses off as she threw her large arms around him.

Michael smiled weakly. He knew her as the Pincher—and, sure enough, she reached out and tweaked his cheek.

"The last time I saw you, you were only this big," she gestured, "and you were sliding all over the dance floor at your cousin's wedding, remember?"

Michael nodded.

Then, shifting moods, she said solemnly, "So sad what happened to your little sister. How're you doing?"

"Fine," he replied.

"That's good. Remember, you're the big boy in the family. You have to be the strong one, for your mother and father, right?"

Michael nodded. How many times had he heard that already? Ah, Sadie meant well. Such a tragic figure. After losing her husband last year, she recently received news that her only child, Roberto, was missing in action.

One afternoon, some of Michael's classmates came by as a group, all decked out in school uniforms. Led by Sister Medina, they said a decade of the rosary. Then, quietly, as if they were in church, they recessed out the back door and down the stairs. Michael wished he were going with them, back to school.

Michael felt most afraid, and vulnerable, late at night when all the visitors had gone home. He would sit at the edge of his bed and look down into the front room. There was mama combing Christina's hair and straightening her clothes as Aunt Loretta-Loretta, hands on hips, pleaded for her sister to come to bed. This was a scene Michael, an avid movie fan, played over and over again in his mind as he tried to fall asleep that night, and in the nights that followed.

These were long, torturous days. By the time Father Toomey came to the wake on the third and final night to lead the mourners in prayer, everyone was exhausted. Everyone except Anna, who seemed energized at nighttime when the crowds were heaviest. Michael leaned against his mother, while Christopher, who was asleep now, nestled under Camille's arm. For Father Toomey, this was just another ritual in a long pastoral ministry, but he could sense the great loss and pain in the room as he began The Lord's Prayer. He had to say something more meaningful tonight.

The prayer ended, the priest turned to Anna and Arturo. "I know these are difficult days for you and your family, but try to remember: Christina is at peace with the Lord and all His saints and is filled with love and joy. I'm sure she's playing and dancing with the angels right now." Slowly, the mourners started filing past the coffin one more time. Knees bent, the last visitor made the sign of the cross, and the wake was over.

The next day, Father Toomey looked out from the sacristy and was surprised by the size of the congregation on hand for the funeral service. The crowd consisted mainly of women, many in black, but there was a fair sprinkling of men, several in uniform, along with three sizable groups of schoolchildren, nuns, and priests.

Among the more familiar faces in the pews were Mr. and Mrs. Clooney—the bartender and his wife—who were all done up in a way Father Toomey had never seen them before. Mrs. Wood and her daughter Dottie were also there, both portraits of grief. Sitting nearby was the generous Mrs. Fucito, so stylish in that black dress. There was the nurse Father Toomey met at the wake the previous evening; she was working in the hospital and tried to console Anna the day her daughter died. On hand, too, were a few local politicians and the regular neighborhood mourners along with Leo the policeman, who had been walking the Tenth Avenue beat since who knows when. It was time to begin the service.

Father Toomey wiped beads of perspiration from his brow as he watched the pallbearers lead the little white coffin and a procession of family, relatives, and friends down the center aisle. Over the next 45 minutes, the old priest and a bereaved congregation pleaded the case for Christina and the redemption of her immortal soul before the altar of God with prayers, incense, song, and tears. How many wondered what sins this five-year-old could possibly have committed? Was not Christina already an angel in the House of the Lord? *Requiescat in pacem.*

Following the church service, Father Toomey, in the first limousine, led a procession of funeral cars and other vehicles to Calvary Cemetery on Long Island. There were only a few clouds in the sky when family and friends arrived at the grave site. The trees were green and full and swayed gently in the breeze. Birds were chirping gratefully.

Mama and papa, arm in arm, got out of their limo and slowly walked toward a large mound of earth in the middle of rows of tombstones. They seemed older by years today. Christopher wanted to see how deep the hole in the ground went and walked to the edge of the grave site. Michael gently pulled him back from the precipice. Aunt Loretta-Loretta came over to Camille, who was shaking from head to foot, and whispered something about being strong because she was the oldest. Michael would always remember the spoiled smell of freshly turned soil.

Father Toomey read a famous psalm with a conviction that belied his familiarity with the oft-said verses:

> *The Lord is my shepherd; I shall not want.*
> *In verdant pastures he gives me repose;*
> *Beside restful waters he leads me;*
> *He refreshes my soul....*

The priest gave the final blessing. And then the little white casket was lowered into the ground. Each mourner tossed a flower into the grave. There were some final hugs, a few outbursts, more tears. Anna looked back one more time before moving into the back seat of the limousine. Arturo gave a deep sigh and followed her into the funeral car. Christopher brushed past Camille and wiggled between mama and papa. His sister was about to say something, but didn't. "Sorry," said Christopher. Camille patted him on the knee as she got into one of the jump seats. Michael hopped into the other jump seat, squinting into a bright sun at the pile of dirt next to his sister's grave and a small group of grave diggers nearby.

Aunt Loretta-Loretta insisted on staying with her sister and family for another day, then she would return home to Long Island. It was rare for her two sons, Salvatore and Rocco, to be on furlough from the army together. Sal was headed for England, then who knew where; Rocco was ordered to fly west for duty somewhere in the Pacific.

It was time for the Terranovas to begin life without Christina, on their own.

CHAPTER 5

▼

Arturo reopened the store the afternoon he buried his daughter, but he couldn't face the endless stream of sympathetic customers for long, so he closed up shop and went home early. Anna and the children, along with Aunt Loretta-Loretta, were just finishing supper when he opened the front door and walked into the dining room.

Seeing his father, Christopher jumped up from the table, ran to him, and hugged him around the legs. Papa picked up the boy, held him longer than usual, and kissed him on the cheek. Despite Christopher's tendency to get into family scraps from time to time, there was a special bond between father and his youngest son. Perhaps Arturo liked Christopher's spirit of freedom and independence and wished he had shown more of it growing up in his strict Italian household. Michael was next to welcome his father, and papa responded by patting him on the head and kissing him on the cheek. *How could you not love this boy? Such a kind and gentle boy, my Michael.*

"Hello, papa," Camille waved from the kitchen. She didn't ask why he had closed the store so early tonight; nor did anyone else. This had been a very special day for the family, one each member would never forget. "Sit down, Arturo, I make you a plate," Aunt Loretta-Loretta said. "No, No, I am not so hungry. Just a glass of wine," said papa. Mama drew one of her special glasses from the china closet and poured some Burgundy in it.

Arturo sat down heavily and began gulping the wine. "So many people come by to express sympathy. I could take it no more," he explained, pouring himself some more wine. Everyone around the table was staring at him, their eyes riveted on his every word. Suddenly, he pounded the table with his fist, and everyone jumped. He continued, "Sometimes, I think: How did this thing happen? Why? Why to us? What else could we have done to save that poor girl? Maybe we should went to see another doctor or take her to the hospital sooner? Could this happen again? Please, God, no! Why did we move? Maybe we should go back to Fifty-sixth Street with the gypsies, the junk store, and the dogs in hallway."

"Please, Arturo, the children," Anna whispered.

"You torture yourself," Aunt Loretta-Loretta added consolingly. "You did all you could do, and more. It was just the time for the child."

"NO! NO!" he shouted, his face reddened by anger and the wine. "No one should…No one should die when they are so young." Christopher started crying; Michael and Camille filled up and exchanged worried glances.

"Please, please, Arturo, think, the children," Anna repeated.

"The children, they should ask their teachers why such things happen. Maybe they know in Catholic school. Maybe you know, Anna."

"I do not know," she said. "What I know is we come here to America to find the better life, and we will find it. No matter what you say, this is good home we make here."

He waved his hand in disgust and was about to continue his tirade when Aunt Loretta-Loretta interrupted him. "*Abasta!* Stop this! Stop now before you say things you regret, and I call the police and have you arrested," she said, a playful smile crossing her face. Arturo always had respect for his wife's sister. Two miscarriages, one stillborn, and two grown children headed for dangerous assignments abroad, and she always bounced back, stronger and as optimistic as ever.

Above all, Aunt Loretta-Loretta was kind and generous to the Terranova family. She never forgot the children's birthdays; she let them run and play all over her house during the family's frequent visits to her home on Long Island; and she gave them each a loaf of blessed bread from her *San Giuseppe* house shrine every year.

Arturo got up from the table and went into the kitchen to wash his face and hands. "I think I eat now," he announced.

"Sit down, I fix you something," said Aunt Loretta-Loretta.

"Not too much," he pleaded.

In the weeks that followed, Arturo seemed to lose his business focus and drive. Once known for his punctuality, he followed an erratic schedule opening and closing the store, he was late calling in his orders and making payments to wholesalers, and he was beginning to let the store's appearance—once a source of great pride—slip into disarray. Then one day, his old friend Mrs. Fucito, who came to his rescue that cold winter day when he was refused a seat on the bus for carrying a bushel of fish, stopped by to do some shopping. She waited until she was the only customer in the store before approaching Arturo.

"I can't believe this is your place, Arturo," she finally said.

"What do you mean, Mrs. Fucito?"

"I mean you always took such pride in your business. Look at the fruit, the vegetables. They look like somebody stepped on them. And the cold cuts...."

"Please, Mrs. Fucito, I have great respect for you, but...."

"Let me finish, Arturo, please. We have been friends a long time. I know how important this business is to you. I remember you telling me, right in my home, that someday you will own your own place and get the respect you deserve. Remember?"

"Yes."

"One more thing, and I'll shut up. When my husband died, I could have let the business go to pot. But, thank God, I didn't. I learned as much as I could about it and worked hard to make it successful. I think I did a pretty good job."

"Yes, you did."

"Don't make your business go to pot, Arturo." There was a moment of silence between them. "Okay, let's do some business. Can you have my order delivered?"

"Of course, Mrs. Fucito."

It was a hard lesson, but one he had to learn now, before it was too late. In his grief and anguish, he had lost his way and his motivation, and, in so doing, he stood to lose all that he had built from scratch. As Mrs. Fucito suggested, he just couldn't let his business go to pot.

Anna seemed lost without her little girl. On the surface, she was her old self—involved, hardworking, in charge—but the zest, the spirit, perhaps even the life, had gone out of her. Often, she drifted off in her own thoughts when someone was talking to her, giving the appearance she wasn't listening or didn't care. For long periods, Anna sat in the front room and stared out the window at the apartments across the street. She would sit there sometimes and hold a piece of clothing—a dress, a sweater, a blouse—Christina used to wear. Sometimes when all of the children were gathered around the dinner table arguing or yelling at one another, she would walk away and go lie down in her bed. Once she went up to the roof. Camille and Michael, fearing the worst, rushed up to try and find her and bring her back home.

"Stay here, Christopher," said Camille anxiously.

"No, I'm coming," he pouted.

"Okay, then hold my hand."

The three of them ran up the last two flights of stairs and pushed open the roof door. They were frantic when they didn't see mama immediately, their heads spinning in all directions. Then they spotted her on the far side of the building facing downtown. Overhead, a blue and white sky, inflamed in the West with splashes of purple and orange, was getting ready for a spectacular sunset.

"MOM! We were looking for you," cried Camille, the leader of the search party. "What are you doing on the roof?"

"I come here, and think. It is quiet, just the birds. No one is screaming or fighting."

"We were worried," Camille went on.

Mama could see the concern in their faces. "What do you think I do?" she asked. No one answered. Then, turning to her oldest son, she repeated the question. "What do you think, Michael?"

Michael shrugged his shoulders, tears welling in his eyes. Mama opened her arms. "Come here, all of you." She embraced them like a great eagle guarding her young. "Like papa say, we are family. We take care one another, not fight and yell."

"We'll try, mama," said Michael.

"Look at that big building," mama observed, pointing to the Empire State Building. "I no think I want to work up there."

"Me, too," said Christopher.

Another time they would have all laughed at that comment. "Let's go home," said Camille, a hint of weariness in her voice.

Until that day, Anna had no idea how much the children worried about her. She would have to make some changes so they wouldn't feel that way again. One thing for sure: She had to get out of the house and spend more time with people. The next afternoon, Anna started going down to the store with Christopher, and she continued the practice throughout the summer and into the fall. The contact with customers, along with the many other activities she performed—preparing food for the lunch crowd, talking to sales people, working side by side with Arturo on new shipments—helped lift her spirits. It was the therapy she needed.

Nervous and worried about everyone, especially mama, Camille went into a free-fall when she learned she had a book report to finish in order to graduate. Ben Stern, who dropped by one day with his Benny Goodman records, offered her one solution. "I can help. I'm a very good reader. What's the book?"

"*The Red Badge of Courage.*"

"Oh, one of my favorites, by Stephen Crane."

"I think Sister likes the boys better than the girls."

"So that's why she assigned it?"

"Yes."

"My cousin Elena loved it," said Ben, quickly adding, "It's a war story, you know."

"I know."

"Actually," Ben continued, "it's an anti-war story. I think we can work together on it."

And they did. With Ben's help, Camille managed to complete her assignment on time. But there was one final hurdle: The graduation dress turned out to be too large. Camille had lost a lot of weight following Christina's death, and mama had to tuck in the dress at the last minute.

The events of the past weeks were just too overwhelming. Camille was crying and shaking when she walked across the stage to receive her diploma from Monsignor Lonier. She was thankful that friends like Dottie Wood and Harry Slovich were there to help her get through the day.

When Michael returned to school, he felt like a stranger, as if he were returning from a long trip or illness. Everyone seemed so distant. While his classmates were polite to him when they saw him, they were not very friendly. Nor did they invite him into their homes or ask him to play games with them. Only Casey Russell, the Black kid from Fifty-third Street everyone in class avoided, made an attempt to reach out. Perhaps he knew what it felt like to be alone and lonely.

Casey's feeling of loneliness grew even more intense earlier in the year when his father left home one morning and never came back, and his mother began working nights.

"Wanna listen to the ball game with me?" Casey asked after school one day.

"Who's playing?" Michael inquired.

"Dodgers and Cardinals."

"I'm a Yankee fan."

"So...you got nothin' to lose," Casey reasoned.

That was the beginning of a friendship

When they arrived at Casey's house, Mrs. Russell told Michael she was sorry to hear about his sister, gave the boys some cream soda and chips, and sat down and listened to the ball game with them for awhile. For the first time in days, Michael felt secure and calm. This was better than going home and facing, alone, that awful vision in the front room.

In September, Christopher started school, in nearby Sacred Heart. Michael moved up to the fifth grade at St. Paul's. Camille was taking the crosstown bus to Julia Richman High School. The children seemed to bounce back first, although they were yet to face some of the darker corners of Christina's death. Arturo again talked about expanding the business. Anna seemed to draw strength from the people around her, especially her children, and from friends and neighbors she came in contact with each day. She also found loving support from Aunt Loretta-Loretta and Uncle Tony, who were frequent visitors, and her brothers Pietro and Rafaello, who kept in touch, as they said they would. Even her younger brother Giovanni managed to send a few words of encouragement, through the Red Cross, from war-torn Italy.

More for the sake of the children than for anyone else, Anna and Arturo put on a brave face. And they knew deep down that they didn't cross an ocean, marry, raise a family, and build a business in a great land now engaged in a world war only to see their dreams and family shattered.

Abroad, clashing armies were moving toward a monumental climax. By the time 1944 ended, the Allies had liberated Paris, and, despite a major German counteroffensive in the Ardennes, continued advancing toward Germany, while the Red Army swept through the Balkans. In the Pacific, General MacArthur lived up to a promise made in 1942 and returned to the Philippines, while the Allies continued to hop successfully from island to island.

There were many signs the end was near. President Roosevelt won a fourth term. A group of German officers tried to kill Hitler, but failed. Mussolini was on the run. And, in Japan, Prime Minister and chief of staff Tojo and his cabinet were ousted for a more traditional form of government.

The Terranovas would emerge from the war wounded and scarred by tragedy. Yet they grew closer than ever, fearful but still confident about the future, wary yet willing to take reasonable risks. Finally, they were on their way again to being a family.

1951

CHAPTER 6

▼

Nineteen-year-old Camille Terranova didn't know how it happened. It just happened. Here it was—October 1951—and she and Harry Slovich were writing love letters to each other, she from Fiftieth Street in New York City, he from an army tent in a rugged, distant land known as Korea.

"Did I tell you how much I love you today?" she always began her bright, uplifting letters.

His letters were more serious, but bravely comforting, and always ended with the words: "P.S., did I tell you how beautiful you are today?"

As she sat down to write her letter this night, she wondered how their friendship had blossomed into a love that reached across thousands of miles....

For years, Camille had regarded Harry as merely a close friend, the tall, thin guy with the bright blue eyes who made her laugh when he told a story. And he always was there when she needed him. When Christina died, Harry seldom left Camille's side during the wake, and he was a frequent visitor to her home in the weeks that followed. For a while, mama set a place for him at the Sunday afternoon table, and the family treated him as one of their own.

Camille was thankful and proud when Harry took a special interest in her brothers, especially Christopher, who always seemed to be getting into trouble. His advice to the boys covered a broad range of subjects, including the best way to study for exams, how to train roof pigeons, and what you have to do in order to win in cards. "Rule Number One when you play cards," he told Christopher, "is make sure you know who you're playing with."

With the arrival of the telephone in the Terranova household, Camille found another way to stay in touch with Harry. There followed long, usually one-way phone conversations in which she recounted, in detail, what happened each day in high school. Harry mostly just listened.

"Remember Lucy Lucas, the one I told you about?" Camille began one day.

"Uh-huh."

"I don't know what's wrong with her. One day she's my friend, the next day she's not," she went on.

"Uh-huh."

"I mean, we walk home together, and we're talking and laughing, and the next day in school, it's like she doesn't know me."

"Weird."

"Yeah," said Camille, "and to top it off, the other day she says I'm her best friend. Figure that one."

"I'm sure it's nothing you're doing," Harry commented. "Maybe you should ask her why she acts that way in school."

"What, and ruin a beautiful friendship?"

Four years of high school went by quickly, and the conversations soon drifted into new areas, namely careers and jobs. Camille was overwhelmed with fear the day before she was to begin her first job, as a member of the secretarial pool at the Metropolitan Life Insurance Company. Once again, Harry was there—this time in person—to listen.

As someone who had just started working himself—at a pet store—he tried to offer some calming words of advice, sometimes with a twinkle in his eye. "It's just a job." "You're a smart cookie." "It'll get better, you'll see." Camille's first-job fears dissipated after a week or two, and she became more confident with each passing day. She always had more strength and talent than she realized.

Camille may not have been able to tell you how it happened, but she could pinpoint the day her relationship with Harry changed. They were at a local dance, sometimes known as "a beer racket" to neighborhood residents. They were sitting around a table with several of their friends, including Dottie Wood and Maxie Myers. Maxie was telling some spicy Knock-Knock jokes and kidding with Dottie, as he often did. "Whatdayasay we crash out of here and get ourselves a room?" whispered Maxie, loud enough for everyone to hear. "Why? Did your mother throw you out of yours?" said Dottie, to the laughter of everyone within earshot, including Maxie.

Camille knew Maxie was in his glory when he was the center of attraction, and she was glad for him. Besides being in the spotlight, the short, wiry young man loved to make people laugh. He inherited his sense of humor from his father, a stagehand and numbers runner, who had high hopes for his son. "Someday, we'll all have to wipe our feet on the carpet before we go into his office," his father often boasted. In his mother's view, there was nothing her boy could not do. "Come on, Maxie, do that imitation of Mickey Rooney," she urged him whenever there was any kind of crowd (two or more) around to listen.

Yet, despite all the pampering, Maxie was no spoiled brat. He loved his parents and worried about them. There was that business about a brother who died in a fire before he was born, along with his mother's retreats into depression and his father's long battle with booze. He would do anything to make them happy. The same with his friends. And, of all his friends—and he had many—Maxie was especially close to Harry. Long into the night on many occasions, they mapped out plans to open, together, a new kind of pet store, where every animal was treated with compassion.

"Hey, how about we give all the pets names and have the customers *adopt* them?" said Maxie during one brainstorming session.

Harry couldn't help laughing. "The fish too?" he asked.

At the neighborhood dance, someone went up to the microphone and announced that this would be "the last dance," and the music started playing. Camille and Harry looked at each other and, in one flowing motion, got up to dance. "Goodnight Irene" by the Weavers was never an easy song to dance to, especially since it was a waltz, but, tonight, Camille and Harry glided with the music. Harry leaned down and gently placed his cheek against Camille's. She raised her head for a moment and gazed into his eyes, then placed her cheek snugly back against his. She wondered. *What was so different about this night? Why is this dance so special? How is it that I didn't notice before how beautiful Harry's eyes are?* She wanted to continue dancing—no, it was more like floating in some serene space and time—but the music came to an end.

Later, in the ladies' room, Camille, still glowing from her magical dance, made her announcement to Dottie: "I think I'm in love."

"With who?"

"Harry," Camille beamed.

Dottie couldn't believe it. "Get out. Good old Harry?"

"Yeah. Ever notice how gorgeous his eyes are, or how well he dances, and how gentle he is?"

"If you say so...Oh, brother, I think you got it bad."

When Harry took her home that night, she *knew* there was something different between them. They hardly said a word, just held hands all the way home. He walked her up the front steps and into the hallway, where he muttered something about his having a nice time at the dance. They stood there for what seemed like an eternity staring into each other's eyes.

"I want to kiss you," he finally said.

"I don't mind," she replied.

They kissed, briefly at first, then long and passionately. As if pleased with the results, they both smiled broadly.

"Can you beat this?" Harry began excitedly. "I love you, Camille. I guess I always have. I just didn't know it 'til tonight."

Camille was crying and laughing all at once. "And I love you, Harry. What a wonderful surprise!"

They kissed one more time, and again, tenderly at first, then passionately. Maybe it was an echo of an old parental warning or her parochial school upbringing. Something told Camille to stop this beautiful, but potentially dangerous, spiral before it was too late.

"I really gotta go, Harry. You know, my mother's waiting, and I'm sure papa's up, too. I'll see you tomorrow," she promised awkwardly and ran up the stairs.

She was past the first landing when he replied. "Yeah, tomorrow."

On the third floor, she looked down through the opening and waved to let him know she had reached her landing safely, then disappeared into her apartment.

Camille did see Harry the next day, and the next and the next, and they discovered they could remain friends as they became lovers. Over the next few months, they were inseparable. They shared their hopes and passions and began talking about creating a life together.

Camille could see that Harry's dream of owning a pet store with Maxie Myers was no empty wish, and he told her about his other goals: "a nice home, with lots of trees," along with "two or three kids," "a dog and other assorted pets," and "a station wagon to take the family all over the country." Camille also wanted it all—a higher-paying secretarial job now, then someday "a home in the country" and a family ("not too big, not too small").

They seemed to have the same items on their wish lists. If there was anything to prevent them from reaching their goals, they weren't aware of it.

When the Communist bombardment began and elements of 90,000 North Korean soldiers invaded the Republic of South Korea one rainy Sunday morning in late June 1950, Camille and Harry, like most Americans, were more concerned about making all their dreams come true than fighting another war. After all, these were generally upbeat times for the country, and it had not been quite five years since the end of World War II. Besides, what business was it of ours to police the actions of countries so far away?

It was left to President Harry Truman and other world leaders to explain why, in their opinion, it was so important to prevent South Korea from being gobbled up by Communist North Korea. After all, hadn't Mussolini, Hitler, and the Japanese warlords—not long before—moved from conquest to conquest, confident no one would dare resist them? This latest power grab couldn't be allowed to happen again, Truman argued, and the United Nations Security Council, in the Soviet Union's unexplained absence, voted "to repel the armed attack and to restore international peace and security in the area."

As noble as his cause appeared, the President did not, at first, win the hearts and minds of Americans by committing military support to the South Korea. Unlike World War II, the Korean War, which the Administration preferred to call a "police action," could not arouse an impassioned or patriotic show of support from ordinary citizens.

Like most Americans, Camille and Harry thought the crisis would pass. It didn't. In fact, it only intensified with the advance and retreat of both armies. Behind the war news was the growing realization that America was facing a new type of aggression in Communism. Fears mounted as national leaders like Senator Eugene McCarthy warned of a widespread Communist threat—"a Red under every bed"—that could lead to the awesome unleashing of nuclear warfare.

Early in 1951, Harry did the unthinkable. He enlisted in the army, rather than wait to be called. A couple of days later, Maxie Myers decided to join his friend and enlisted, too.

The night before the two men left for boot camp, Camille sat with Harry in the front room listening to music and talking.

She wanted this moment to last forever.

"When I get back, we'll start making some plans, big plans," he whispered.

"I know, I know. We'll have plenty of time to plan. Just promise me one thing now."

"What's that?"

"That you don't do anything foolish and you take care of yourself."

"That's two things."

She started sobbing. "And you make sure you come back to me."

"I will, I will." They kissed. Out of the radio floated the heartfelt voice of Tony Bennett singing "Because of You."

She smiled bravely through tears. "Wanna dance, soldier?"

Once again, just as they did that magical night at the neighborhood dance, they glided around the floor, occasionally looking into each other's eyes. From the kitchen, mama saw them dancing, but, respecting their privacy, turned away and continued cooking. "Did I tell you how beautiful you are today?" Harry whispered. An hour later, he was gone.

Camille was stunned by how fast things were moving. Within three months, both Harry and Maxie were shipped out to Korea—Harry to an infantry division, Maxie to a tank corps. She tried to stay in touch with both of them, and they, with her, but it was difficult. The two men were constantly in motion, reaching positions deep within North Korea. Then the Chinese Communists entered the war on the side of the North Koreans and pushed the UN troops back down the peninsula.

In the confusing months that followed, President Truman dismissed General Douglas MacArthur, commander of the Allied troops, for attacking the Administration's policy of trying to contain the war to the Korean peninsula and for promoting a wider war in Asia. Many Americans opposed Truman's action, a testament to MacArthur's wide popularity, but others thought the President had made a gutsy move, and the right one. As the momentum in the war shifted back and forth, new truce talks were begun between the two sides. It seemed like this was a war no one could win or lose—or turn their backs on.

Now here it was, October 1951, and Camille was writing another letter to Harry, who, last she heard, was somewhere slightly north of the 38th parallel, while Maxie's division hunkered down north of Seoul. As usual, she would try to be cheerful and playful—and loving, of course—in her letter. "Did I tell you how much I love you today?" she began once again.

She wrote quickly and confidently, telling him about work, the latest neighborhood scuttle-butt, what she watched on TV, and the family especially Christopher, and she told him about a beautiful house in New Jersey she saw in a magazine. In her heart, she pondered the age-old mysteries of war and peace. *Why are you there, and I'm here? Why can't we be together in a world at peace, if that's what I want and that's what you want and that's what most people want? Haven't we seen enough war?*

CHAPTER 7

▼

Within the Terranova household, mama had watched the changing relationship between her daughter and Harry with intense, but secret, interest. In general, she approved. This was, after all, good old Harry, a loyal friend of the family, and Camille was a young woman ready to move onto the next stage of her life. Still, Anna would prefer that they wait a couple of years before doing anything serious such as get married. She knew Arturo also felt they should wait, but for a different reason. He liked Harry, but he clung to the hope that she would meet someone with higher, more professional ambitions who would lift his daughter to a lifestyle the Terranova family only dreamed was possible.

When Harry left for basic training, both Anna and Arturo were worried that he might be sent to fight in this dreary new war, but they also were relieved that Camille and Harry would not be seeing each other for awhile. Now there was time for everyone to relax, cool off. *Then we see what happens.* Somehow, Anna had blocked out the memory of an earlier time: She was 18 going on 19, she was in America less than two years, and she was about to get married to this confident young man from her province whom she met at her sister's home in Queens. Back then, her parents, writing from Italy, had urged her to wait a couple of years. She didn't follow their advice.

But these were different times. Watching her children grow up—and one of them die—during wartime, Anna had become more protective and cautious than ever of their well-being, and she smothered them with concerns about everything, from the clothes they wore to school grades to the state of their teeth. Though occasionally annoyed by this showering of attention, the children went along with it, and sometimes embraced it. Why not? Who could not stand being fussed over in a large family?

None of the children fell outside mama's radar screen when it came to their health:

If Christopher woke up sniffling or sneezing, she would tell him, "Better you stay home from school today, I make some soup."

One nice, fall evening, Michael was getting ready to go over to a friend's house. Michael was in good health, but that night mama felt the need to remind him, "Please, put on your sweater. You want to catch a cold?"

Another evening, when Camille was preparing to go out with her friends, mama warned her, "Please, no wash your hair—you catch pneumonia."

She had a litany of advisories. "*Mangia*, eat, you feel better....Watch out for drafts....No sit on the stoop, you catch something." Always, in mama's eyes, there was that dreaded intruder—fever—lurking in the shadows, ready to pounce.

There were times Anna relaxed, and she seemed like her old self. This was especially true when they were all together, which was becoming rarer as the children got older. Her favorite pastime was playing cards with the family after Sunday dinner—her kind of cards, which usually meant an occasional, small breach of the rules. She masked a competitive spirit to win.

She also loved to have friends and relatives drop by on Sunday. Somehow, she always found a place for them at the table. A special late Sunday afternoon treat was a trip with her old friend Grace from Fifty-sixth Street, or more recently with Camille, to the old Tivoli theater on Eighth Avenue to catch a good movie, preferably a comedy or a love story. No war movies or horror shows, please.

During the week Anna followed a busy schedule. After she saw the kids off to school or work in the morning, she went down to the store to make sandwiches for the lunch crowd, stack the shelves, wait on customers, and prepare for the next day. Sometimes, during a quiet spell in the afternoons, she shared a cup of coffee and talked with Arturo. The conversation was usually about the family and its problems. Increasingly, it was centering around Christopher, now 12, who, Anna learned, was palling around with a tough group of boys from the neighborhood.

"I tell you, Arturo, I worry sick. I am so afraid. I no like those boys, Christopher's new friends," she began one day.

"What do you mean?" Arturo asked.

"Those boys—Jimmy D., Roger and his brother, one they call Falcon—they are nothing but trouble," she replied.

"How you know, Anna?"

"I hear, I have friends."

"What you hear?"

"Mrs. Clooney tell me those boys are always on the roof, and climb down fire escapes. God know what they do there." She started to cry, caught herself. She was in the store. "Please, Arturo, seal your lips. No say nothing to Mrs. Clooney. She is good friend."

"No worry."

"Mrs. Clooney say some people missing things, she think maybe those boys steal those things," she continued.

Arturo grew angrier as she spoke, finally slamming his fist on a bag of potatoes. The pain shot up his arm.

"Those boys heading for big packs of trouble," Anna concluded.

"Did you talk to Christopher?" he asked.

"I talk to him, sure, but he say they all good boys. No problems."

"Does Michael know?"

"Yes, I tell him," Anna replied, blowing her nose with a handkerchief. "I ask him to keep eye on things."

"And he does?"

"What you expect, Arturo? Michael has his high school and his homework, and he has his own friends." She paused, then continued, "He has new friend. Her name is Josephine, they call her Jo. Nice girl, very intelligent. They do the homework together. Once in a while, they go to movies or ice cream parlor." In the background, the radio was playing. Nat King Cole was singing "Too Young."

"Michael has girlfriend now? He is only 15."

"Where you been, Arturo?" said Anna. "This is 1951."

Arturo shook his head in disbelief. "I speak to Christopher. Tonight. No fail."

"Okay, do not be so crazy. You promise?"

"No worry. I promise."

Later that afternoon, as she did every day during the week, Anna went home to prepare supper for the children, who these days seemed to be eating on a staggered system. As she cut up some vegetables, she prayed Arturo would not lose his temper, which he sometimes did, when he spoke to Christopher.

No fail, papa would talk with Christopher when the boy stopped by the store before going home. This business of being on roofs and climbing down fire escapes had to stop now. In the meantime, Arturo had his own problems—bum checks from the laundry people down the block that were piling up. The bills were coming in faster than ever, it seemed, and he wasn't ready to pay them. More and more, he was asking for credit. Arturo impassionedly slapped his hands together and said a silent prayer to the saint in the black cassock on the cross beam.

The phone rang, bringing him back to earth. He tried to collect himself as he greeted the caller. "Hello, Arturo Terranova."

"Oh, hello, Mr. Terranova," said a man on the other line in a clip, but friendly, voice.

"Sergeant Reilly, 17th Precinct, here. I have your son Christopher here, along with three of his pals. We're gonna hold them until their parents pick them up."

"What they do, sergeant?"

"They were on the roof and climbing down a fire escape when we picked them up. Don't know what they were doing. They say they were playing 'follow the leader.' Don't know. We've had some robbery complaints. If I were you, I'd keep my eye on Christopher. Seems like a nice kid. The rest of them…forget it. Oh, by the way, did you know your son smokes? Found a pack of cigarettes on him. Philip Morris."

Arturo was trembling with fright and anger, but he tried to stay in control. "Be right down there. Thank you, sergeant."

At the police station, a police officer led Arturo to a detention area where all four of the boys were waiting to be picked up by their parents. "You know, they're not out of the woods yet," said the policeman. "They're free to go now, but they're all under suspicion. We know it's a tough neighborhood, but if I were you, I'd keep a close eye on your boy, Mr. Terranova."

"Absolutely, officer," said Arturo.

When Christopher first saw his father, he broke out in a smile which quickly disintegrated into a look of concern and fear. "Hello, papa." Without responding, Arturo waited for Christopher to come out of the holding area, a painful look greeting his son. He didn't look at his three friends.

Outside the police station and heading home, papa wanted to cuff his son soundly for the trouble he caused, but he thought better of it. This was too serious, he needed to find out what was going on, and Anna would not like it if he lost his temper. He took a deep breath. "What you doing on the roof?"

"Just playing," said Christopher, almost in a whisper.

Papa's accent was thick, but his message was loud and clear. "Bullashit! I know what you do up there."

"Really, papa, we just hang out there."

"Do not be so smart," said Arturo, his voice rising again.

Christopher fell silent, and he started dusting off his pants and jacket. Walking away from the police station, papa recognized the man walking toward him. It was one of his customers. Arturo put on a friendly smile. "Hello, Mr. Heinz."

"Oh, hello, Artie. Nice day."

"Yes, beautiful." Arturo was smiling again. "How you been?"

"Fine, fine, thanks."

"Say hello to Mrs. Heinz."

Out of range of Mr. Heinz, papa felt the blood rushing and bubbling to the top of his head, and with it came an uncontrollable urge to strike someone or something. He dared not, however, remembering his promise to Anna not to go crazy. Then, in a paroxysm of rage, he did the only thing he felt he could do under the circumstances: He started biting his own hand.

Christopher stared at his father in disbelief. "Why're you doing that?"

"*Camminare*...walk, walk," said papa in measured tones. "See, see, the whole neighborhood know you steal," he said, his blood slowly returning to normal levels. "You and those boys heading for lots of trouble. It gotta stop. Now. *Capisco?*"

"Sure, papa, whatever you say."

"I say, from now on, you come down the store and stay with me after school."

"Ah, papa, I have hockey practice in the school yard."

"No hockey for one month, then we see."

Christopher shook his head disconsolately.

"No Falcon and those other guys, too—and no more Philip."

"Philip?"

"Yes, Philip Morris. You know how your mother feel about smoking."

Christopher looked surprised that he knew so much. "Okay, okay," he said weakly.

"Look at you, a mess," papa continued. "You look like you just come from the war. Maybe it would be better you were in Korea."

"Why, so I could get killed or something?"

"No, so you grow up and be a man."

"Are you going to tell mama what happened?"

"What you think? She take one look, she know."

Christopher tucked in his shirt and zipped up his jacket. There was defiance in his mouth, but papa thought he saw tears in his son's eyes.

Not that Michael lacked compassion for Christopher and his troubles. In fact, he loved his younger brother and he was always worrying about him. But these days there were other things on his mind, as well. High school. Homework, tons of it. Getting a social life. And Jo Trudell.

Michael met Jo in the local public library at the beginning of the school year when they lunged for the same reference book at the same time. Rather than tear it in half, as Jo jokingly offered to do, they decided to share it, and a friendship began. After several more library meetings, Michael one afternoon invited Jo to finish her homework at home with him. Weighing the alternative—a cramped apartment with four noisy brothers—she accepted the invitation.

From the beginning, Michael thought Jo was someone special, and the more he learned about her, the more he liked counting her as a friend. The eldest of five kids, Jo—or Josephine, as she was known to her parents—seemed older than 14, with a strong sense of responsibility beyond her years. Her parents were the superintendents of the building where they lived, but since Mr. Trudell worked two jobs that kept him away from home most of the day, the super's chores usually fell upon Mrs. Trudell and Josephine, with some help from the boys.

Mrs. Trudell often said it was a blessing that she had someone like Josephine to help sweep the hallways or shovel the sidewalk out front when it snowed, and the girl did her chores around the apartment, as well, all without constant reminders. That same sense of responsibility carried through wherever she was. Once, on a crosstown bus going to school, she helped revive a fellow student who went into convulsions. She even climbed the fence and came to the rescue of a kitten that wandered near the railroad tracks between Tenth and Eleventh Avenues.

Pretty and bright, Jo was always eager to share her opinions on a variety of issues. All you had to do was look at the slight turn in her light blue eyes, and you knew Jo was one smart cookie. Her narrow, metal-framed glasses only accented her intelligence, which, combined with a sparkling sense of humor, made her fun to be with, yet slightly intimidating.

"What did MacArthur mean when he said, 'Old soldiers never die, they just fade away'?" she asked Michael one day when they were doing homework together.

"Don't know," Michael replied. "I almost fell asleep on my desk when they played his speech over the public address system in school. It's an old West Point ballad or something."

"Yeah, but what does it mean? A bit dramatic, don't you think?"

"I guess."

"You know what I think, Michael?" Jo went on, combing her long, honeyed hair. "I think he was trying to send the country a secret message. You know, 'You ain't seen nothin' yet, folks. I shall return.' Bet he runs for President someday."

Michael stopped writing. "He'll have to wait his turn."

"Who do the Republicans have? McCarthy?"

"Why not?"

Jo smiled slyly, her eyes sparkling. "Oh, brother! Why not Howdy Doody?"

In the following days, Michael invited Jo up to the house a number of times. Most of the time, mama was there when they came home. When she wasn't, and the homework could wait, Jo and Michael played house. Michael would explain how to make English muffin pizzas or peppers and eggs or some other casual Italian dish. Jo would show him how to make biscuits or bacon and eggs or curly french fries. Making pancakes was a joint enterprise, but a messy one. They tried to clean up before mama arrived, but Anna always knew when someone was in her kitchen. She really didn't mind the intrusion.

Sometimes Jo would stay for dinner. When she did, she helped mama prepare the meal, set the table, and clean up afterwards. During dinner, she took notice of how respectful and behaved the family was around the table, and she told Michael as much one evening, "What, did you all go to military school for good table manners?" With four brothers ranging in age from four to eleven, it was a daily fight for every morsel in the Trudell household. When he wasn't working one of his two jobs, Mr. Trudell kept the boys in check. In his absence, mom had her hands full, "trying to keep the boys from killing each other," as she explained to Michael one day. With Josephine's help, mom managed.

Michael liked the way Jo got along with his family, especially Camille, the working girl. Sometimes after dinner, Jo and Camille would sit in the front room listening to records or just talking about a wide range of subjects, including school, work, music, and boys. Jo listened quietly when Camille, her eyes aglow, talked about the latest letter she received from Harry. Camille was impressed by Jo's knowledge of current affairs. "She knows her beans," she told Michael after Jo left one evening.

It seemed Christopher also liked Jo, and she liked him. But they hardly spoke to each other, even though she tried to draw him out. He appeared to be preoccupied most of the time, as if he had a deep, dark secret. When the phone rang one day, Christopher ran to pick it up before it rang a second time. "I'll get it!" he shouted. Mama glanced over at Michael. No one had to tell Jo there was a problem.

Mama did not say anything until after Jo went home. Then she asked Michael what was going on with Christopher.

"I don't know, mama," said Michael, a tinge of frustration in his voice.

"He up to no good, I just know."

"What do you want me to say, mama?" said Michael. "He probably is, but what else can I do? I sleep with him. I get up with him. I meet him after school. I make sure he goes down to the store, just like papa wants. And I talk to him all the time. I can't be with him 24 hours a day, mama."

"I am so afraid Christopher get into big trouble, Michael." She started to cry.

"Mom, don't." He had to say it, "You know, I have a life, too."

"I know, I know, Michael," she said. "I wish Harry were here."

"So do I, mama."

She continued, "You are the sensible one, *figlio mio,* and we are family, and he need your help."

"I'll try, mama, but I can't promise."

CHAPTER 8

▼

The morning sky was overcast, and there was a preview of winter in the air, complete with a few snow flurries. By the time the Macy's Thanksgiving Day parade began, however, the sun had broken through and slithered down into the city's canyons. Thankfully, Michael and Jo had found a prime location between Fiftieth and Fifty-first Streets for her brother Matthew to watch the colorful assortment of bands, floats and balloons parade down Broadway.

This was the traditional beginning of the holiday season in the city. Michael always loved this time of year, and sharing it with Jo made it even more special.

"Someday, maybe, we'll bring our kid to see the big parade," he blurted out in his enthusiasm.

Jo seemed both surprised and pleased by the comment. "Yeah, why not?" She laughed nervously, her face reddening. He had never seen her blush before.

By the time Santa made his climactic appearance down the avenue, Matthew was tired but managed a wan wave at the bearded man in the huge sleigh. And suddenly the parade was over for them. Jo bundled her brother in her arms and headed home. Halfway down the block, Michael took over. When they reached Jo's building, Michael slid the sleeping boy over to his sister once more and kissed her quickly. It was the first time they kissed. Michael liked the feel of her cool, soft lips. She blushed again.

"See you later," said Michael as he started walking away.

"Thanks for a nice time," she said tenderly

He was blushing now. "Yeah, thanks."

When he got home, Michael felt the festive mood immediately. Even Christopher seemed to be caught up in it. He joined in the blessings, talked and laughed with everyone around the table, and later helped clear the table for a game of Parcheesi. Michael quietly noticed the change in his brother, and was happy for mama, but surprised, and a bit suspicious. Christopher seemed just a little too amiable and helpful.

As it grew dark, Michael left for Jo's house, and Camille went to the movies with Dottie. While mama finished up in the kitchen, papa turned on the TV and began nodding in his favorite chair. When he had fallen asleep, Christopher slipped out the front door and down the stairs into the street.

It was dark now and raining lightly when Christopher got to the meeting spot, a roof overlooking Tenth Avenue. A light snow was in the forecast. Roger and his brother Tim, the one they called Falcon, were already there. Roger took a long swallow from a bottle of Schaefer beer and offered it to Christopher.

"Nah," Christopher said, then changed his mind. "Where's Jimmy?" he asked before taking a gulp.

Impatiently, Falcon blew out a cloud of cigarette smoke into the chilly air. "Not here yet. What a pussy!"

"Easy, brother, easy," said Roger, trying to calm down a rage that was apparently building. "Must be good reason. It's Thanksgiving, for cryin' out loud, remember?"

"Yeah, like I give a shit," said Falcon, spitting out a fleck of tobacco.

"Ah, shut up, Tim," said Roger.

Christopher handed the bottle to Falcon and leaned against one of the chimneys. He dug deep into his pocket for a loose cigarette, found one, and lit it. Then, his back against the chimney, he slid down the brick wall. "What, didn't you guys have any turkey?"

"Who needs it?" Falcon barked, chugging down some beer. "Who needs damn turkey?"

"Jesus!" said Roger. "Want the whole neighborhood to know we're up here?"

"I hate turkey," boomed Falcon, finishing his thought. "I'd rather have a hamburger any fucking day."

"You're an ass hole, you know, Tim," said Roger with a menacing glare.

"I think I see him," said Christopher, eager to change the conversation.

Two roofs away, a huddled figure in an oversized pea jacket moved slowly toward them.

"That's it, take your stupid time," cried Falcon.

"Eat me, Falcon," said Jimmy D. as he drew near. He stuffed a hand in his jacket and pulled out an almost empty pack of Camels. "Shit, it's cold. Hey, what'll we do tonight, guys?"

"We can sneak into the movies again. *Mutiny on the Bounty*'s playing on Forty-second Street," Roger suggested.

"Nah, seen it, five times. 'Mr. Christian, Mr. Christian,'" said Jimmy D. in his best Charles Laughton imitation. "The movie's so old it crackles. How 'bout we play some cards?"

"In the rain?" said Falcon. "What about the cards?"

Jimmy D. raised his eyes in disbelief at Falcon's concern. "No problem. How 'bout we climb down and play cards in Mrs. Kahn's apartment? She went away to her sister's for the weekend."

Except for Falcon, they all laughed.

Once more Christopher came to the rescue. "I'm broke anyway."

Falcon glared at Jimmy D. "What about you and me play King of the Roof? First one off loses."

Jimmy D. ignored the challenge, searching his pocket for a match.

"Chicken?" Falcon persisted.

"Up yours, Falcon!"

At that, Falcon made a lunge for Jimmy D. and knocked him down with a thud. Despite his oversized pea jacket, Jimmy D. grabbed Falcon around the waist and wrestled him to the tar surface. Slipping and sliding across the roof, they exchanged desperate blows, most of them missing their mark. As they rolled toward the edge of the building, Christopher and Roger became more anxious and moved in to break up the combatants.

Just then, the door to the roof flew open, and out came Mr. Baker, a long flashlight in his hand. "Hey, what're you kids doin' up here?" he shouted. They didn't answer, but scrambled onto the roof of the attached building. "I catch you up here again, I call the cops!" the super screamed after them.

They kept running, losing their footing on the rain-slicked roof. One by one, they jumped over a shaftway separating two buildings. Christopher, the last to leap, didn't quite catch the other side and slipped, almost falling five stories into the dark abyss. The others didn't stop running as Christopher worked desperately to pull himself up onto the ledge.

With strength he didn't know he had, he finally boosted himself onto the rim of the shaftway, squirmed onto the roof, and hobbled away as fast as he could toward the nearest door.

Christopher knew he would catch hell for leaving without telling his parents, but he was never so glad to be back home. As expected, mama leaped out of the chair when she saw him, dirty and disheveled, the tears in his pants revealing bloodied knees. He tried to hide a slight limp as he slithered through the front door, but didn't do a good job of it. "*Madonna mia,* what happen to you?" she screamed.

"Nothing," he replied. "Just playing."

"Playing, my foot! Where were you?"

"Out…out with the guys," he explained.

"And not say one word to us?"

"Everyone else left—Camille, Michael—and you didn't say nothing," he argued.

"Yes, but I know where they go. You sneak out like a snake."

Just then, a voice boomed from the far bedroom, "Anna, Anna, is that Christopher?" It was papa, who was already in bed. He had an early day; for some reason, he always found the day after Thanksgiving one of his busiest.

"Yes, yes."

"You tell him I talk to him tomorrow," he barked.

"Okay, Arturo. Now go to sleep." She turned to Christopher. "You are so lucky your father go to bed early."

"I'm sorry."

"You always sorry, Christopher." She sighed. "What is the trouble with your foot?"

"I was running, goofing around, and I fell. I think I sprained it."

"*Mama mia,* look at your knees. Take off your pants. I take a look."

That night in bed, Christopher thought about what had happened, could have happened, on the roof, and he started sweating. The fighting. The punching. The kicking. In his mind was the image of these four young bodies, all twisted together, falling over the edge of the building. Once again he saw himself struggling onto the ledge of the shaftway, no one around to help him. It was crazy and scary, even thrilling and a little funny now, when he thought about it. He wondered whether he should call Jimmy D. and Roger tomorrow and relive the experience. On the other hand, maybe it would be best not to contact those guys for a few days.

"Smells like mercurochrome or iodine in here," said Michael as he climbed into bed with Christopher a little later.

"I fell," Christopher explained.

"What happened?"

Christopher was busting to tell the story to someone, but he wasn't quite sure he should say anything to Michael. He tossed out a crumb. "Horsing around."

"Yeah, so I heard," said Michael.

"What did you hear?" asked Christopher, surprised and worried.

"I heard there was a rumble on the roof, and you were there. News travels fast in this neighborhood."

Christopher fell into a faint whisper. "Please, please, don't tell mama or papa, and I'll tell you the story."

"Tell me the story."

Christopher did, in broad terms, omitting some of the details, like the smoking and the beer drinking. "And, when Mr. Baker came out, we all started running," he concluded. "There was this shaftway, and we tried to jump over it. The others made it. I almost missed, but I managed to pull myself up, and, well, I'm here."

"Jesus, Christopher, you could have been killed." They pondered the thought; neither said anything. "We could have been preparing for *your* wake in the front room," Michael finally concluded.

Christopher laughed at the absurdity of it all.

"It's not funny. For once in your life, get serious. Think of someone beside yourself."

"Hey, I am," said Christopher, muffling laughter. "Did you know that papa bites his hand when he gets mad?"

"Yeah, so?"

"I think it's an Italian thing."

"No, it's a papa thing," said Michael. "I saw him do it once after this wise-guy customer came into the store and asked for a hero; only, he called it 'a guinea hero.'"

"What did papa say?"

"He said, 'We no sell guinea hero.'"

They both laughed. Michael continued, "And when the guy left the store, without his sandwich, papa started biting his hand. Wow, was he angry!"

There were many things to mull over that night before the boys fell asleep. Once again, Christopher thought about the near tragedy on the roof. Somehow, Harry—his old mentor—came to mind. He was playing cards with him in a foxhole in Korea. *The Number One rule when you're playing cards is know who you're playing with.*

The following week, Christopher didn't see his roof buddies, and, according to papa's "orders," he made sure he went directly to the store after school. Although news about the incident on the roof was all over the neighborhood, Anna and Arturo didn't learn about it until two weeks later. By then, the holiday season was in full swing, and papa and mama were busier than ever in the store. "I talk to him after the holidays," he told Anna.

One afternoon before Christmas, Christopher was on his way home from the store when he ran into Roger and Falcon.

"Well, look at you, man," said Roger. "Where've you been?"

"Been busy, school, working in the store, that sort of stuff," Christopher explained.

"Last time I saw you, you were hanging by your fingernails in the shaftway," said Falcon, an odd smile creeping across his face.

"Yeah, thanks for coming to my rescue," Christopher countered. "Where're you guys headed?" he quickly added.

"Jimmy D.'s," Roger replied. Apparently, Falcon and Jimmy D. had ironed out whatever differences stood between them. "Wanna come?"

Christopher's answer came quickly. "Yeah, why not?"

CHAPTER 9

▼

As the Christmas season peaked, truce talks between the United Nations forces and the Communists were resumed. There was a feeling that peace on earth, or at least in Korea, was achievable and that the troops would be coming home soon, perhaps by Christmas. That hope was short-lived, while the talks continued amid much wrangling and little progress.

By the end of the year, fighting broke out again. The intensity of the Communist attacks convinced the Americans and their UN allies that they had been suckered into the conference at Panmunjom. Clearly, all the Communists wanted was time to take the heat off themselves and rebuild their troop strength and fortifications. They also had thought that all the arguing and haggling in Panmunjom—the so-called Talking War—would test the Americans' will to fight and force them to bow out of a war that was becoming more unpopular. They were mistaken.

In the weeks that followed the resumption of the Shooting War, Camille stopped receiving letters from Harry, although she kept on writing. Rumors spread around the neighborhood about this soldier and that soldier being wounded, killed, or missing in action. It was a terribly tense time for families and friends. In fact, however, there was only one confirmed casualty, news of which swept through the neighborhood like an old tenement building on fire. It was the death by mortar shell of Maxie Myers on January 15, 1952.

Camille took the news hard, and immediately went to pay her respects to the Myers family. Maxie's mom and dad were sitting at the table drinking coffee when Camille arrived. They didn't say anything when they saw Camille. They merely got up, hugged her, and cried together. Mrs. Myers went to the china closet and took out a cup, brought it to the table, and poured some coffee into it. Camille added some milk and sugar and began stirring, searching for the right words for a grieving family.

"I'll miss him, we'll all miss him," Camille finally said. "What a great guy, funniest person I ever knew."

"Yeah, did you ever hear him do Mickey Rooney?" Mrs. Myers added.

They all smiled briefly. On the table was a telegram, which Maxie's family apparently had been reading over and over again. *We regret to inform you that your son, Maximillian Myers....*

Mrs. Myers picked up the telegram, folded it neatly, and put it in her apron pocket.

Three weeks after news about Maxie hit the neighborhood, Harry Slovich ducked under a field tent to avoid the cold, slashing rain. He pulled two letters out of his fatigue jacket and sat down on a bench. He read the letter from Maxie Myers first. Dated January 14, 1952, it told about how much Maxie loved the tank corps, and, to Harry's surprise, Maxie said that he was thinking of making a career of the service "when this thing is over."

The second letter, dated a week later, was from Camille. She was briefer than she normally was, and her natural cheerfulness was missing.

Dear Harry,

I love you so much, and I wish I were there with you right now. How much you must be hurting after hearing that Maxie was killed in action on January 15! I know how close the two of you were. Oh, how I'll miss him. Please take care of yourself. Did I tell you how much I love you today?

Camille

Harry folded the letter in half, then opened it and began reading it again. Had he not just received a letter from his friend? Slowly, it dawned on him that Maxie's letter was one of the last he had written before he was killed. When Harry left the tent for his platoon, he didn't give a damn if the rain sliced him in half.

Back in the States, Camille began to understand the therapeutic value of work. She dug into a variety of tasks, hoping to ease the pain over Maxie's death and the letters that stopped coming from Harry. As the days wore on, she was leaving work later and later. She arrived home dead tired each night. There was a quiet "Hello, any mail today?" and a "No, sorry, honey." Maybe, at mama's persistence, she took some soup or a sandwich, then off to bed she went. Sometimes she would call Harry's mother to see if she had heard anything. No. No. Always No.

Then, after a restless night, it was time to get up for another long day of hard work and disappointment.

By the end of January, Camille still had not heard from Harry, and the strain was starting to show. The life was drained from her beautiful hazel eyes, and her dark brown hair, usually bright and shiny, fell dully on her shoulders. She didn't seem to care how she looked or what she wore. Her friends at work began to notice the change in her, and they stopped asking whether she had received any mail from Harry. Even her boss, Nate McDaniel, told her to take some time off. "You're working too damn hard. You're making us all look bad," he kidded her.

"I can't, I need this," she told him.

One night, coming home from work after another long day, she opened the door to find her mother, hands on hips, waiting for her. "There's someone for you in the front room," said mama, a big smile on her face.

"Who is it?" said Camille, ripping off her overcoat. Her heart was pounding.

"Old friend. Go see."

Hoping, praying, Camille ran into the front room. It was not Harry.

"I'm going to kill you, mama," cried Camille as she reached out and hugged Ben Stern.

"I told you old friend," mama shouted back.

For a long time, Camille and Ben stood holding each other.

"Some greeting!" said Ben, a handsome young man with laughing, charcoal eyes. "You'd think I just came back from Korea, instead of law school."

"So great to see you again, Ben," cried Camille.

"How long has it been, two years?"

"Seems like more," she responded. "You look great."

"So do you," he gleamed.

"Liar!" It felt good for her to laugh.

Over the next couple of weeks, Camille saw Ben several more times. They had dinner in a small ristorante near her job, and they met for a late-night snack at a

West Side diner. Most of the time, they just walked and talked, and when it got too cold they ducked into a cafe for coffee. She told him about Harry and how they fell in love and what they were planning together, before he joined the army with his best friend Maxie.

"But then poor Maxie was killed in action, and there followed this awful silence! I mean, nothing! It's been almost three months since anyone received a letter from Harry," she told Ben one Saturday afternoon as they watched the skaters at Rockefeller Center. Ben was a good listener, and Camille needed to talk, but he began to feel uneasy when she went back over some of the details, especially the part about the magical night at the dance.

"I have a feeling he's fine," said Ben finally. "He just needs time away from everyone, after what happened to Maxie. Maybe he even feels partly responsible."

"How so?"

"If he didn't join the army—you know—maybe Maxie wouldn't have joined."

"You think that's it?"

"I'm positive," he replied. "Do I know guilt or do I know guilt?"

She laughed.

"Hey, you'll see," he continued. "You'll hear from him soon, lucky stiff."

"Thanks, Ben. Thanks for the encouraging words. Now, tell me what's going on in your life."

Ever since his father sold the building that housed the Terranova family two years ago, Ben had been going to law school at Columbia. He was hoping to be a trial lawyer handling civil rights cases. He was a counselor last year at a summer camp in Upstate New York, where he met a young woman named Judy Castle, and they had been dating, on and off, since then. He was certain this mutual attraction would fade away, like all the others, but, he said, he's "not so sure now."

"What changed your mind?" Camille asked.

"You."

"Me?"

"Yeah, you," said Ben. "I guess you never knew I had a crush on you."

"Oh, Ben."

It was time for him to let it all out. "I came back to see you, to find out whether there was any chance, any chance at all, and there isn't, not for me, not now. I see this guy in Korea, who hasn't written to you in a while, looming large in your future."

"Oh, Ben, what can I say? You'll always be very special to me."

"Yeah, but not special enough."

Tears in her eyes, Camille reached out and threw her arms around him. They stood holding each other as the skaters swirled beneath them.

"I think I'd better go," he said.

"Call me, please," she pleaded quietly.

"I will, but not for a while," he said. "I'd better hit the books."

As she walked home, it was getting cold, and the light was starting to fade. The hope that was renewed by Ben's return in her life seemed to flicker, and she felt alone again. She could only imagine how Ben felt. Later, she felt the urge to call him, but she didn't. Instead, she pulled out some old letters from Harry and started reading them, and cried.

A week later, Camille got a letter. She was so excited she almost tore it apart before reading it. Sobbing uncontrollably, she ran into the toilet and closed the door. Mama stood guard outside to prevent any interruptions. The letter began:

Dear Camille,

Remember me? I hope you didn't forget me, because I haven't been writing. But I never forgot you. I'm sorry for not answering you sooner, but between the 12-hour guard shifts and the patrols, this war has kept me busy, and on top of everything I've been doing a lot of thinking, mostly about Maxie. When he died, part of me and my dreams died, too. He was a beautiful person, a great friend, and one funny guy.

The letter went on to recall how Harry and Maxie had planned to open their own pet store someday, but then Maxie had a change of heart when he joined the tank corps.

It surprised the hell out of me, but he loved the tank corps and he talked about making a career out of the service when this damn war is over. At least he died doing something he loved, but I'll never forgive myself for leading him into the service in the first place.

Camille thought about what Ben had said about the guilt Harry might be feeling. She continued reading the letter.

> *I know he'd want me to pursue something I love, too, but right now, I don't know what I'd like to do when this thing is over except to be with you.*
>
> *Again, please forgive me for not writing to you sooner. I had a lot on my mind, but I'm alright now. Stay well and say hello to everyone.*
>
> *Love, H.*

Camille looked for the familiar ending—*By the way, did I tell you how beautiful you are today?* It wasn't there. Then this news:

> *P.S. Look for me to come home in two months. I'll write with the details.*

Camille wanted to share the news with everyone. Mama's eyes filled with tears when she heard. On her way over to see Harry's mother she stopped by to see papa. "I am so happy for you," he beamed.

Mrs. Slovich was not one to show her emotions, but she started filling up when Camille told her. "About time," Harry's mother concluded. "We have no business being there. Sit down, my dear. Have a cup of tea." Camille, bursting with joy to tell the world, didn't have the heart to say no.

Harry Slovich came back from Korea, as he said he would. But he was not the same man who left more than a year earlier. A walking skeleton, he was more quiet and serious, and the sparkle in his eyes was gone. Camille noticed the change in him right away, but she made up her mind to be patient, not to say anything. After all, the man just came back from a war.

One day, Harry went out and bought a dog, a mixed breed with a heavy collie influence, which he called Max. Just like that! Camille was struck by how quickly he decided to buy the dog. She also wondered why he stopped talking about opening a pet store, or their plans for the future. Yes, she would just have to be patient. Time would heal his wounds, she thought.

Ben didn't call her.

Meanwhile, political events on the national scene were accelerating. First, President Truman did something that had the potential to change the course of history and the war. He announced he would not run for President again. Because the Constitutional amendment limiting the President to two terms was adopted during his time in office, he could have run for a third term, but he chose not to do that.

Stepping in as the Democratic Presidential candidate was Governor Adlai E. Stevenson of Illinois, an erudite, upright man who valiantly sought to make up in integrity what he lacked in charisma. The Republicans turned to the extremely popular Dwight D. Eisenhower, better known as Ike, the World War II Supreme Allied Commander and hero-general who pledged to "go to Korea" and, by implication, put an end to the war.

Overwhelmingly, Americans liked Ike and voted him into office. The result was a widespread feeling in the land that the new President would act decisively. In fact, despite an occasional foray here and there, both sides were getting sick of this war. On the morning of July 27, 1953, an agreement between the warring sides was signed, and the fighting stopped.

Christopher celebrated by sharing a bottle of beer with his friends on a roof overlooking Tenth Avenue. For Christopher, there was no better way to mark the occasion. He loved looking out over the city from the rooftop of a neighborhood building. Besides giving him a feeling of the energy and power of the city, he could sense the vastness of the world beyond Tenth Avenue, and in that vastness were limitless opportunities ready to be tapped. He knew in his heart that one of those opportunities—perhaps a nice, little place like papa's store—was waiting for him.

Looking over the edge of the building today, Christopher spotted Harry Slovich in the street below. Hunched over, with a vacant look in his pale, solemn face, Harry looked like a pitiful figure as he slowly walked his dog along the avenue. Christopher wondered why his old mentor had not stopped by the house lately. He took another long swallow of beer.

1968

CHAPTER 10

▼

Not far away, a fishing boat signaled its arrival with a long, loud blast of the horn. The noise woke Christopher, and he sat up from the stained, faded rug that had served as his bed. Opening his light brown eyes, he tried to figure out where he had slept the night. Gradually it came to him. He was in Cal's place in San Francisco. Christopher Terranova—Arturo's boy from the West Side in New York City—was doing something he vowed he would do 24 years ago when Christina died: He was living in California.

He looked around the room, a shabby reflection of its former Victorian middle-class self. The night before, this place was jammed with party-goers, rock music, strobe lights, and clouds of tobacco and marijuana smoke. It was all quiet now. Sleeping nearby on a love seat that had seen better days and nights were a man and a woman, a tangle of legs and arms and hair. In the corner, turning restlessly from side to side under a dark green, woolly blanket was a woman with long, braided hair. Christopher recognized her as the soulful-eyed one who had claimed her name was "Mary Magdalene." On a pullout bed was a lone figure in army fatigue pants who Christopher surmised was Cal, the tenant and party host.

A light bulb hung lifeless from the textured ceiling over a large, squat wooden table. On the table were empty bottles and glasses, the stub of a large patchouli candle, and some drug paraphernalia—remnants from the New Year's Eve party the night before, welcoming 1968. A cat moped in from the other room, stared at Christopher, and hopped on the bed. The boat horn blared again, and the cat hardly stirred.

Christopher tried to steady himself as he raised his thin frame from the floor and wobbled into the other room, which turned out to be the kitchen. On a wooden bench next to a long picnic table sat a bare-breasted woman nursing an infant. Christopher smiled weakly at her and headed for the sink.

"Bloody boats," moaned the woman in an English accent.

"Yeah." Christopher splashed some water from the kitchen sink on his face.

"Maybe we should do something."

"You mean organize a protest against boat horns?" he asked.

"Yes, why not?"

Looking up at the clock on the wall, he said, "It's 1:30 in the afternoon. Don't you think it's late enough for boats to blow horns?"

The woman took the infant from her breast. Then, with a little annoyance, she said, "I don't know about you. What's your name again?"

"We don't need to protest everything that moves. My name's Christopher. What's yours?" The baby burped.

"Good boy, Jason. I was christened Elizabeth. My friends call me Lace."

"Nice names, both of them—Jason, too." Christopher opened the refrigerator and searched for something to drink.

Cal entered the room. "Help yourself, man," he said hoarsely.

"Thanks…. Cal, right? A beer would be gr…groovy." Christopher couldn't believe he had said that. Although he was at the epicenter of the hippie world, the West Side native really didn't feel like a flower child. Of course, he was now firmly opposed to the war, and he went along with some of the trappings of the Age of Aquarius—the music, the open sex, and the drugs, or, more to his preference, the booze. But somehow he couldn't see himself in combat boots, with flowers in his hair, twirling peace signs in the air—not yet anyway. As for doe-eyed hippie gals with long, gauzy dresses dancing in the sun, no one from the neighborhood reminded him of them except the old woman with five dogs who lived in the basement on Forty-eighth Street.

A scream erupted from the other room. Cal and Christopher were almost tripped up by the cat when they sprang to see what was happening. The woman with the long, braided hair was shaking and picking at imaginary things on the dark green blanket. "Jesus, sweet Jesus!" she screeched.

Cal turned to Christopher. "Bad shit, bad trip. It's happening more and more."

"Give her some chamomile," the woman with the baby suggested. "It'll calm her down."

Shoeless, "Mary Magdalene" ran past everyone and out the door. She was screaming all the way down the stairs.

"That your friend?" Cal asked the couple on the love seat. "You better see if you can help her." They sat up quickly and started putting on their shoes.

Christopher thought it was a good time to leave, too. "Hey, thanks," he told Cal after gulping down the last of the beer. "Great party! Had a blast." He placed a wrinkled $10 bill on the kitchen table and walked toward the door. "Peace!"

Only six months before, Christopher had been sitting and watching television with his friend Jimmy D. in a gin mill on Ninth Avenue. Life was good. He was 28, military service—free of any armed conflict—was behind him, and he had a job, in the sampling department of a textile firm. Not bad for someone who survived a troubled adolescence with two petty theft charges and one charge of possession of stolen goods, all of which were dismissed, thanks to the savvy of a lawyer recommended by the local Democratic club.

So what if the textile sampling job was not one of the best positions in the city? It was a foot in the door, and he kept his expenses down by living with his parents on Fiftieth Street. While there was no sustained love interest in his life, he had occasional dates and one-night stands, sometimes with someone from work, sometimes with strangers. He never lost touch with his neighborhood pals, or whoever managed to escape the draft, regularly frequenting local gin mills.

If there was a persistent problem, it was that Christopher drank too much; only, he never admitted to it. His drinking, however, was a growing source of concern and irritation to his parents. Mama constantly urged him to find a nice girl and settle down, just like his brother Michael did when he married Jo, and Christopher would say, "I'm looking, mom, I'm looking."

Like so many Americans, Christopher had become transfixed by the scenes of young men, like himself, under fire and dying in the jungles of South Vietnam, that flashed on the TV screen night after night. In the summer of 1967, the war was escalating. American troops were ballooning to the 500,000 level, and the human and economic toll was reaching new heights. Students, teachers, Blacks, hippies, celebrities, and ordinary citizens all demonstrated against the war in growing numbers in big cities and small, and on campuses throughout the country.

At first, Christopher couldn't connect with the ragtag bands of war protesters who nightly marched, shouted, carried protest signs, burned draft cards, and even set American flags afire on the TV screen. Somehow, since he had completed his tour of military duty before the situation over there had worsened, he had felt out of it, like he had missed the big parade. He also couldn't help thinking how the GIs over there and former GIs felt about the war protests. *Are we dishonoring them? I wonder what Aunt Loretta-Loretta's son Sal, who wound up a prisoner of war in World War II, thinks when he sees the antiwar demonstrations? And what about Harry Slovich, who fought in the Korean War, and Maxie Myers, who paid the ultimate price?*

But the war, which had seemed so far away, was beginning to hit home with increasing ferocity. Christopher's old buddy, Falcon, was one of the early casualties: Dead by sniper fire near Pleiku. Falcon's brother, Roger, who had decided to make a career out of the Army was shelled near Da Nang. He was still recuperating in an army hospital. The latest casualty was Reggie Ryan, who some say had a chance to play pro hockey, perhaps for the New York Rangers. He was wounded badly near the demilitarized zone—the DMZ—and taken to Hue, where he was treated by Patricia Espinosa, Patsy to her friends, a nurse from the neighborhood. And so the stories went. Gradually, Christopher became more open to the antiwar movement.

It was the "summer of love" that finally pushed him over the edge. As he watched thousands gather in San Francisco's Haight-Ashbury for a summer of peace and brotherhood, along with some good times—sex, rock and roll, and drugs without parental oversight—Christopher made up his mind to go to California. When he told Michael about his plans, his brother tried to talk him out of going, but Christopher was unshakable.

Michael pleaded a strong, sensible case based on past experience. "Why do you need to go out there, Christopher? Do you really have to place yourself in harm's way? With all of those temptations, who'll be around to bail you out if you need help?"

Christopher took a position that seemed more in tune with the times. "Oh, come on, Michael. Why do you always have to be so cautious? Isn't this the Age of Aquarius, brother—a time for love, peace, brotherhood, and good times?"

Going to California was a dream long in the works for Christopher, and he was determined to make it happen now. More for the good times than anything else, Jimmy D. decided to go along with him.

So, one muggy summer morning, they left. Mama stood on the stoop watching until the '62 Corvair, which they bought for the trip, rode out of sight. Christopher saw mama fade out of his life through the rearview mirror.

About four weeks later, Christopher and Jimmy D. arrived in California, minus the Corvair, which had burned out somewhere in the desert. Each carrying one bag, they had hitchhiked the last leg of their trip.

Their first stop in California was Los Angeles. Jimmy D. decided to stay there rather than push on to San Francisco. He wanted to check out the job possibilities in the movies. Christopher went on to San Francisco according to the original plan.

When he arrived, he didn't come wearing flowers in his hair, as singer Scott McKenzie had suggested, but he was excited and optimistic. Over the next few months, both the excitement and the optimism began to fade. The realities of living in a big city without a permanent address, with only temporary work here and there, intruded on his plans to change the world and have a good time doing it. But he never stopped believing.

Now here it was the first day of the new year. Music was everywhere as Christopher left Cal's place and headed for Golden Gate Park. From some apartment, Aretha Franklin's rich, gospel voice was demanding "R-E-S-P-E-C-T." Further on, the Beatles were heard singing their anthem to the peace movement—"All You Need Is Love"—from a psychedelic store selling hippie paraphernalia. As he passed the store, Christopher was greeted by a man with a full face and head of hair. "Happy new year, brother." Christopher was startled by the greeting. He had forgotten it was New Year's Day. "Yeah, sure, peace, man!"

When he entered the park, Christopher could hear at least two bands playing in the afternoon sun. The closest was offering a heavy-handed version of "Light My Fire" by The Doors. Christopher listened briefly, then moved on. People were everywhere. Some were stretched out on the grass, apparently asleep, the acid haze of the night before hovering above their heads. A small coterie sat listening to a guru in Indian dress, with a sitar, expounding on the virtues of meditation.

A larger group milled around a folding table, preparing for yet another demonstration. Behind the table sat a graying woman in a frilly, cream-colored dress explaining the new march route. Near her was a huge, bearded man in army fatigues. Christopher recognized him as the man he had met the night before and learned was a phony Vietnam veteran now involved in organizing peace demonstrations.

Christopher sat under a tree and pulled a letter out of his back pocket. Since he didn't have a permanent address now, letters came infrequently. When they did come, they came through a friend of a friend who agreed to accept his mail while he was in the city. Once again, he read the letter from his sister Camille, lingering over the ending:

You really need to write or call mama and papa. They miss you so, as we all do. With the kids and all, I don't see them every day, but we visit them as much as we can. Papa hasn't been well. Doctor says it's his blood pressure.

We're trying to convince him to retire and take a nice vacation to Italy with mama, but so far he just laughs and says, "Who will take care of my customers?"

Imagine that? He closed his store last year and took a job as the produce manager of the local supermarket, and he's still thinking of his customers.

Anyway, little brother, I think of you constantly. You remember how we used to fight all the time when we were kids? I never stopped loving you, and worrying about you. Take care of yourself, and don't forget to write.

Love,

Camille

Christopher folded the letter carefully and put it back in his pocket. He leaned against the tree and closed his eyes. The air was heavy with the burnt-rope smell of pot, but he caught a whiff of something sweet like perfume or incense.

A shadow crossed his eyes. He opened them to see a tall, thin woman standing over him. "You never know who you'll meet in the park these days," she commented before flopping down next to him. She kissed him on the cheek. "Happy New Year!"

"Same to you, Carol," he said, returning the kiss. "Missed you last night."

"I was there, you weren't," she said with mock seriousness. "You checked out early."

"Sorry about that," moaned Christopher.

Dark circles under her light blue eyes betrayed a heavy night of partying. She lit up a long cigarette and blew out a cloud of smoke and coughed. "I stayed up as long as I could. This guy kept bugging me about going fishing with him. I finally had to tell him I don't fish on New Year's for ecological reasons. He was puzzled by that, but I think he got the message. I don't know what time it was when I decided to go home and call my folks back East."

Carol Decker was from New Jersey. Her father had a real estate business waiting for her when she left Rutgers last year, but, straight out of school, she went to California to join the peace movement. A magna cum laude graduate, she became convinced that Vietnam was the wrong war at the wrong time in the wrong place and was sapping the country's youth. Friendly and easygoing, with a devilish sense of humor, Carol was one of the first people Christopher met when he arrived in Haight-Ashbury. Since they had lived in neighboring states back East, they became close friends, like brother and sister. Once in a while, he even slept in her small apartment, which she shared with two women.

"And how's everything back in Jersey?" he asked.

"As advertised. Everyone's mad as hell at me, but they were glad to hear from me. My father wants to retire and move to New Mexico with his new wife. My mother, who lives a few blocks away in our old house, says she met a nice man in the supermarket. They have a date to go shopping together next week. My kid brother David is against both relationships."

"And you?"

Carol took another drag on her cigarette. "I say, let it be. Bless them all—the long, the short, and the tall."

Christopher laughed.

"And what about you?" she continued. "How many times are you going to read that letter? When are you going to call home?"

He got up off the ground awkwardly and dusted the back of his pants. "You're getting to sound like my mom every day. I think they're ready to go. You marching today?"

"No, I'm dead."

"This'll be my fourth march this week."

"I lost count."

"Do you think they make a difference—the demonstrations I mean?" He really didn't expect her to answer.

"Drop by my place when you're finished. We're having spaghetti, a *Cucina Decker* specialty." She smiled and kissed him again. She looked so tired and fragile as she walked away.

"You bet. Save some for me." He loved that girl. What would he do without her?

The protest march down Geary Street served notice that the peace movement would continue into the new year, but it was a more quiet demonstration than usual. The signs said it all. "Make love, not war!" "Get out of Vietnam now!" "Peace on earth!" The marchers ended up in Union Square, where a real Vietnam vet urged government leaders to end the war now. Christopher listened, cheered appropriately, and, when the march broke up, headed anxiously toward Carol's apartment.

He suddenly realized he hadn't eaten anything all day, and Carol Decker made some of the best pasta sauce west of the Mississippi. Christopher picked up the pace. As he did, he heard fire engines wailing somewhere in the city. The closer he came to Carol's place, the louder they became, and the faster he walked.

When he reached Clayton Street, puffs of white smoke were still billowing out of the upper floor apartment where Carol lived. Christopher rushed up to the front door, but he was stopped from entering by a police officer. "Can't go in there now," said the policeman. "It's not safe yet." He motioned Christopher over to a police barricade, where he spotted Carol's two roommates holding each other and crying. When he walked over to them, they reached out and hugged him, trembling with grief.

Diane tried to explain. "Carol fell asleep smoking. That's what the police said. The cigarette fell out of her hand and into a waste basket. When the firemen came, the apartment was full of smoke. Carol was still in the bed. They managed to get her out of there, but...."

"It was too late," Rita added. "They took her to the morgue. Fortunately, the fire didn't spread to any other apartment."

"No one else was hurt," Diane continued.

Rita picked up the story. "The fire engines were already here when we both came home from work. You should have seen the smoke pouring out of the window. They did a great job containing the fire."

"No one else was hurt," Diane repeated.

"I don't know what we'll do tonight," Rita said.

"I was just talking to her this afternoon," Diane added.

"So was I," said Christopher.

He walked away. He felt like he was being sucked into a dark chasm he had only a faint memory of descending into a long time ago. He longed for something that once had been a part of him, and then was ripped away. There was that terrible loneliness and fear again, and the deep sadness. *For Christ's sake, she was like a sister to me.*

CHAPTER 11

▼

It was called "the war unlike any other war," but in many ways it was like all of them. There were tactics, both offensive and defensive. Opposing armies attacked and counterattacked. There were major battles and small skirmishes. Among the many heroic deeds, there were acts of cowardice. The casualties continued to climb each year as the number of troops increased. On the American side alone, for example, there were 1,350 killed and 5,300 wounded in 1965, when the U.S. started the big buildup and committed 180,000 troops to Vietnam. Two years later, when American troop strength reached 500,000, 9,353 were killed and 99,742 wounded.

If there was one factor that separated Vietnam from other wars, it was the volume of antiwar sentiment surrounding it. As wars go, World War II was a popular war. There were plenty of good reasons to be in it, although that was not what anyone would want to tell the troops engaged in some of the bloodiest battles in Europe and the Pacific. Korea was not a popular war in the U.S., coming so soon after World War II. Called the Forgotten War, it was a quiet war by comparison to what came before and after it, finally reaching a stalemated conclusion. Vietnam was the noisiest. Wrapped in a message of love and peace, the drumbeat against America's involvement grew louder and louder and, while annoying to many, won over increasing numbers of supporters as the war continued.

At the end of 1967, polls continued to show that the majority of Americans stood by U.S. military actions to stop the spread of Communism in Vietnam. Against the backdrop of compelling, daily TV reports from the front, however, the protesters were being heard, and felt. And on January 30, 1968—as Vietnamese revelers took to the streets in towns and cities to celebrate Tet, the lunar new year—close to 70,000 Viet Cong and North Vietnamese troops attacked seven major cities and 30 provincial capitals across South Vietnam, even breaking onto the grounds of the American embassy in Saigon. The attack on the embassy was quickly repelled by a platoon of American airborne troops, and so were the attacks throughout South Vietnam.

Nevertheless, the Tet offensive hit home with devastating impact. After being told that the countryside in South Vietnam had been secured, Americans were stunned by the enemy's show of force. By the end of March, President Lyndon Johnson replaced General William C. Westmoreland as commander of U.S. troops in Vietnam, announced his intention not to run for re-election, and ordered a halt to air and naval bombardments except in the DMZ. Like so many other Americans, the Terranovas—from the top of the family on down—were torn apart by the war.

Anna Terranova saw no room for war, ever. Her abhorrence of armed conflict was personal and went back a long way, to when she was little Anna Rubino in her small village in Bari. She remembered the day it actually began. Her oldest brother Christopho came in from the field, hitched old Marti the donkey to a post, packed a few things, including some figs and pears, in a satchel, and left to fight the Germans. This being the height of the picking season, mama and papa never came in from the field to see their boy off. Years later, Anna remembered running after her brother, crying uncontrollably, as he faded out of sight. He never came back.

Christopho's decision to leave the village was the first great tear in the family fabric that had remained basically intact for generations. When he was mowed down by machine gun fire in one of the last, senseless battles of the war, his death set off a series of disruptions in the Rubino household.

First, after the Armistice was declared, Anna's brother Pietro emigrated to America in search of better economic opportunities. Following him six months later was Rafaello, who became Ralphie in his adopted country. Two years later, when the brothers were settled in New York City, they asked Loretta to join them. She eventually did. Anna, who was very close to her older sister, was the next to emigrate. Young Giovanni thought about it many times, but decided to stay. Mama and papa never quite recovered from the breakup of their family, but there was a sense of pride mingled with sadness as they watched their children leave and begin their journey to America.

Now, as 1968 began, Anna felt fortunate. There had been a couple of major scares on the Cold War stage, such as the Berlin blockade and the Cuban missile crisis, but Michael and Christopher had managed to escape hot wars. Still, Anna didn't stop worrying about her boys or the other children from the neighborhood. Whenever she met someone she knew with a son, or daughter, in Vietnam, she promised with a pat on the arm, "I say novena."

With her ingrained hate and fear of war, Anna quietly came to support the Vietnam protesters, no matter how caustic or crude they could get, but she wouldn't allow herself to openly side with the demonstrators. She watched and listened to the news and wondered. It was just too big a leap for her to think that these young protesters could change the course of history.

Occasionally, Arturo would meet an old customer who didn't know he had closed his store, and once again he'd have to explain why he was now the produce manager of the local supermarket.

"Bum checks," Arturo told Mr. Kagan, a neighborhood realtor, one day. "You would not believe how many nice people have such bad checks."

"That's too bad, Mr. Terranova. You took such pride," said Mr. Kagan.

Arturo shrugged. "Eh, what can I say? This job, is not so bad. It is steady. It is inside work. No one bothers me. And I have no worries about the bad checks anymore. You know what I say?"

"Sure, that must be a good feeling," Mr. Kagan agreed. "But if you're ever looking for a new location for a store, just let me know."

Arturo laughed. "You think I would open another store? No, no, I am too old, but thanks for obliging me with such a nice offer. I keep in mind, Mr. Kagan." He laughed again. Something didn't ring true in his laughter.

Truth was, nearing 65, Arturo hardly ever stopped thinking of opening another store in the neighborhood. Buried deep in his heart, it was something he kept hidden from everyone except Anna. The key to making it happen was Christopher, not Michael. Michael was already settled in his publishing career. Christopher could be involved, as a partner, from the start, and when Arturo was through working, it would all pass on to his youngest son, or so Arturo thought. Christopher, however, appeared to have other plans.

For the life of him, Arturo could not understand why his son would want to leave a nice home and a good job—and, of course, his family and friends—and go all the way to California and march with those damn hippie people against the war. As far as Arturo was concerned, if the President and his advisors think we should be in Vietnam, then, like good, patriotic Americans, we should be behind them. *Tet offensive or not, we must be supportive and strong.*

Arturo also knew, firsthand, the importance of backing the soldier in battle. In the first Great War, he was merely a teenager, but he managed to follow his father to the front and to become an ambulance driver. One morning, he stopped to pick up two wounded soldiers, one of whom turned out to be his father. When Arturo saw his father, he started to cry, but behind cold, almost lifeless eyes his father reprimanded him. *"Sei uno soldato e uno uomo."* In other words, be a soldier and be a man. Arturo never forgot that message.

After the war, Arturo, an only child, took over most of the chores around the family's small farm. Never fully recovered from his wounds, his father died about a year after the Armistice was declared. Not long afterwards, Arturo and his mother decided to set sail for the United States.

The long voyage over a hostile ocean to an unknown future was racked with fear, but once the Terranovas landed, they were eager to establish roots in their new land. Despite running up against some ugly bias and hostility from time to time in America, Arturo tried to blend in with his new country and compatriots. At the same time, he tried to stay close to the people from the old province who shared the same heritage and language. Through personal, physical, and economic hardship, he worked hard to be a good American, and, here in 1968, he wasn't about to lose what took him so long to accomplish. *Loyalty to country is* Numero Uno.

Arturo and Anna each knew and respected where the other one stood on Vietnam. For peace in the family, they tried to avoid confrontation. It wasn't easy. Occasionally, after watching the news, they couldn't help but argue, sometimes heatedly, usually in two languages. After the President announced in March that he would not run again, they stopped watching the news at night and started going to bed earlier. Better that way. Less aggravating. It was a lesson Michael and his wife Jo might have been persuaded to consider before it was too late.

At first, Michael really believed that the Vietnam war was justified to stop the spread of Communism, and, like his father, he found it difficult to take a stand against the President. To him, that was a form of betrayal to the country and the troops. But as a young professional making his way in New York City, he heard the arguments against America's involvement, and they were starting to make sense to him. So, after a while, rather than voice his opinion in support of the Administration in Washington, he thought it best not to say anything.

One of the so-called silent majority, he continued to support America's efforts in Vietnam to contain Communism, but he was less vocal about his views than he had been. His focus was turned almost entirely on his family and his job, rather than changing the world. Michael also loved his uptown apartment overlooking the Hudson River and nothing made him happier than when the family was together there. But getting everyone in one place at the same time was becoming increasingly difficult to do. Michael traveled frequently and often worked late. His wife, too, was constantly on the run.

Jo always had strong opinions about the world, the country, and the political process, which became even more intense after President John Kennedy was assassinated in 1963. Then, when the country began boosting its troop strength in Vietnam under President Johnson and when two of her brothers were enlisted to fight there, Jo became immersed in the peace movement. A dedicated member of an antiwar organization from Greenwich Village with a growing agenda, she organized rallies against the war with other groups throughout the area.

After Martin Luther King was murdered in April 1968, she also became engaged in campaigns to promote civil rights. And, with the assassination of Senator Robert Kennedy in June, she attacked a political process that was about to nominate Presidential candidates she could not support, rallying behind peace candidate Senator Eugene McCarthy. At the same time, she continued her antiwar marches and other activities, which became a growing source of tension between her and Michael.

As a substitute teacher during the day and an antiwar organizer, political activist, and civil rights proponent whenever she could fit it in, Jo spent much of her time away from the family. And, if she were to go back to teaching, full-time, as she planned to do, she would be spending even less time with Michael and John. But what could she do? Her causes, all of them, were too important to her and to the world.

CHAPTER 12

▼

Huddled across the street from his son John's school, Michael wondered if the sun would ever show itself again. It had been raining on and off for the past four days. And now here it was Friday afternoon—a week before the end of the school year—and it looked like the rain might continue through the weekend. Michael had so hoped they could do something together as a family, such as go to the Bronx Zoo. *If there's a God, this rain will stop. This family really needs time together.*

Michael leaned back as close to the building as he could without crushing his large, black umbrella. When another class, but not John's, was dismissed from school he sighed for the umpteenth time. *Where the hell is 1C?* Something told him to be patient. Think positive.

Against the steady patter of the rain above him, his thoughts turned to a happier time when the sun was shining. Jo was 17, he was 18. They were sitting on the beach at Brighton Beach one late afternoon in August. Michael was trying to read *Crime and Punishment,* and Jo, behind enormous sunglasses that screamed for attention, was staring out into the ocean. It seemed that every time Michael read a few sentences, some muscle-bound colossus would kick sand in his direction. After the fourth sand-kicker went by, Michael turned to Jo and said, "I'm no Charles Atlas, but if one more guy kicks sand in my face, I'm going to start kicking…."

Jo laughed. "My hero!"

"I mean I've been on this one page for the past hour."

Jo laughed again.

"What's so funny?" he asked, puzzled by the source of her humor.

Jo got up and started brushing the sand off her bathing suit. "They're not kicking sand at you." With that, she headed toward the water. "I'm going in for one last dip."

Michael watched as this lithe figure walked into the sea, her smooth, round hips swaying gently in the sun. Nearby, two of the colossuses were also watching. This may have been the first time Michael realized that Jo was moving out of the pretty, but awkward, teenage stage and becoming a beautiful, young woman with her own personality and style. Michael decided that Dostoievsky could wait. He closed the book and went in for one more dip, too.

From then on, Michael and Jo were always together, or so it seemed. Even when they went to New York University—he in pursuit of an English degree, she as a political science major with an eye to becoming a teacher—they managed to take a few classes together. One teacher thought they were married and offered to rent them his cottage in Cape Cod. When they told him they were just good friends, he said, "Well, do you want to rent it anyway?"

Outside John's school, a taxi went by and splashed water across Michael's pants. He gave a futile "Hey!" to the driver and remembered that it was raining that day, too, when he and Jo were married. Piercing rain. Drenching rain. Unrelenting rain. When the couple met at the altar to exchange vows, they were dripping wet and worried. What next? They anticipated the worst for the rest of the day, but they were filled with love and hope for their future. Father Corrigan joked at the end of the ceremony about how he should have added another line to the wedding vows—"for wetter or dryer"—and everyone clapped and laughed as the couple made their way down the aisle. Outside the church, no one stayed around long enough to throw rice or take pictures. They all scattered, many beating it to the wedding banquet. When the band from New Jersey didn't show up because of flooding, Jo's father found a local band to take its place. Halfway through the reception, the band from New Jersey arrived and started playing alongside the other group. In the end, a fun time was had by all, or most, including Michael and Jo, who earlier in the day sensed a disaster in the making. They were thrilled when so many guests told them that theirs was the best wedding they ever attended, whether it was true or not. For a long time after that, Michael and Jo enjoyed talking about "their wedding from hell."

In the early years, Michael and Jo shared many happy and proud moments. Among the most memorable were Jo's first teaching assignment, Michael's various promotions at the publishing house, and, of course, the birth of their son John—their crowning achievement who arrived four years into their marriage. Although both Michael and Jo led active lives, they managed to find the humor in their life experiences which they loved to share at the end of a long day. Many of those experiences had to do with John's accomplishments—his first step, his first word, his first tooth, his first real food, his first potty contribution, his first anything.

So, how did it happen? Michael asked himself as he waited for five-year-old John to come out of school. When did the fun and laughter stop? How did Michael and Jo start drifting apart and into different worlds? More and more, he blamed it on the war.

Finally, Michael recognized Mrs. Gomez, John's first-grade teacher, and he charged across the street with more than a dozen other umbrella carriers.

John seemed surprised when he saw his father. "Dad, dad, what're you doing here?"

"Your mom asked me to pick you up today. Okay?"

"It's okay. Where's mom?"

"Mom has a meeting this afternoon. They're planning a big antiwar march on Wall Street next week. Didn't she tell you?"

"Oh, yeah, I forgot. Mrs. Gomez talked about protest marches today. Mom's really upset about the war, isn't she?"

"Sure is, isn't everyone?" Michael said. It started to come down hard again. "Stay under the umbrella before you get soaked, John. I'll try to hail a cab."

"A cab? Where're we going?"

"Oh, surprise," Michael replied. "You're going to grandma's for dinner. Friday at Terranovas, how's that?"

"Wow, that's great. What about you, dad? Are you going back to work?"

"No. Luckily, I was able to get out early today."

Actually, luck had little to do with it. His annual budget numbers were submitted to his company, on time, as usual, and they were excellent. What's more, as editor of a group of professional and trade magazines, he enjoyed some flexibility that enabled him to handle a personal matter during business hours, whether it be to pick up a son at school or to save a marriage.

The apartment on Fiftieth Street was exploding with delicious culinary smells when Michael and John arrived. Mama had made foods they both liked—*maccheroni e spinaci* flavored with olive oil and garlic; breaded fried jumbo shrimp; and *focaccia barese,* the one-inch-thick kind you could eat hot or cold. On a side table was a Parcheesi game and a deck of cards, for later, and a new toy jumbo jet. Grandma knew that the boy, named for her youngest brother who did not emigrate to America, loved airplanes.

John could see that mama was excited when she opened the door and welcomed them.

"Well, look who is here, for Pete sake," Anna gushed.

"My name is John," said the boy, trying to set the record straight.

"I know, I know," said Anna. "You think I do not know?"

"You said Pete."

Anna and Michael laughed. She tried to explain "That is just a…how do you say, Michael?"

Her son came to the rescue. "An expression…. Give grandma a nice hug."

"Oh, I am so happy you come visit me, John. Pretty soon, I see you all the time."

The plan was for John to stay with grandma during the day while Jo taught summer school. Anna was looking forward to her summer visitor.

"You want to see what I made in school today?"

"Sure."

He handed her a coloring of an American flag. "My mama's at a meeting. She marches against the war, grandma."

"I know, I know, John," said Anna. "Your mother does important work." For a moment, her eyes met Michael's, then they backed away from each other.

"When's papa coming home?" asked Michael.

It kept raining, occasionally pouring, all evening. After dinner, they played Parcheesi—grandpa, too—and later settled down to watching TV in the dining room. A boomer broke the silence, briefly rousing John, who had fallen asleep on the couch.

"Well, I think I go to bed," said Arturo. "Another early day tomorrow."

Michael got up from the end of the couch. "I think we better head home."

"Don't be silly," said Anna. "Leave the boy here tonight. This is Friday. You pick him up tomorrow."

Michael got up, stretched, and yawned. "I don't know, mama. Jo will be expecting him home tonight."

"Is raining hard," Anna argued. "Where will you find a taxi now?"

"Yes, let the boy stay," Arturo agreed.

"Okay. I think you're right." Michael gently kissed John, then his parents. Before leaving, he couldn't help glancing once more into the front room. It was turning dark, but the old vision was as discernible as when he first saw it. There was mama, leaning over the coffin, combing Christina's hair and straightening her clothes, while Aunt Loretta-Loretta, hands on hips, pleaded for her sister to come to bed. *Did that really happen? It was so long ago.*

"Goodnight, mama. Goodnight, papa."

When Michael got home, the apartment was in darkness except for a small lamp Jo kept lit in the foyer. He headed straight for it, clicked it off, and began turning on ceiling lights throughout the apartment. There was something comforting to him about light. Michael opened the refrigerator, bypassed a bottle of half-filled Chablis, and selected a can of low-cal cream soda. Flopping down on the couch near the window in the living room, he drank his soda slowly and waited. The rain cast a glassy curtain over the scene outside, but Michael was able to make out the lights of a tugboat chugging down river.

He leaned back in the chair. His mind drifted back to his days growing up on Fiftieth Street. Christina had recently died, and they were all there—Camille, Christopher, Michael, and, of course, mama and papa. *We were always together. Through good times and bad. It was our source of strength, our foundation as a family. What happened to that closeness in families?*

His eyes were starting to close when he heard the front-door latch turning, followed by several clicks. Jo was home. Entering the apartment, she started undoing everything Michael had done She snapped on the small lamp in the foyer and began turning off the ceiling lights in the other rooms. When she saw that John wasn't in his bed, she was surprised and went looking for him. Clutching a bundle of flyers under one arm, Jo entered the living room. Michael was sitting at the edge of his chair.

"He's not here," he explained, catching the fear in Jo's eyes. "He's alright," he continued. "He's staying overnight with my parents. It got late, and he fell asleep, and with the rain coming down so hard, I thought it best he stay there. He'll be fine."

"I know, I know." said Jo. "It's just that I wanted to take him downtown to the office with me first thing in the morning."

"I was thinking we could all go to the Bronx Zoo," said Michael.

Jo decided not to seek a resolution to that conflict now. "What are you doing up?" she sighed, plopping herself and her things down on a nearby couch.

"Waiting for you," he replied. "We need to talk."

"Oh, Michael, please, not now. It's been a long day, and it's not over yet. I have to change the date of the march on all of these flyers."

"I'm sorry for you, Jo, but we've got to talk," said Michael.

"Can't it wait?"

"No."

"Talk."

Now that he had the front stage, he didn't know how to begin. "What's happening to us?" he finally said. Jo sensed that he was heading down a familiar path, and she started shaking her head.

"Please! Give me a chance," he continued.

"Go ahead."

He went on, "It's like we're living in two different worlds, and John is somewhere in the middle, between us. I mean I hate this damn war, too...."

"If you're asking me to give up the downtown group, I can't," she jumped in, rising from the chair. "I'm too involved. It's too important. If you haven't noticed, this country is coming apart at the seams."

"But do you have to be the one to put it together?"

"Why do *you* do what *you* have to do?" she replied. "Come on, Michael. I'm not alone in this. There are a lot of people out there like me. Why don't you try to get involved?"

"I am involved. I'm involved in living. I'm involved in my family. I'm involved in my work."

"Oh, come on, Michael. It's a big world out there."

Michael fell silent for a moment. "What about John and me? What do we do while you're organizing marches down Wall Street?"

Jo drew in a deep breath. "My family is the reason I'm marching down Wall Street."

Michael shook his head in frustration and stretched out on the couch. He knew this would be where he would be sleeping tonight. "Don't mind my Tenth Avenue, but that's bullshit."

Jo snapped the light off as she left the room. She needed to take a shower before tackling the flyers.

CHAPTER 13

▼

This was the good life, and Camille knew it. It came with being Mrs. Ben Stern, and she was only now starting to enjoy it. Nevertheless, she still felt a twinge of guilt whenever she excused herself from her many household and community activities, as she was doing this August afternoon. As many times as she read and reread the opening of this new book, she just couldn't get into it. Finally, she put it down on the little glass-topped table and sighed.

From her cushiony lawn chair on the cedar deck, Camille watched her two-year-old twins, David and Jeffrey, playing in the shallow pool that Ben had set up on the lush, manicured lawn behind their suburban New Jersey home. On a nearby lawn chair, her ten-year-old daughter Loretta was slapping away at a mosquito on her leg. When it seemed to be a lost cause, the girl got up from the chair and flopped down in the narrow pool between the twins.

"Jeffrey, stop splashing," whined Loretta.

Jeffrey turned, saw Loretta, and after a brief stoppage resumed his watery slam-dunks, causing David to retaliate.

"MOM!" Loretta pleaded for intervention.

"Stop splashing, boys." They did.

"When are we going to get a grown-up pool?" Loretta asked. "We have room."

"Your father wants to wait until the twins get older," Camille explained.

"Jennie Lewis just got one."

"Good for Jennie. She has no younger brothers or sisters," her mother said.

"Oh, come on, mom."

"Who knows?" Camille confided. "Someday, maybe we'll move into a bigger house with a pool already built into the ground."

"When? Christmas?"

Camille ignored the comment.

The sun hid behind the clouds and a breeze crept in from the northeast. Camille looked up at a tall spruce gently swaying over the rambling flower bed at the edge of the lawn. She wondered how long it had been standing there. *Maybe it will be selected someday to be the Christmas tree overlooking the Rockefeller Center skating rink in New York City.*

Camille often thought of the city, and the people she left there, especially her parents, who still lived in the building on Fiftieth Street. They presided over their five-room apartment as if nothing had changed since they moved in nearly 25 years ago. Camille and Ben visited them whenever they could, and she was glad Michael and Jo lived nearby in case of emergency. Meanwhile, the old neighborhood was changing. Young families, Latinos, the upwardly mobile, and others brought new life to the area, but drugs and new, more violent criminal elements, along with pockets of poverty, were slowing the progress.

Most of her friends were out on Long Island now, or in New Jersey, but some of them remained in the neighborhood, many in high-rises that sprang up on Tenth and Eleventh Avenues. Dottie Wood had an apartment in one of them. And there was, of course, Harry. He was still living in his old apartment. His mother had died. So did Maxie the dog, but Harry had two new dogs now and a cat, and once in a while he would treat Dottie to dinner in a local Italian restaurant at Forty-sixth Street and Ninth Avenue. Camille, who stayed in touch with Dottie, knew all about that, and any other important neighborhood change.

Camille had long ago come to the terms with what happened with Harry, but she couldn't help thinking of him, her first great love, from time to time. There they were, a couple on the verge of getting married when he went away to Korea. Then something happened. Camille knew something was wrong when Harry came home. He wasn't the same person she kissed that night in the front room before he left for boot camp. The sparkle in his beautiful blue eyes was missing, and there was a sadness about him he couldn't seem to shake.

Camille had thought he needed more time to readjust to civilian life. Six months passed. Almost a year. She tried to talk about their future together, as they had done so many times before, but he would just say, "Yeah, that would be nice," and change the subject. Then, just like that, it was over. Camille remembered the day it happened. She had just come home from work when her mother told her that "someone" was waiting for her in the front room.

"Is it Ben?" she asked, strangely aglow with anticipation.

"No," said mama, "what do you think? It's Harry. I told him to play some records."

Camille peeled off her coat and kicked off her shoes as she headed for the front room. The sweet sounds of "Glow Worm" grew louder and louder.

"Oh, I see you found it," she said, kissing him gently on the lips. She was referring to the record by the Mills Brothers, one of Harry's favorites.

"Yeah, great song."

She picked up a slight tremor in his voice. "You okay?"

"Yeah sure," he replied.

"I didn't hear from you all day."

"I have some news," he went on. Then, after a slight pause, he added, "I got a job, in the city Sanitation Department."

She didn't know he was interested in that line of work. "Oh."

"It's a good job," he continued. "Good benefits. Pension. Security and all that stuff."

Camille tried to smile but couldn't. She even found it difficult looking him straight in the eyes. "What about your dream of opening a pet shop?" she finally said.

"That's gone…dead," he replied dully. "I left it on a hill in Korea."

She could feel the terrible fear welling up from the core of her being. "And what about our dream of making a life together?"

"There is no one I love, or will ever love, more than you, Camille," he said sadly, "but I left that dream in Korea, too."

Camille could no longer hold back the tears and reached out to throw her arms around him.

"Please, please, Camille," he said, picking up his jacket from the sofa. "I think I better go." He paused before he said what he said next. "I think it's better we don't see each other anymore. I'm sorry." With that, he put on his jacket and walked out of her life. Just like that.

It was as if she was struck by a train, but, miraculously, was still alive. Inconsolable at first, Camille became immobilized. She couldn't get out of bed. She couldn't dress. She couldn't eat. She couldn't go back to work. Her mother tried everything to console her and lift her spirits. "It is the war, that lousy war, not you," mama explained. "It take the life out of him." Very gradually Camille came to agree, and she went back to work and started seeing a few close friends like Dottie Wood. In the meantime, her mother kept urging her to call Ben. "Have cup of coffee, talk, laugh. He is good friend." She would have none of it. As it turned out, Ben called her—not once or twice, but three times. Finally, she agreed to meet him.

By then, Ben had broken up with Judy Castle, and he was just beginning his law practice. When they met, once again Ben did most of the listening as she rambled on about Harry. Until one night they found themselves in a little restaurant near where she worked.

"Enough, enough already about Harry," said Ben. "Remember this place?"

"Yes, yes I do," she answered, almost surprised that she did. "It's the place we used to meet when I didn't hear from Harry during the war."

"Now *there's* progress. Finally, a 'we'—you and me."

"What do you mean?"

"I mean it's not all about Harry. It's nice we share some things in common, too," he replied. "You know how I've always felt about you. I'm really very fond of you, Camille." She started getting nervous.

"Don't worry," he continued. "I'm not going to make a scene and knock over the linguini, or anything like that."

She looked into his dark eyes to see if he was kidding. "You're my friend, Ben. You'll always be my friend."

"I want to be more than your friend," he said.

She started moving her salad aimlessly around with her fork. "I need time."

"How's three months?" he concluded. She smiled. "Case closed. Now let's eat."

Within a year they were married. It was the first mixed marriage outside the Terranova and Rubino families. Anna liked Ben, always did, and she knew that in time the rest of the family would like him, too. Papa was delighted with his son-in-law, the lawyer.

The phone rang, and Camille was back to August 1968. "Watch the boys," she told Loretta as she dashed into the house.

"Hello."

"Hi, it's me."

"Oh, Ben. You coming home?"

"Yes, but I'm going right out. I'm going to Chicago. I'm sure there are some people out there who need a lawyer who knows something about civil liberties." He was referring to the demonstrators who converged on the Democratic Party's national convention to protest the war, racism, and the political system. Some of the demonstrators threw rocks, and many of them were beaten and jailed by the Chicago police in front of an international TV audience.

"Oh, Ben, please, don't go," Camille pleaded. "It's a mess out there."

"I can't just sit here while all that…is going on."

She recalled the television pictures of demonstrators being roughed up as they were hustled into patrol wagons. "We saw it—the violence in the streets. It was unbelievable. Please, honey, you might get hurt, or worse."

Ben paused. "Those people, the demonstrators, need the kind of help I can provide."

Camille knew he wasn't about to change his mind. "What do you want me to do?"

"You know my small carry-on bag. Put my blue suit in it, and my blazer, a couple of shirts, and some underwear. My flight out of Newark doesn't give me much time. Sorry, Camille."

"I know. I hope you have enough time to eat something."

The boys were still splashing, and Loretta was slapping mosquitoes off her legs in the lawn chair when Camille returned to the deck and announced, "Come on, boys, out of the pool, into the shower." Loretta looked to her mother to explain why the pool was closed. There was still some sun left in the afternoon. "Your father's going away tonight," Camille said. "We're going to have dinner together before he goes."

Streaks of light poured through the spruce as the sun prepared to make its last stand in the west. Camille looked around once more before heading into the house. *How do you explain it? So much peace and beauty here, and out there, in Vietnam and Chicago and so many other places, the world is exploding with violence. God help him.*

When Ben got home, there wasn't much time for anything more than a tuna sandwich and a glass of white wine. Jacket and briefcase in one hand and carry-on in the other, he kissed everyone goodbye before dashing for the cab that would take him to the airport. At the end of the driveway, he turned and looked at Camille. "Don't worry. I'll be back in a couple of days."

In fact, it was almost three weeks before he returned. He was hell-bent on helping the battered demonstrators any way he could. He came back more committed than ever to ending that damn war.

CHAPTER 14

▼

Christopher seemed less committed to the peace movement after Carol Decker died. He went on a few marches, but his heart didn't seem to be in them. Steve Wylie, one of the march organizers, noticed and decided to have a talk with him after one of the demonstrations. "Hey, man, I know you're hurtin'," he told Christopher. "She was a great gal. Why don't you go off on your own and take some time to get it together? If you need some space, you can stay with me."

Strange, how people we hardly know feel for us and we don't even know it. Up to that time, Christopher hadn't said two words to Steve, who some marchers secretly referred to as Boss Wylie. Steve, a native of Chicago who had moved to San Francisco to pursue a gay lifestyle, was a taskmaster, always making demands, calling for volunteers, encouraging the troops.

"Thanks, Steve," said Christopher. "I just might take you up on that offer." He did. After moving into Wylie's place, Christopher moped around the apartment for a while. When he got bored, he ventured out and drifted around the city, finally applying for a job on a fishing boat, which he landed on the strength of his limited boating experience in Sheepshead Bay, Brooklyn.

Over the next couple of months, life settled into a rhythm that Christopher accepted as normal. He fished all morning, drank all afternoon, and slept all night. Once when he was out to sea, he caught his foot in some rope and nearly fell overboard. Another time, high seas sent him crashing into the bow, wrenching his neck. "Rookie mistakes," said the captain. Christopher's answer to these incidents was that he needed a drink.

Once again Steve Wylie intervened. "You gotta stop this now. You're killin' yourself," he told Christopher one afternoon. "I'm no psychologist, but I think you have a drinking problem. Tell me to jump off the Golden Gate Bridge if you like, but you need help. Maybe it's time you went home, know what I'm sayin'?"

"If you want me to get out, just say so," said Christopher.

Steve sighed, blew out some air. "I'm not chasin' you, man, but you can't go on like this. If you don't stop, they'll find you washed up on Alcatraz."

"Sure…sure…I know what you're saying."

Christopher didn't. The next day, he packed, wrote a thank-you note to Steve, and caught an afternoon flight back east.

Just as in the biblical story of the prodigal son, Christopher was welcomed with open arms when he returned from California. Mama and papa were so happy they threw a party for him at their apartment on Fiftieth Street. Everyone, it seemed, was there.

Camille arrived with her daughter Loretta and the twins, all dressed up in their holiday best. Ben came later after a long day shuttling between court and his office downtown. Michael and Jo also came to the party, separately. No one asked why, but they knew. There are no secrets in a close family. Jo brought little John, who was a bit shy greeting everyone at first. It didn't take him long to find the twins and go sliding on the linoleum.

Roger Foster, Christopher's buddy from the roof days, limped in with Patsy Espinosa, the beautiful, dark-eyed nurse who, like Roger, recently returned from Vietnam. They were just friends, a fact that did not escape Christopher who liked the way Patsy's face lit up when she smiled.

Harry Slovich was going to come, but decided not to. Quiet, little Dottie Wood was not so quiet or little anymore. She let out joyful screams when she spotted someone she hadn't seen in a while.

"Hear from Jimmy D. lately?" Roger asked Christopher.

"Last I heard he was up for a bit part in a Charlton Heston movie."

"What movie's that? *The Ten Commandments—Part Two?*"

"Yeah, 'Introducing James DiBlasio.'"

The dining room table was loaded with lots of mama Terranova treats, including lasagna and inch-thick *focaccia,* along with some American favorites for the kids, including hot dogs and hamburgers. Within reach of the festive table, Arturo enjoyed greeting the guests, or just listening to conversations, or playing with the kids. Occasionally, Anna or Camille would admonish him for devouring something that they deemed was not healthy for him. "Papa, you know about salt." "Arturo, no wine!" "Stay away from the hot stuff."

Papa was so happy to see Christopher, and just before the guests arrived he let it slip that he was interested in opening another grocery store. Christopher didn't take the bait, however, and Arturo thought it best to wait before approaching his son again about forming a retail partnership.

Christopher looked spectacular in his California tan as he roamed the rooms renewing friendships. Maybe it was the dark circles under his eyes or how he kept popping Rheingold after Rheingold and then spilling the contents as he spoke excitedly to one of his friends, but not everyone was impressed.

He tried to make light of the spillage. "Hey, I always knew I'd make a big splash someday."

Everyone laughed. Everyone except mama and Patsy the nurse.

On a gray afternoon in early December three weeks later, two grave diggers in heavy boots crunched up a snow-laden road in Calvary Cemetery in Queens, Long Island. They didn't speak to each other, apparently saving their energy for the work that lay ahead. Almost in synchronization, they turned off the road and walked toward a grave site they were assigned to dig. As they neared it, they both noticed a large green clump on a nearby grave which one of the grave diggers later said he thought was an evergreen grave blanket. The clump turned out to be a young man in a green parka stretched, face down, across a snowy grave. Next to the man on the ground was an almost empty bottle of scotch whisky and several empty cans of beer. In one of the man's hands was a full can of beer. The other hand was resting against a tombstone bearing the inscription:

**Terranova,
Christine
1939–1944**

One of the grave diggers went for help. The other felt for a pulse, but couldn't find one. Out of desperation, he turned the man around, zippered up his jacket, and started rubbing and slapping his face and hands.

When Christopher was brought to the hospital, he was still unconscious. His face was a battered mess, apparently from a fall, and his feet and hands were dangerously close to being frostbitten. He was treated for shock and hypothermia, and his stomach was pumped.

When the tubes were removed, a head nurse tried talking to him. Somehow she knew his name. "Come on, Christopher. Talk to me, Christopher." Silence. Again: "Come on, Christopher. Say something, Christopher." Finally, the young man opened his eyes and tried to scream. Nothing at first, but then in a hoarse but clear voice he shouted: "Mother fucker! Don't touch me!" The head nurse looked startled, then smiled. "I think he'll be okay now. Let's find him a room."

The next day, in a pool of sweat, Christopher slowly opened his eyes and looked around. The light pouring in from the nearby window nearly blinded him. When he turned his head away, he saw an old man with scraggy pepper-and-salt whiskers snoring in the bed next to his. Christopher tried to shield his eyes and ears with his arm and hands. The stench of whisky and beer mixed with bile was sickening, and his head was pounding. The pain and pressure in his face were so intense it was as if he were wearing a lead mask, and he felt as if he had been kicked in his throat and stomach.

When the room suddenly grew darker, he opened his eyes again and noticed someone, apparently a nurse, pulling down the blinds. When she turned around, he saw it was Patsy Espinosa. She smiled, and it was as if the whole room lit up again.

"I'm going to tell your mother to wash your mouth out with soap," she said, her dark eyes sparkling in their playfulness.

As sick as he felt, Christopher went along with the joke. "Was I that bad?"

"You were so bad they gave you and your friend here your own room."

"I don't remember a thing."

"Why would you?" said Patsy. "You were out cold, literally speaking, when they brought you to the emergency room."

"You were there?"

"I had to be. I'm the head ER nurse."

"Oh, great."

Patsy reached for his wrist to feel his pulse. "How are you feeling?"

"Like shit, pardon my language.".

Patsy shook her head. "You consumed an awful lot of alcohol."

"I remember, I think."

"Your alcohol blood level was between 300 and 400."

He didn't respond. Obviously, the numbers were too high.

She continued. "Do you remember where you were?"

He thought for a moment. "I think I was headed to the cemetery to visit my sister's grave."

"If it's any consolation, you made it. That's where two grave diggers found you in the snow."

"I must have blacked out."

"You were unconscious." Patsy let the seriousness of the situation sink in. "You know, if you're interested, the hospital runs an excellent program for anyone with a drinking problem."

He looked at her suspiciously.

She lit up the room with her smile again. "Pardon the commercial. Like I said, I work for ER, not PR."

"Aren't you supposed to be in the ER now?" he asked.

"Yeah, I just stopped by for a visit. Here, let me fix your pillow."

Over the next few days, Christopher saw Patsy on a daily basis. She stayed just long enough to see how he was doing, tell him a joke she heard in ER, and fix his pillow. By the fourth day, Christopher was looking forward to her daily visits. As he started feeling better, they talked about the neighborhood and the people they knew there, their families, and themselves.

Compared to Christopher, Patsy was a newcomer to the West Side. Her family moved there only five years ago. It was a good move. Patsy was headed for a pack of trouble as a reluctant member of a Bronx gang. Instead, she enlisted in the army, where she became a nurse and did a tour of duty in Vietnam. Her experiences over there proved invaluable when she returned home and picked up her career in civilian life, wiser and more compassionate but scarred for life by the terrible pain and misery she saw in Vietnam. She now had her own little apartment on the West Side, separate from her parents' place.

Over the next several days, Christopher learned that Patsy's parents emigrated from Puerto Rico in the early fifties; she had a younger brother named Ricardo; and there was a soldier from Georgia she almost married. Christopher was glad that chapter in her life was over, and he wondered what it would be like to continue his conversations with Patsy outside the hospital. The day before he was scheduled to be released, he decided to ask.

"You know, tomorrow's the day," he began.

"I know."

"Do you mind…can I see you tomorrow night when you get off?" he continued. "Maybe we can have some…coffee or something."

"I prefer cocoa this time of year."

"Hmm, cocoa. Who would have thought?"

Next day, Christopher was sitting in the back of a diner on Eleventh Avenue, not quite ready to face the world, when Patsy walked in the front door. He waved when he saw her, and she waved back, a vision of vibrant beauty in her blue parka and wool tam. Christopher didn't know whether he should shake hands or kiss her. She resolved the issue, kissing him on the cheek.

"Sorry, I didn't have time to change," she said, revealing her white nurse's outfit under the jacket. "Last-minute emergency."

"Now, why doesn't that surprise me?" said Christopher with a wry smile.

"My life seems like one long emergency sometimes," she added, stuffing her hat in her bag.

"Have a cocoa."

She looked up at him and laughed. "I could use some real food, too."

"Best meat loaf in town here."

Over the next two hours, they sipped cocoa, ate meat loaf, and talked, mostly about the neighborhood and, of course, the war.

"I just missed it, the war, did you know that?" asked Christopher.

"I heard," she replied. "You were lucky."

"I guess I was, getting out when I did, but sometimes I feel guilty." He tried to laugh, but was unsuccessful. "Knowing some of my friends died there…."

She reached across the table and held his hand. "Don't, don't feel guilty. I thank God you weren't there."

They continued seeing each other in the following weeks, and the conversations took an even more personal turn—to their family, hopes, fears, desires, and plans for the future. As their friendship grew, they fell in love. Two months after they met in the diner, Christopher was introduced to Patsy's parents, and she had dinner with his.

There were feelings all around that this was a good match, so the shock was minimal when Christopher moved in with Patsy. Christopher found a decent job in textiles, but he didn't close the door when papa approached him again about opening a new store. Papa had just the site in mind, on Ninth Avenue near the Port Authority, and Christopher listened with respect and some interest.

The future seemed promising for Christopher and Patsy. Then a series of events shook their lives. Papa Terranova had a minor stroke and was persuaded by mama to retire. Patsy's brother Ricardo was busted for possession of pot. Reggie Ryan, a friend of Patsy's, who lost a leg in Vietnam, was killed by a hit-and-run driver on Twelfth Avenue. Christopher's old buddies called him almost every night and asked him to meet them for drinks. He turned them down at first, even hung up on them, but then decided a couple of beers wouldn't hurt. Knowing what she did about addiction, Patsy pleaded with him to stay home, but he went anyway.

In the world beyond Tenth Avenue, Richard Nixon was elected to succeed Lyndon Johnson as President and pledged to bring an honorable end to the war. In fact, an agreement ending the war was not signed for another four years, and it would be another two years before the last 1,000 Americans, along with thousands of Vietnamese, were evacuated from Saigon.

Vietnam was a costly experience. Between 1964 and 1973, more than 57,000 Americans lost their lives, while upwards of 313,000 were wounded. The toll of this war on the lives and psyche of Americans on the home front could not be measured and was still to be reckoned with as 1968 came to a close.

1991

CHAPTER 15

▼

Gloria Terranova couldn't believe she was finally here—here being a small hospital room on Long Island—to give birth to her first child. There were times during the past eight-and-a-half months she thought the day would never come. And now, five hours after entering the hospital, she wondered whether her time was really near. It had been a long afternoon.

When someone screamed behind the door to the adjoining room, she glanced over at Tom Dempsey and sat up in bed. He patted the sweat off her brow while making light of the loud, penetrating cry. "Sounds like baby is coming next door. Maybe we'll be next."

Gloria's dark, sunken eyes darted around the birthing room one more time and settled on a chart of cervical openings. "I hope I won't be too loud," she whispered.

"You be as loud as you want, honey," Tom said, his eyes dancing with excitement. "If anyone has a problem with the noise, they have to answer to me." Gloria let a brief smile cross her face. She always liked his swagger and his sense of humor. "What would I do without you, Tom Dempsey?" She leaned over and kissed him.

What a year it had been! In that time, they met, fell in love, and began living together, and now they were about to have a baby. Gloria tried to focus on that reality. *We're not husband and wife in the traditional sense, but we're one in heart and spirit, and we're about to start our own family. Whether you know it or not, you'll be a great dad, Tom Dempsey, and I think I'll be a pretty good mom.*

They felt a joy and a hope that any new parents would feel. But at the same time, there was that other, darker reality—the impending war in the Persian

Gulf—and it refused to go away. Gloria was worried, especially since there were reports that Tom's army reserve unit might be activated at any time. *I can't afford to have you marching off to war, Tom Dempsey. Not now. What would we do without you?*

Tom returned the kiss just as Gloria's obstetrician, Dr. Sylvia Allen, walked into the room. She was all business. "Let's take another look-see, guys. I think we're almost there," she said. Behind her was a flushed, round-faced nurse who looked as if she had a train or bus to catch. She cracked a weak smile and started taking Gloria's blood pressure. Gloria thought of her mom, who recently returned to nursing, part-time, after a long career turn into motherhood. She wished she were here with her now.

"I think we'll start pushing in about half an hour," Dr. Allen concluded.

Gloria wondered why the doctor used the first person plural pronoun to refer to an action *she* alone would be taking, but she didn't say anything. "Can I make a call?" she asked. "I'd like to speak to my mother."

The doctor put a finger to her lips—a request for silence—and continued examining Gloria with her stethoscope. "Sure, but make it brief," she said, her probing completed. "I'll be back in a bit. Buzz me if you need me." After the doctor and nurse left the room, Tom picked up the phone and started dialing for Gloria.

Christopher picked up the phone on the other end. "Hello."

Tom appeared surprised to hear his voice. "Oh, hi…er, Mr. Terranova. This is Tom. Tom Dempsey."

"Hi, Tom, what's up? Everything okay?"

"Sure, fine," Tom replied. "I thought you were at work."

"Early day. I have some paperwork to do. Besides, it's my birthday."

"Good for you. Happy birthday. Wait a second, Gloria wants to talk to you." She took the phone. "Hi, daddy. Where's mom?"

"Out shopping, buying me a present, I think. She should be back soon."

"Happy birthday, daddy. I have a present for you, too."

"Oh, you didn't have to do that," said Christopher.

Gloria paused, drew a breath. "Oh, yes, I did. I'm in the hospital. They want me to start pushing in half an hour."

"Pushing? Pushing what?"

"Pushing for the baby." Christopher went silent. She continued, "When my water broke, we came right over. I've been having contractions for the past two hours, but the cervical opening isn't the right size yet, so they have to wait. But Dr. Allen says I'm almost there."

Christopher decided to ignore the medical details. "That's great, sweetie. As soon as mom gets back, we'll head over. Are you sure you're okay?"

"I'm fine, daddy. Don't worry."

"And Tom?"

"He's good, too." Neither mentioned anything about the army reserves, although Christopher had been anxiously following newscasts about the war.

He did some calculations in his mind. The baby was due near the end of January, and here it was the first week of January 1991. "You're early," he concluded.

"I know. Since when was I on time?"

Christopher smiled, remembering the times his daughter waited until the last minute to complete school projects. "Well, at least you're not late," he replied. "Thanks, sweetie. What a wonderful birthday present! Best ever!"

As Christopher waited for Patsy to come home, he tried to absorb what was happening. Gloria was going to be a mother! She was only 18, still his little girl with the great big heart, but she was maturing right before his eyes.

And Tom? Cocky son of a gun, but Christopher liked his confidence and his enthusiasm. Reminded him of someone he knew, namely himself. Tom was only 19, but he was trying hard to make it work with Gloria. He was an assistant supermarket manager by day and helped out at Christopher's gas station in the evening. He really wanted to be a fireman, and he had started the application process to reach that goal.

From a small apartment over a bakery near Gloria's parents out on the Island, the young couple spun their dreams. Christopher encouraged the young couple's hopes, and although he preferred that they face the future married, he said nothing. It would have been hypocritical for him to do otherwise.

When he thought about those days when he and Patsy lived together before they were married, Christopher smiled, shook his head, and wondered how they had managed to get through that period in their lives. Their apartment off Tenth Avenue on Forty-seventh Street was so small and cramped they had to keep some of their clothes at their parents' apartments. And thank heaven they didn't have a cat or a dog, let alone a child! Christopher was not yet working in the early days, so it was his job to keep the place in order, take care of the laundry, and cook supper—no small tasks for someone who didn't have a clue about such home-making details when he was growing up.

Being together in such close quarters also gave them an opportunity to learn more about each other, the good habits and the bad. Sometimes the learning process was fun, as was the case when Christopher discovered Patsy's uppity way of eating soup. With outstretched pinky, she tilted the bowl away from her to spoon up the remnants. Christopher tried not to laugh when he saw her doing it, but he couldn't help himself, and he had this kind of machine-gun laugh that sent others into spasms. Patsy was no exception. Among his oddest habits, Christopher, who was slightly hypochondriacal, used to keep medical supplies, including Bengay and Band-Aids, in the headboard of the bed. Her mother offered one explanation for his stash to Patsy: "Maybe he is opening a drugstore."

After several months, Christopher began showing a darker side to his nature. Occasionally, he would get moody and restless and started complaining about minor lapses such as a missing sock or a cup of coffee that turned cold. Once, when he felt that way, he went for a long walk and met a couple of his old pals, who had been calling him regularly. They went for a drink, and that was the start of it.

Over the next few weeks, Christopher seemed to forget that grim memory of the man in the green parka lying dead-drunk and unconscious across his sister's grave, and his drinking got heavier. Patsy never forgot what had happened that December day, and she encouraged him to attend 12-Step meetings. He said he would go, but didn't. He started hitting the bars right after work. When he finally arrived home late, he would listen dutifully to Patsy, who was getting louder each time; then he'd kick off his shoes and announce, "You done? I've got to go to work in the morning."

Then, one night, Christopher didn't come home. Patsy became worried and phoned Michael, who immediately called his brother's workplace and was told that Christopher was "out sick." Next, Michael scoured the neighborhood. None of Christopher's friends, it seemed, had seen him in days. Bartenders, too, had no idea where he could be.

As dusk arrived, Michael was about to file a report with the police when he suddenly had this idea and ran toward his mother's apartment building on Fiftieth Street. Bounding up five flights of stairs, he swung open the door and walked onto the roof, Christopher's old hangout. Michael looked around, but saw no one. He clambered onto the roofs of the adjoining buildings. Nothing. He was heading back to his mother's place when he saw something in the fading light—a disheveled figure smoking a cigarette slouched against the wall of a shaftway. Michael moved closer. It was Christopher. Quietly, almost as if this was a chance meeting in the park, Michael sat down next to him.

"Hey, buddy, where've you been?"

Christopher didn't answer.

"You want to go home?"

Christopher glanced at his brother. "I can't."

"Patsy's so worried about you."

"I can't. I can't face her," said Christopher, dropping his head into his knees. "I'm so ashamed."

Michael put his arm around his brother.

Christopher started sobbing. "I think I need help, Michael."

"We'll help you. You know your family's always there for you."

This was Christopher's first step toward rehabilitation. He learned other steps in a drug and alcohol rehab program that he began the following day. Smooth sailing from then on, it was not. With all of the temptations out there, there were slips and near-slips along the way, an arrest for driving under the influence, and another visit to the emergency room. But there were also 12-Step meetings to pick him up when he fell. Christopher kept getting back up until his sobriety stretched out from days to weeks and then to months and years. As he came to understand, addiction was a lifelong condition that required constant, almost selfish, vigilance, reinforcement, and support.

Patsy was proud of his progress, and nearly three years after they met they were married. First came Gloria, and they moved to a modest home in Bayside, Queens. Five years later, Anthony was born, and they found a larger home in Hicksville. Over the years, Christopher tried many jobs. From textiles he moved into retail sales and then computers. When an opportunity to buy a small auto repair shop near home came along, he grabbed it, with financial help from the local bank and Michael.

Anxious to share the news about Gloria and Tom, Christopher cracked his leg against the end table twice when he jumped up from the sofa to look out the window. First home, from school, was Anthony, his 13-year-old son. If Gloria was the apple of his eye, Anthony was its sparkle. Energetic and enthusiastic, he seemed to do everything on the run. He was outgoing and made friends easily. Although he was short and struggled with his weight and his school work, he had a big heart that was always ready to help someone. "See you in fifteen minutes," he shouted to his friend Timmy before bursting through the front door.

"I got a B in math today," he announced.

"That's great, Anthony." Christopher was always anxious to praise his son whenever he could.

Suddenly, the boy noticed who was standing there. "What're you doing home so early?"

"I took a day off. It's my birthday."

"I know, mom told me. Happy birthday. Where's mom?"

"Shopping," Christopher said. "I have some news."

"Are you and mom splitting?"

Christopher shook his head in disbelief, but he had an idea why his son would say such a thing. Several of Anthony's friends were from families with divorced parents.

Anthony continued, "Is grandma okay?"

Christopher knew his son had a special bond with grandma Terranova. Despite the language barriers, they talked regularly on the phone. Usually it was just small talk, a joke Anthony heard in school, or something he wanted to tell her in private, knowing full well she could keep a secret. "You sure are a cheery soul," said Christopher. "Grandma's fine."

"Then what?" Anthony demanded.

"Would you believe your sister is having a baby?"

"Now?"

"Yes, now."

"Here?"

"No…in the hospital."

Anthony tried to weigh the enormity of the situation while he thought about what he needed for the hockey game. He ripped off his coat and tossed it on the sofa. "Do I have to go? I have a big game this afternoon."

"No," said Christopher, "but your mom and I will be going. Just so you know when you come home. Don't be late."

Christopher nodded. "Is it a boy or a girl?"

"I don't know. We'll find out when we get there."

"Can I hold the baby?"

"Sure, Anthony. Just be careful and…."

"I know, wash my hands. Mom already told me." He ran up the stairs to finish changing.

Twenty minutes later, a car pulled into the driveway and came to a halt just before a pile of old snow near the garage. Christopher felt his heart leap with excitement, but he didn't want to frighten Patsy. He was standing in the foyer, a smile on his face, when she opened the door. "Don't take your coat off," he said. "Baby's coming."

Concern quickly gave way to excitement in Patsy's glowing face. "Where is she?"

"If you mean Gloria, she's at the hospital."

"Is she alright?"

"Everyone's fine, grandma. She wants us there."

"Let's go!"

By the time they got to the hospital, the baby—a boy weighing in at slightly less than seven pounds—had already arrived. When they were told that the baby would be called Thomas Christopher Dempsey, Christopher and Patsy filled up and hugged the new parents. Seeing his grandchild for the first time, Christopher noticed how much the baby resembled him, yet he could not deny the resemblance to Tom Dempsey. For a fleeting moment, he thought again about the impending war in the Persian Gulf.

CHAPTER 16

▼

After Vietnam, Americans wanted no part of war again, and when the Berlin Wall—or at least large chunks of it—came tumbling down in 1989, they were jubilant. Many thought that the threat of major war was over and that a long period of peace would follow, allowing concerned members of the world community to concentrate on eradicating such scourges as AIDS, malnutrition, and ignorance and on keeping up with the information technology revolution that was changing the way people lived their lives and did things.

Then along came Saddam Hussein. As Iraq's dictator, he ruled his country with an iron fist, using torture, terror, and chemical warfare to subdue and control his people. Partially with the help of Western powers, he also built an army that at its zenith lay claim to being the fourth largest in the world. During the 1980s, he led that army into a war with neighboring Iran that lasted eight years. That futile conflict left Saddam in foreign debt for billions. If he was to realize his dreams of regional dominance, he had to find a way to pay off his debt and expand his coffers. That way turned out to be the invasion—on August 2, 1990—of Kuwait, Iraq's small, oil-rich neighbor to the south.

President George Herbert Walker Bush moved quickly to galvanize the United States and prevent what he felt might be a repeat of the appeasing policies that led dictators like Hitler to gobble up their neighbors. He organized a diplomatic and economic counterattack that won the support of more than 30 nations, including Russia. As part of what he called Desert Shield, President Bush sent 125,000 American troops to Saudi Arabia in a "wholly defensive" gesture.

When the United States saw that economic sanctions and diplomatic moves weren't working, it shifted into high military gear, with the blessings of the UN

Security Council. Some 250,000 American land troops were deployed to the Persian Gulf area, and an attack was set for mid-January 1991. No gradual escalation this time around. Hit them hard, hit them in force.

Seared into the minds of many Americans at that time were those nightmarish TV pictures of the last helicopter pulling away from the roof of the U.S. embassy in Saigon some 15 years earlier. To those citizens, war was not an option, and they formed and joined antiwar coalitions to make their case. The coalitions consisted of veterans of the Vietnam peace movement, pacifist groups, extremists on the left and right, civil libertarians, conspiracy theorists, and others. Among those leading the charge against the coming war was Jo Trudell Terranova.

After her separation from Michael, Jo found a new life for herself in Greenwich Village, where she and her son John took up residence. She continued to teach school and participate in activist causes. Michael stayed in the apartment uptown as he continued to move up the corporate ladder at the publishing company, reaching an executive vice-president position. Both of them dated others from time to time, but for a long time there were no serious matches in their lives, and they stayed in touch with each other, mainly for the sake of their son John.

Eventually, Jo did find someone special. He was Larry Mazur, a furniture salesman, animal shelter helper, and part-time poet, whom she met at a Save the Neighborhood meeting. She immediately felt a kinship with him. Both of them had been married, with children, both were involved in a variety of causes for some time, and both were ready for something of a more lasting relationship. After 10 years of living separately, Jo asked Michael for a divorce, and he reluctantly agreed. Their decision was a devastating blow to John, who retreated into his room, burying himself in schoolwork. It also saddened their parents and mutual friends, who believed that these childhood sweethearts were destined to stay together forever.

After John moved out to pursue a career in the naval air force, Jo moved in with Larry in his Village apartment. A tall, spindly man, Larry proved to be a capable partner in the furtherance of the antiwar movement and other causes. Except for an occasional outburst of temper, which was usually directed to the outside world—namely, the President, conservative members of Congress, all local politicians, and neo-Nazis—Larry was good to Jo.

Like most antiwar protesters, Jo wanted Iraq to get out of Kuwait, but she preferred to persuade Saddam to leave through economic and political pressure rather than by military force. "Sanctions, not war" was the rallying cry of the protesters and some members of Congress. However, the Iraqis, who were used to economic hardship after the eight-year war with Iran, didn't bite and continued to rally around their Father-Leader.

The more involved she became the more she realized that the conflict in the Persian Gulf would be no Vietnam. Peace would be difficult to sell this time around. The atrocities and military actions of the Iraqi leader could not be ignored. What's more, the presence of her son John in the war zone complicated things personally for Jo. Like any mother, she was worried about John's safety. Why he decided to join the military in a familial atmosphere so opposed to war was beyond her, but this was his choice, and she always encouraged him to make his own decisions. For that, she took pride in his service to country and kept a picture of him in full uniform by her bedside.

Even before the shooting started, Lieutenant John Terranova was flying alerts off a carrier in the Persian Gulf, partially to survey the Kuwait-Iraq terrain, partially to unnerve the enemy. Life aboard the carrier was a mixture of routine activities and adventurous, highly dangerous pursuits for Jo and Michael's son. When he wasn't flying F-15s over unfamiliar or hostile territory, John ate, slept, attended briefings, watched TV, or wrote letters to family and friends.

At first, the letters were very general and unemotional, reflecting his general calmness and confidence about life and his work. But as the attack date drew near, they became more personal and emotional and charged with a fair amount of excitement and nervousness. In the final hours before the launchings, John wrote a long, loving letter to his wife Eloise in Virginia, he wrote a brief, nostalgic note to grandma Terranova recalling the wonderful summer they spent together when he was a little boy, and he wrote a moving message to his divorced parents. What he had to say could be addressed to both:

Dear Mom and Dad,

If you're wondering why I'm writing one letter, it's not that I'm trying to save money on paper or postage. It's just that these days I think a lot of both of you, together.

It's little things that come to mind. Like when you both took me to the top of the Empire State Building, and Dad lost his cap in the wind. I wonder if someone is still wearing it.

Then there was grandpa Terranova's 70th birthday party when Dad let me drink some wine. I never told you but Uncle Tony also gave me some of his wine. I think I took a nap right after that

I don't remember where it was, maybe it was church on Sunday, but in my mind's eye I see the three of us walking hand in hand down a long corridor, and you know what? We're all smiling. And why not? We had some great times together. A few rocky times, too, for sure, but both of you never gave me anything but your unconditional love. For that, I am eternally grateful.

I love you both.

John

Now it was time to go to war.

Jo had weighed the idea of sitting this one out, but her commitment to peace was too strong to let her do that, so she stayed involved. Every week, she led meetings rallying already committed members of the peace movement and laying out protest march ideas and other demonstration plans. "Hey, we did it before, we can do it again," she told dwindling congregations. "We can nip this thing before it starts."

When she got John's letter, however, her attitude changed. She was immobilized for three days. A full-time teacher now, she called in sick at work and arranged for a substitute teacher to take her class. She hardly ate anything, and she couldn't sleep. All she did was lie in bed and stare at John's picture. Larry became worried and took over her meeting for that week. By the fourth day, she was ready to go back to work and resume her life, but some of the zest was gone. She decided to back out of this antiwar campaign.

When Michael received a copy of John's letter from Jo, he read it three times, trying to catch all the nuances. The hidden message behind the words was clear: Here was a young man on the brink of war, and he was scared—and whom did he turn to at this critical hour? His family, of course.

Michael, too, had a photograph of John in uniform, which he displayed by the window overlooking the river. He picked up the picture and stared into his son's deep blue eyes. "God bless you," Michael whispered. John's letter came with a brief, dispassionate note from Jo: "This is for you, too, Michael. I suppose we should answer with separate letters. Hope all is well. Jo." Michael read her note again, as well.

In his mid-fifties now, Michael was growing older gracefully. The twice-a-week workouts in the gym made him look trim and fit and younger than his years, despite the gray hairs that were spreading beyond the temples. Nevertheless, the pain of separation and the feeling of failure continued to haunt him. Hardly a day passed when he didn't ask himself, What the hell happened? He couldn't get Jo out of his mind. After the divorce became official, Michael buried himself in his work. It was better that way. When John began pursuing his career in the navy after getting his degree at Fordham, Michael plunged into a broad range of work-related issues. His weekdays were filled with meetings, both one-on-ones and group sessions. There were meetings to review current editorial strategy and to map out budgets. He saved the weekends for more long-range strategic planning.

As the 1990s began, technological advances such as the computer and the Internet threatened to disrupt old systems of doing things and threw his company and, in fact, the entire publishing world into a soul-searching frenzy. Michael tried to make sense of it all. He took management courses. He attended media and technology workshops in the U.S. and abroad. He invited technologically savvy individuals to come to the company and explain what was happening. Most of all, he listened, and then, gradually, he acted—two traits that were in short supply in many publishing houses looking to survive in a time of tremendous change.

The day after he received the letter from John, Michael was looking forward to hearing from a team of three techies—partners in their own software venture—who were visiting the office to discuss the virtues of establishing Web sites for magazines. Just prior to the presentation, Michael was shaking hands and introducing himself to the speakers when he discovered he knew one of them.

"Casey Russell? Fifty-third Street?" Michael quietly inquired.

"Yes…yes," said Casey. "I'll be damned. I thought your name sounded familiar. Michael Terranova, from Fiftieth Street, Ninth and Tenth Avenues, right?"

They shook hands and hugged. "Right," said Michael, "but don't tell anyone around here. They don't know I'm from Hell's Kitchen."

"The last time we saw each other I bumped into you at the Museum of Natural History," said Casey.

"I remember, a few months after you moved uptown," Michael agreed. "We promised to stay in touch."

"We didn't. Sorry about that. How the hell are you?"

"Fine…well, pretty good."

"Which is it?" said Casey, a smile across his handsome, dark face. "Fine or pretty good?" They agreed they had a lot of catching up to do and set a lunch date.

At the Four Seasons a couple of days later, neither felt much like eating—they would have preferred to just talk and talk, and listen—but they managed to order as they paused to catch their breath. Casey picked up the story of his life after he left Hell's Kitchen with his mom, who, by the way, was still alive and, for a long time, asked about "that nice boy Michael from Fiftieth Street." After moving uptown, Casey went on to finish his elementary curriculum at a public school, and, with some encouragement and persuasion from his mother and maternal grandparents, he went on to graduate from Cardinal Hayes High School. He then attended New York University, where he majored in business administration. His first job out of college was with a small ethnic advertising agency, where he rose to an account supervisor position, and, more important, met Jill St. Lawrence, a woman he eventually married. A series of jobs in corporate marketing followed before he decided to investigate the exploding new world of technology. He and Jill had two children—Rhonda, a medical intern who was completing her final year, and Tanya, who joined the army air corps a few years back and was currently flying helicopters out of Saudi Arabia.

"Get out of here!" said Michael.

"What? What did I say?"

"My son's there, too," Michael explained. "He's flying F-15s out of the Gulf."

"No shit!" Casey looked around the restaurant's famous Pool Room. One of the power brokers gave him a side glance. "Excuse my French."

Michael explained that John had been stationed in the Persian Gulf for the past month and was likely to see battle if—rather, when—the Allies went on the attack. He told Casey how proud he was of his son, as he knew Casey must be of his daughters, but, like any parent, he was worried. "Out of my bloody skull. Now, pardon my English," said Michael. The power broker looked over once again

"And what about your wife?" Casey whispered. "What was her name?"

"Jo…Jo Trudell. You remember her?"

Casey responded immediately. "Oh, sure. Blond, blue eyes, big family, sharp as a tack."

"That's right," said Michael. "We're divorced…haven't talked with her in a while."

"Sorry about that. I'm sure she's worried, too, with John so close to the action." Casey thought about what he was about to say next. "Maybe you should give her a call."

"Yeah," said Michael. "I guess I should."

After lunch was over, both Michael and Casey exchanged phone numbers and e-mail addresses and agreed to stay in touch. As he headed back to the office, Michael thought about Casey's suggestion. *Yes, Jo must be worried sick, too. I'll call her today.*

CHAPTER 17

▼

Ben Stern didn't like to tell anyone he was partially retired. He preferred to say he was cutting back on his office hours. Basically, what that meant was that he was spending less time traveling into Manhattan, where he maintained his office, and was working more out of his "beautiful hacienda" in Ridgewood, New Jersey, he told anyone who wanted to know. Wherever he was, Ben focused his energies on a few long-time clients as well as a selected group of non-profit organizations and *pro bonos*. A fitness disciple, he also continued to work out in the gym three days a week and was one of the more visible walkers around town.

When Ben did go into the city, he sometimes traveled by limo, accompanied by his twin sons, David and Jeffrey, both of whom still lived at home and recently started working in the World Trade Center. Since they usually took the bus into New York City, they welcomed a change in the way they traveled to work, especially when a limo was the option.

Ben's daughter Loretta had worked with her father at the law firm until she married Alex Conway, a high school teacher. The mother of one-year-old Arthur, she was a full-time homemaker now living in a small house on a cliff facing the Manhattan skyline in Edgewater, New Jersey.

Ben was glad he was not going into the city this January morning. With a shove from a northeast wind, temperatures had fallen into the teens. He turned on the TV, which was filled with news about the imminent war. As he did, a phone began ringing somewhere in the house, but he didn't jump up to answer it. He was absorbed in a newscast about troop deployments to the Persian Gulf area.

Always one to look at the big picture, he thought about the impact of war on the country. There was good reason, it seemed to him, for America, the undisputed world leader now, to take action against Iraq's takeover of its smaller, oil-rich neighbor. But, except for some minor armed conflicts in Grenada and Panama and a retaliatory air raid on Libya, it had been a long time since the United States was involved in a major war. Ever since Vietnam, there was a deep-seated reluctance by Americans to go to war again. It would take a tremendous catastrophe on the order of a Pearl Harbor to make them fighting mad again.

Ben also thought about the impact of war on the Middle East, especially Israel—the hotbed of so much turmoil in the area—which he had visited with Camille twice. He knew several people there, including an old school friend from Columbia University.

Finally, what about the world alliance that had rallied around the American leadership against Iraq? Suppose the war lasted for months or even years. Could that alliance be sustained, or would individual nations start bailing out?

Camille came into the room and sat down. When she saw what was on TV, she sighed.

"Why do you keep watching this stuff, Ben?"

"Why not?" he said. "This is the world we live in."

"Some world."

Ben nodded in agreement. "How's your mother?'

Camille sighed again. "It's getting harder to get her going in the morning."

"Come on, let me make you some breakfast."

For Anna, living with Camille and Ben in New Jersey was like wearing a fancy pair of shoes that just did not quite fit. It was not that she disliked her daughter and son-in-law. In fact, she loved them dearly, and the home was lovely and spacious. It was just that for Anna there was no place like her own place, and that place for more than 35 years was the apartment on Manhattan's West Side.

Looking around her new bedroom, she couldn't believe she had access to—or needed—"all this stuff," including a sofa, a table, a king-sized bed, two end tables, a bureau, plus a TV set, a phone, and a walk-in closet. In the old bedroom on Fiftieth Street, there was room for only a single bureau, one drawer of which contained the boys' underwear.

Even so, Anna liked sitting on the sofa for a while before getting her breakfast. Inspired by pictures of the Sacred Heart and Mother Cabrini on facing walls, she had time to collect her thoughts and to pray. All around her were reminders of her life. On one end of the bureau was a grainy photo of Anna's mother and father at their small farm in southern Italy; on the other end was a picture of Christina two months before she died. Between them were smaller pictures of her grandchildren. Displayed on the long table were wedding pictures of Camille, Michael, and Christopher, along with an enlarged black-and-white photograph of Anna and Arturo on their wedding day. She often looked at that image, remembering the hardworking man and their early years together. *Such a handsome man. What a beautiful couple we were.*

It was more than 12 years since Arturo had suffered a cerebral hemorrhage and died. Anna long ago had forgiven herself for his death, but she often wondered whether he might have lived longer if she hadn't agreed to take that trip back to Italy. Everyone insisted that they return to their roots. They said it would be good for both of them, especially papa, who was not in the best of health and whose dream of opening a new store with Christopher had all but disappeared.

Anna and Arturo took off for Rome in mid-October. With them on the trip was their granddaughter Loretta, then in her early twenties, who was instructed by her mother Camille "to keep an eye on them, especially grandpa," who already had taken a mild stroke, and "watch out for those Italian boys—they pinch behinds."

The first half of the trip was magnificent. Rome, the Vatican, Florence. So much beauty and culture and religious fervor in one country—and mama was right: One bold young man did pinch Loretta. They next boarded a train headed south, where they planned to see some old relatives and friends, whoever was still living. By prearrangement, they were to stay at the home of a nephew, Vito Rubino, and his wife Maria. He was the son of Anna's brother, Giovanni, now deceased, who had decided to stay in Italy during the great migration after World War I.

It was an emotional journey. As they came into Bari, both Anna and Arturo noticed changes that had taken place in the area, but they also recognized parts of the countryside along with familiar towns, and a flood of memories deluged them. This was a private moment, and Loretta let them enjoy it without saying anything. Anna reached for Arturo's pills in her bag and gave him one.

When they got to the terminal, they were met by Vito Rubino, a short, affable man who was dressed up for the occasion with a light tan suit and tie. With him was his teenage son Giancarlo, who immediately eyed Loretta and smiled. *"Buongiorno,"* said Vito with a flourish. "Welcome." There were hugs all around. Loretta made an awkward reach for Giancarlo, who was still smiling broadly. She later learned he was looking for a wife and would have walked on coals for an American partner.

Vito's house was in the same town where Anna was born. When they arrived, there were more hugs, from Vito's wife Maria, a courtly woman with a bright smile, and the rest of the family. A few friends and neighbors came later, bringing food and wine and other tasty treats. The feast lasted through the rest of the day.

The next day, Vito drove the three visitors to Arturo's village, where he was reunited with a couple of his old friends and a distant cousin. Another, smaller feast ensued. In fact, there were celebrations every day they were in the area. Both Anna and Loretta tried to get Arturo to rest, but he refused. It was very satisfying to be so welcomed. Besides, he didn't want to insult his hosts.

On the day they were headed back to Rome, Arturo felt as if he were losing his balance and stumbled as he was about to board the train. Once inside, he started slurring his words. Both Anna and Loretta became alarmed, but they tried not to show it. They just wanted to get home as quickly as possible. When they returned to the hotel, they confirmed their flight back to the States and started packing. The flight home the next day was a quiet one. Arturo slept most of the way.

There was no doubt that he had suffered another stroke, said his doctor, who immediately placed him in the hospital for a battery of tests. While he was there, five days after returning from his beloved Italy, Arturo Terranova—immigrant, husband, father, and store owner—suffered a massive cerebral hemorrhage. Two days later, his family at his side, he died.

Anna tried to keep the apartment on Fiftieth Street after her husband died, but the stairs became too much for her. Two years after Arturo died, she accepted Camille and Ben's invitation to live with them in New Jersey.

Now here it was, 1991. Anna wished Ben and Camille good morning when she walked into the large, modern kitchen, and they returned the greeting. Camille got up to turn on the gas under the kettle for mama.

Anna glanced at the TV. "Do you think we have another war?"

"I'm afraid so," Ben replied.

She waved her hand in disgust, then shuffled off to the bread basket where she located a slice of cinnamon raisin bread and placed it in the toaster. "When do they learn?"

In the newscast, a U.S. reconnaissance plane took off from Dhahran in Saudi Arabia, and Anna watched the plane soar into the sky. She thought about her grandson, Navy Air Force lieutenant John Terranova, and his parents, and a worried look came over her face. *What a nice young man, little John is, and now he must go to war. I give Michael and Jo a call. They must be so worried sick.*

Desert Shield became Desert Storm on January 16, 1991. For the first six weeks, the war was fought in the air and by sea. Evading radar, stealth bombers were the first to go on the attack, hitting communications centers with seemingly high-precision impunity. They were followed by waves of Allied fighters that sent Iraq's Soviet-made jets crashing into the ground or scurrying into nearby Iran for sanctuary. The fighters cleared the way for more bombers to destroy air-defense installations, military bases, Scud missile launching pads, and other targets. With the help of jets equipped to detect and neutralize enemy radar, the Allies quickly gained air supremacy. At the same time, Tomahawk cruise missiles were unleashed from carriers in the Gulf, traveling at speeds of 550 miles per hour.

With CNN leading the charge, the news media provided continuous coverage. By the looks of it, the smart bombs were striking their targets without causing too much collateral damage. Whether that was always true or the Pentagon was releasing only film of bombs that had hit their mark, the air and missile attacks displayed the awesome technological power of the Allies and underscored the stunning emergence of strategic bombing.

Tom Dempsey was not surprised when his reserve unit was called up, but he was caught off guard by the swiftness with which he was sent to join American forces in the Persian Gulf. In his mind's eye, he could still see his wife Gloria, the baby in her arms, kissing him goodbye and telling *him* not to worry. If only he could see her again. From a tent in the desert, he wrote her:

If I'm worried about anything, it's how you and the baby will manage while I'm way. I know your Mom and Dad will help, and that's great. But I'm not planning to be over here very long. We got a bunch of gung-ho guys who don't take crap from nobody, and we'll all be back before you know it. As far as I can see, this war in Arabia is a piece of cake.

In Saudi Arabia, Tom waited, and trained, for his turn to join the battle. For weeks, he practiced attacks on simulated enemy fortifications, wondering, like everyone else, when the land war would begin. As he watched Allied air forces pound a host of targets, he knew the time was drawing near when his outfit would be entering the war. Though he wouldn't admit it to anyone, he hoped the pilots had done a thorough job of clearing the way and reducing the strength of the enemy force that the foot soldier would have to face.

There was no telling what would happen next. Were the Iraq troops playing possum and holding out until the ground offensive began? Would the bloodbath many predicted now begin? Was there any truth to the rumor that 60,000 body bags were ordered for the confrontation?

The ground offensive began in the early morning of February 24. Allied soldiers in camouflage suits and carrying gear to protect themselves against chemical warfare attacked along a 300-mile front. U.S. marine and army divisions and British armored units, along with Saudi, Egyptian, and Syrian troops, stormed into Kuwait, while American and French airborne forces struck inside southern Iraq. Iraqi soldiers surrendered in droves, but there was no time to high-five a buddy in victory celebration.

"Keep moving, keep moving!" Tom's unit was told. With lightning speed, it pushed forward, as did the entire Allied force. All of a sudden, he found himself in a swirling sand storm that clouded his vision. Adding to the confusion were burning, bombed out tanks and other vehicles which were strewn all over the place along with the bodies of Iraqi military personnel.

Turning around to his rear, Tom saw three Iraqi soldiers coming over a dune, and he dropped to the ground and took aim. The Iraqis released their gear and raised their arms in surrender. What happened next was mostly a blur. Tom heard the blast, but that's all he remembered. Later in the hospital he learned that a bomb killed one of his buddies and the three Iraqi soldiers and wounded several others, including himself. He also learned that the missile was an errant bomb from an Allied war plane, what is referred to as friendly fire. Just as quickly as he was called to fight, the war was over for Tom.

And in a few days, the war was over for everyone. By the fourth day of the land battle, Kuwait City was liberated amid joyous celebrations. On February 27, President Bush announced that the two main objectives—the destruction of Iraq's military power and the liberation of Kuwait—had been met and he was suspending ground operations. In the soaring spirits of the moment, he was reported as declaring, "By God, we've kicked the Vietnam syndrome for once and for all!" True to his word, the President began bringing the troops home right away, although some observers argued that he should have finished off Saddam Hussein then and there. He didn't, and Saddam continued to rule Iraq with a tyrannical hand.

CHAPTER 18

▼

One evening a few months after the war was ended, Michael left the office following another long, exhausting day. Meetings and more meetings. Phone calls from hell. Long-winded, unfathomable memos from everyone. And now a growing batch of e-mails. There were the usual problems, some new, some old. Was he going to the managed health care meeting in Washington, D.C.? What to do about a top editor with a drinking problem? Where can he cut ten percent from the editorial budget?

After work, he met Casey Russell at a steakhouse. No pressure. Just two hard-working friends sharing a couple of beers, steak dinners, and some friendly, two-way conversation. Neither of them had a chance to watch the big ticker-tape parade earlier that June day, so Michael and Casey had an extra reason to get together that night: to toast the troops, including their children—John and Tanya—who had survived their first war and were due to return to the States next month.

When he arrived in his apartment later that night, Michael switched on the lights before settling in a chair in the living room and turning on the TV. A reporter was reviewing the victory parade up the Canyon of Heroes on Broadway. Michael tried to spot Tom Dempsey, who was supposed to be among the 12,000 or so soldiers from Desert Storm who marched in the parade, but a deluge of confetti made it almost impossible to find anyone. He made a mental note to call Christopher the next day to confirm whether Tom was there.

Michael was amazed by how far Americans had come in their acceptance of war.

Millions—as high as four million, according to police—lined the sidewalks earlier that day waving flags and banners and shouting "U.S.A.! U.S.A.!" On a smaller scale, victory celebrations were being played out in communities all over America. One can tell the popularity or unpopularity of a war by the way soldiers are treated when they come home, Michael reasoned. What a difference from when the troops came back from Vietnam! He wondered whether the advanced technology of modern weaponry had made war more tolerable.

There was a knock on the door. Michael lowered the TV and backed out of the room, still trying to catch a glimpse of Tom Dempsey and his family in the crowd. When he opened the door, he tried to make out a figure bent over by the side wall.

"Who's that?" Michael asked.

The figure raised its head but didn't answer.

"Jo? Jo, Jesus, is that you?" said Michael.

Jo slumped forward. "Please help me, Michael. I didn't know where else to go."

He lifted her in his arms and carried her into the bedroom. Placing her on the bed, he noticed that her face and arms were bruised and bloodied. Michael decided to put off the questions until he applied some first aid. He could handle the cuts and bruises, but he didn't know what to do about any possible internal injuries. "Are you in a lot of pain?" he asked. She nodded.

"You probably need an X-ray or something," he said. "Let me take you to the hospital."

She sat up in bed, a fierce look of protest in her eyes. "NO, NO, I don't want to cause any problem. Please, Michael."

"Alright, alright, just lie down."

Jo covered her eyes from the glare of the overhead light. Michael snapped off the ceiling light and turned on the lamp. "I just wanted to go home," she continued. "This was the closest place to home I could think of." She wanted to cry but it hurt too much.

"Who did this to you?" Michael finally asked.

"Please, Michael, I don't want any more trouble."

"I know, but who, Jo?" he persisted. "Was it Larry?"

Silence at first. Then slowly she began, "I don't know what happened to him, Michael. It's like he changed overnight. I mean one day he's fine, and we're talking about a vacation to Spain. Then the next day he comes home and throws his dinner plate against the wall."

"Okay, okay, just lie back."

"It had something to do with the war," she continued. "Almost from the start, we knew the movement wasn't getting the support...and I wasn't there to help him."

"Shh, shh, please."

"I couldn't do it this time," she went on. "I mean, our son's flying missions over Iraq. Then John's letter arrives."

Michael nodded his understanding. "So, Larry took over, and the antiwar movement was a bust," he concluded.

"Yes."

"And then the war ended, just like that, and Larry became furious, with himself and the way things worked out."

"Yes."

Neither spoke for several minutes. Jo finally broke the silence. "First, it was just a shove," she continued, almost in a whisper. "I should never have allowed it and walked out then and there. I didn't. In a strange way, I felt sorry for him." She took a deep breath.

"Today was the final straw," she continued. "We were watching the parade on television. He couldn't understand why millions of people came out to cheer the troops. He called them—the spectators—traitors, and he started going berserk. He picked up my picture of John and threw it against the wall. That's it. I had to leave. He told me, 'Go ahead, traitor,' and he punched me, and shoved me out the door, and, when I fell...he kicked me."

Michael felt an anger he hadn't felt since someone called him "Wop!" in high school. "You can't go back there now."

"I know, I know."

"You can stay here."

Jo sobbed, in spite of the stabbing pain.

"Shh, shh, try to rest now. You need your strength."

Sobbing quietly, Jo fell asleep. Michael turned off the lamp and went into the living room.

He knew she needed medical attention, but he didn't know what to do. Then he remembered Casey Russell's daughter was an intern, so he called Casey to see if she might be available for a house call. Within a half-hour, Rhonda was at his apartment, medical bag in hand, ready to exercise her new medical skills.

Later that evening, after Rhonda had left, Michael took another look at the battered woman on the bed and jumped out of his chair. This was a good time to do what he felt he had to do. Jo was sleeping. A man on a mission, he bolted out the front door and down the stairs into the street below. He had no trouble directing the cab driver to Larry's apartment. Michael knew the address from Jo's rare correspondence to him, and once he walked past the building on his day off just to see where she lived. Even though the divorce was final, he'd never gotten over Jo and everything they shared together.

Michael found the apartment number on the mailbox and walked up one flight. He could visualize Larry kicking Jo at the top of the stairs, and he winced. He knocked on the door twice. No answer. He knocked again. Still no answer. Finally, he could hear the lock turning, and the door opened slightly, still linked to the frame by an emergency chain.

Michael didn't wait for the door to be opened completely for him. With a thrust of his well-tuned leg, he kicked it wide open. Larry, in full pajamas, went crashing to the floor behind him. An old woman next door came out to check out the commotion, saw what was happening, and went back into the house. She never liked Larry.

Michael grabbed Larry by the collar and yanked him off the ground. Then punching him with such force that he fell to his knees, he said, "Believe it or not, I'm not a violent man, but if you ever touch Jo again, I'll kill you myself. Understand?"

"Yes," Larry whispered.

"I can't hear you."

"Yes, yes," Larry repeated.

Michael reached over and picked up his glasses, which had fallen on the floor. "I'm going to send someone to get her stuff, all of her stuff. I want no trouble. Understand?"

"Yes, yes."

"Good, good." Michael walked into the bedroom and looked around. When he spotted John's picture on the floor, he picked it out of the shattered frame and headed toward the front door. Larry was sitting up now on the floor and rubbing the back of his head.

"Remember our agreement," said Michael before pulling the door shut.

"Traitors," Larry mumbled.

"What did you say?"

"Nothing, nothing."

Outside, Michael managed to flag down a taxi right away. On the way home, he couldn't believe what had just happened, but he felt no remorse for what he had done. He hoped the ride uptown would be a fast one. Jo was home.

Tom Dempsey's concussion and internal injuries had healed nicely by the time he arrived in New York City. Any uneasiness or fear he had about returning home disappeared when he walked into his apartment and saw Gloria. Such a depth of love and compassion enveloped his wife, and she seemed so much calmer. Considering that she tended to be a bit frenetic at times, especially in a crisis, it was a welcome change. What's more, Tom was amazed by how much Thomas Christopher had grown in such a short time, and the little guy was smiling now, like a real person!

There was something different about Tom, too. It was difficult to tell exactly what it was. A quiet reflection. A trace of melancholy. A mind occasionally set adrift somewhere. The new Tom wasn't bragging about his conquests in Arabia, as the old Tom might have. Gloria noticed the change immediately, but she would not question it. A couple of days after his arrival, she changed her mind.

It was getting dark, and both Gloria and Tom had fallen asleep on the sofa. The TV set was still on, but the sound was low. The air conditioner was humming a monotonous, but refreshing tune. And baby was dry and fast asleep in his crib. Suddenly, Tom sat up and started screaming, "Keep moving, keep moving!" Then, "Hands up, hands up, you bastards!" And, "Oh, no! No!"

Gloria jumped up, her eyes blinking crazily, and she was shaking. "Jesus, what's the matter, Tom?"

"Save him! Save them! Don't let me die!"

Thomas Christopher began crying.

"Tom, please, the baby."

"Help me…somebody!"

Gloria didn't know where to turn. She dashed into the baby's room and tried to calm him down. "Shh, shh, Everything's okay." Gradually, he stopped crying.

Rocking the baby gently in her arms, she came back into the living room. Tom was sitting on the edge of the sofa now, his head in his hands.

"You alright?" said Gloria, the new calmness vanished from her face.

"Just a dream, a bad dream," he explained.

"You scared me."

"I'm sorry. You know me. I usually sleep like a rock. But ever since…."

"Ever since what?"

He got up from the couch and turned off the TV. "I don't want to talk about it."

"Maybe you should."

"Why? Will it bring back Buddy…or those three poor bastards?" He was sweating and trembling.

"Oh, Tom, I'm so sorry." She reached out and held him close with one arm.

"I'm going to bed," he said when he broke away. "Don't worry. It only happens once a night."

The friendly-fire incident came back the next night, and the next, and many nights after that. Gradually, it disappeared except for an occasional thought wave triggered by something as ordinary as a sudden burst of wind, the smell of diesel fuel, or a loud noise. Once in church the loudspeaker started crackling loudly, and he dropped to the floor in panic. Within a month, Tom was given his old job back at the supermarket, and he began working weekends at Christopher's car repair shop. He still hoped to be a fire fighter, and he would complete his tour with the army reserves, which would end next year, but he had a new view of war. He had come to believe that despite its occasional brevity, war was not what it was cracked up to be by its proponents. It made him sick.

Lieutenant John Terranova came to a similar conclusion as he waited for his orders to return home. From his bird's-eye view of the war, he had seen the long, smoking trails of destruction and death in the desert terrain, and he knew he had contributed to the devastation.

From the sky, he saw smoking and burning tanks, trucks, and other carriers, many shattered to pieces by smart bombs and missiles. Littering the desert floor were the stolen treasures of war—TV sets, furniture, toys, carpets, jewelry, clothes, and other precious items—which Iraqi soldiers had hoped to carry home from Kuwait. He saw tank crews abandoning their costly Soviet-built machines and heading home on foot. Hundreds of Iraqi soldiers waved white flags and other articles of surrender and greeted American troops as if they were their liberators rather than their enemies.

Never before had an American victory in a major war been secured with such phenomenal speed and with such technological brilliance. Fewer than 200 American lives were lost, and slightly more than 500 were wounded, while there were approximately 100,000 Iraqi casualties and thousands more who surrendered. Even so, all John wanted to do now was go home. He couldn't wait to hold his wife in his arms again.

In some ways, the waiting—the waiting to go into battle, the waiting to get out of the battle, and the waiting to return home—was the most difficult part of the war for John. Oh, hell, he knew he had nothing to complain about. He had survived his first war, and he would return home to Virginia Beach without any visible scars.

Finally, the day arrived, and he was walking up the steps of his stately home, a gift of Eloise's wealthy parents. His heart skipped a beat in anticipation of seeing his wife again. It was like the first time he saw this stunningly beautiful woman at a pool party and learned that she had postponed plans to be a teacher after graduating from the University of Virginia and, at the urging of some college chums, entered several beauty pageants around the country. As it turned out, Eloise Parker made it to the finals in each case. What's more, she liked the way the beauty pageants made her feel so much she eventually took a job with one of them as a public relations coordinator. That's what she was doing when John met her at his air force buddy's pool party. There followed a torrid romance between them which made her stodgy parents nervous but which culminated in marriage less than a year later.

"Hello, anyone home?" John shouted as he opened the front door. No one answered. He was disappointed Eloise was not home, but he was not surprised. His wife was in constant motion, as if there were just not enough hours in the day for everything she wanted to do. In her absence, he took a shower, poured himself a glass of bourbon, and threw himself across the bed for a much needed nap. When he woke up two hours later, he was not alone in bed.

"Welcome home, fly boy," said Eloise in a sultry, Southern lilt.

"Jesus, you scared me," said John, shaking out the cobwebs. "For a minute, I thought you were one of the guys."

They both laughed as they reached out to embrace each other. They kissed passionately, hungrily. Feeling her softness and warmth again. Catching the aroma of her beautiful body. Renewing an intimacy with her. Looking into her soul again through her loving eyes. It was a moment John had been dreaming about for months.

"Sorry I wasn't here to greet you when you came home," she said, gently touching his face.

"It's okay, champ."

"I met some old friends—Judy and Peter Duffy—and we started talking, and the next thing you know we're having lunch," she explained.

"You gotta eat."

"I get so lonely when you're not here," Eloise continued. "I just want to die."

"Well, I'm here now, and I won't be going anywhere, and I don't want you to die."

"You don't understand, John."

He reached out and kissed her, gently this time. "I do. Maybe we ought to think about having some children to fill up this big, old house."

"Just hold me, hold me tight," Eloise whispered, tears filling her dazzling blue eyes.

"Come here, champ." John felt a vulnerability and longing in her he had never sensed before. "Hey, I'm not going anywhere now."

Over the next week, John and Eloise were inseparable, spending most of their time entertaining and visiting family and friends in the Virginia Beach area. The following week, they headed up to the New York area for a visit with the Terranova and Stern branches of the family. First stop in the city was a visit with Jo and Michael.

John had no idea his parents were back together—or at least living in the same apartment—when he entered Michael's uptown apartment. The fact that his mother was there didn't surprise him, but when she started arranging things around the house, changing her clothes in the bedroom, and cooking supper he became suspicious.

"Okay, am I seeing things or not?" said John. "Are you guys…."

"Living together?" said Michael, completing the thought.

"Yes," said John.

"Yes, we are," Jo replied. "In case you're wondering, Larry and I broke up, called it quits, ended our relationship, whatever you want to call it, and your father was nice enough to take this poor waif into his home."

"You have a problem with that?" Michael added.

John looked over at Eloise. "Did you know?" She was smiling.

"Now don't jump to conclusions," said Jo quickly. "We didn't tie the knot again, or anything like that. We're just an odd couple who happen to be old friends who are living together. Who knows what the future will bring?"

"Whatever you call it, I like it," said John, smiling.

2001

CHAPTER 19

▼

By now Camille was an expert at hosting parties. She had organized enough of them for Ben over the years. This one, however, was making her very nervous. It was mama's 90th birthday, and close to 70 family members, relatives, and friends were scheduled to attend. They were coming to her home in Ridgewood, New Jersey, from as far south as Virginia Beach, Virginia, as far west as Mesa, Arizona, and as far north as Watertown, New York.

The day of the party—Sunday, September 9, 2001—also happened to be Grandparents' Day, which put extra pressure on Camille to get it right. And, weather permitting, Ben's ninety-two-year-old father, Abraham Stern, who had been in seclusion since his wife died last year, was planning to attend. He said he "wouldn't miss Mrs. Terranova's birthday for the world" and he'd be there "with bells on." Both Camille and Ben were overjoyed by his father's decision to come. They arranged to send a limo to bring him to the party and back home to Brooklyn.

Finally, the big day arrived. Hands on hips, hazel-eyed Camille looked through the sliding glass door separating the kitchen from the terrace and garden area behind the house. She was a handsome woman, and, despite a few unwelcome wrinkles around her eyes and mouth, there was plenty of life in the sixty-nine-year-old gal. She was fighting a bit of a weight problem, as she had been doing most of her adult life, but she always carried herself with pride and poise. Generally, the years had been good to Camille. She recovered completely from a partial mastectomy, which had sent her into a tailspin a few years ago, and, except for an occasional arthritis flare-up in her shoulder and some cartilage loss in her right knee, she was in reasonably good health, which she attributed to excellent genes, mainly mama's. What's more, she never lost her innate gentleness and kindness, despite a new toughness that came with living and parenting and being part of a perilous new world filled with threatening events.

Camille decided to check the party area one more time. Sliding back the glass door, she walked out onto a bricked terrace lined with potted plants and shaded by a large maple tree planted by the original owner of the house 35 years earlier. Two bursts of flowers were arranged on a long table where the hors d'oeuvres and drinks would be served. At one end of the terrace were quiet, peaceful nooks with glass-topped tables and black wrought iron chairs. At the other end under the maple was a cluster of cushiony outdoor furniture reserved for the guest of honor and her entourage.

The terrace looked out onto an ample, well-manicured lawn framed by wild flowers that danced around rhododendron and hollyhocks. More tables were set up on the lawn under a tent near a gated pool. Camille gave a tug on the pool gate to make sure it was locked. Everything was in place. Everything except for the food, most of which was being catered. Only a few favorites, including home-made *orecchiette*, plus the inch-thick *focaccia* the kids loved, were not being handled by the caterers. They were being supplied with loving care by grandma Terranova in collaboration with her sister, Aunt Loretta-Loretta. Both were reasonably spry for their ages, although they moved with more deliberateness and caution.

Shaking her head at the absence of the food trays, Camille hobbled as quickly as she could into her spacious, two-story colonial American home. On a marble-topped table in the hallway, she picked up a phone and started dialing. Before she could finish, she heard someone coming down the stairs..

"Are you calling them again?" inquired her daughter Loretta. She had noticed that her mother was a hot potato ready to burst ever since Mass earlier that day.

"Who?" asked Camille with an innocence that failed to mask a trace of guilt.

"You know who, mom," Loretta replied.

"Well, it *is* getting late."

"We have plenty of time, mom. They said they'd be here by noon." Loretta seemed sure the caterers would keep their word. "They don't want to come too early because the food will spoil."

Momentarily deflated, Camille cradled the phone. "I suppose you're right." For the time being, the storm in her subsided. Together they walked down the hallway to the kitchen, where there were some serious deliberations in progress.

At one end of a long, oak table in the large, bright kitchen, Ben was having coffee with Alex, Loretta's husband, and discussing the latest wave of violence in the Mideast. Always in search of an attentive ear on world affairs and politics, Ben found one in Alex Conway, a high school teacher and history buff who had long held that Israel should get out of the captured areas in Palestine, the Gaza Strip, and the Golan Heights. For security reasons, Ben opposed such actions. The Jews had suffered long enough, thought Ben, but at the same time he was sympathetic to the plight of the Palestinian people. While both Ben and Alex were steadfast in defense of their beliefs, they respected each other's opinions. Well, most of the time.

Their discussion was building into a vigorous debate when Camille and Loretta entered the room. "Knock it off, you guys," said Loretta. "This is Sunday, a day of rest."

"I'm Jewish, remember?" said Ben.

"So am I—at least half," Loretta countered. "Besides, it's grandma's birthday."

Sitting quietly at the other end of the table, grandma—Anna Terranova—continued to roll the dough with her thumb into small pieces with short, quick movements. Nearby, her sister rolled a ball of dough into a long string, cut the string into small pieces, and swept the pieces to the side of the wooden baking board or *tavolo* before Anna turned them into "little ears" of dough. Off to the side, eleven-year-old Arthur Conway—Loretta and Alex's son—tried his hand at making the *orecchiette,* but he couldn't quite master the quick sweep of the thumb.

Anna patted her granddaughter on the hand. "Maybe I like to hear, Loretta," said grandma softly. "I get some idea what is happening in the world."

Ben turned to his daughter. "See," he boasted, a smile across his creased face.

Anna glanced out the sliding glass door, then went back to making the *orecchiette.* "I think the caterers, they come now," she said.

Camille leapt off the chair and headed toward the terrace for a conference with the food people. With a sigh, her daughter followed her.

The guests started coming in groups around noon. Among the first to arrive were Jeffrey Stern and his wife Annie, along with their five-year-old son Benjamin, better known as Little Ben, the apple of grandfather Big Ben's eye. They came from downtown Manhattan.

"HERE HE IS," said grandpa Stern, a twinkle in his eye, as he saw his namesake, glued to his mother, gingerly step onto the terrace. Wide-eyed, Little Ben spotted the platters of hors d'oeuvres on a long table decorated with flowers and candles. There was a man in a white jacket and chef's hat carving turkey and ham in the corner. Out on the lawn near the tent, a large assemblage of balloons in many brilliant colors also caught Little Ben's eyes. "What do you say you give grandpa a big hug, then we get you a nice balloon?"

"Don't forget to say hello to grandma," Annie reminded her son. "And where is the birthday girl?" she added. "Oh, there you are. Happy birthday, grandma. My, my, how beautiful you look in that pink dress! It's a real show-stopper."

Grandma Terranova smiled graciously. "Thank you." She always liked Annie. She was loud, a bit overbearing, but she had a big heart.

To Jeffrey, a rather serious and introverted young man, Annie was a beautiful woman who possessed a cheerfulness and spontaneity he always wished he had. He had met Annie at work. While her good looks and charm caught his eye first, it was her compassion at a funeral for an elderly coworker who died a week before he was to retire that made Jeffrey want to know more about this outgoing, caring woman from Mississippi. Eventually, they started going out for lunch, then dinner, even though interoffice relationships were discouraged at the investment firm.

Jeffrey's twin brother David, who worked in the other tower in the World Trade Center, would sometimes join them for lunch. Annie always broke up in tears of pure laughter listening to David's latest dating exploits, and David couldn't stop laughing when Annie told him why she decided to move to the city: To escape the noise and clamor of living with five other siblings, Annie—the next to oldest—came to New York for "some peace and quiet."

Five months after they started dating, Jeffrey and Annie were married. They settled in a modest apartment downtown. While they were making plans to move to a larger place uptown, they discovered Annie was pregnant and decided to stay put. Then Little Ben was born, and, with a few adjustments, they settled down in their downtown apartment.

David Stern was the next to arrive, also from lower Manhattan. With him was a pretty auburn-haired woman named Virginia Snider, from the upper Eighties, whom David had been dating for a few weeks and felt confident enough to bring to the party. Ginny worked as a media planner at a multinational ad agency that was rumored to be going through yet another merger. A faraway look in her light blue eyes betrayed a fear that she would be merged out of a job next week. David thought the party might help take her mind away from any corporate decisions that were in the offing. He was considerate that way.

Though footloose when it came to his social life, David was always ready to lend a helping hand to anyone who needed it. His mother, for one, called on him frequently for "a favor"—taking her to the doctor's office when Ben was unavailable, driving Grandma Terranova to the cemetery, picking up some pastries in the city. And David's strong interest in health care made him the go-to guy in the family for information about a new medicine or some other medical matter.

Christopher and Patsy Terranova decided to take their Dodge Caravan and drive in from Long Island with their daughter Gloria and Tom Dempsey and their ten-year-old son Thomas Christopher. Eight years earlier, Gloria and Tom fulfilled two of their dreams. They were married in a quiet church ceremony, and Tom became a New York City firefighter.

Twenty-three-year-old Anthony, who was the picture of his mother Patsy, came to the party separately in an old Mercury he rebuilt at his father's auto repair shop, where he worked. He hoped someday to be a partner in the business. Nothing would have pleased Christopher more, but he was worried that his son might be following too closely in his footsteps and drinking too much. Recently, there were too many late nights with the boys, and when Anthony did come home, he went straight to bed. Somehow, Anthony always managed to report to work on time the next day.

With some reluctance at first, then more boldly, Christopher asked his son where he had been the night before. The answer was almost always the same: "Just out with the guys. You know, pizza, a couple of brewskies, is all."

Christopher tried to appear cool and calm, "Watch those brewskies, Anthony. They have a way of sneaking up on you. I know a lot about them." It was no secret in the family that Christopher was a recovering alcoholic.

Anthony was always quick with the response. "Don't worry, dad. Everything's under control."

Christopher had an answer, as well. "I thought everything was under control, too."

When Anthony arrived at the party, the first thing he did was throw his arms around grandma Terranova, his phone confidante of many years, and wish her a happy birthday. "You look beautiful, grandma," he said, giving her enthusiastic kisses on both cheeks. The second thing he did was pop open a bottle of beer before going around to greet everyone.

Michael and Jo traveled to the party together. Why not? They were still friends, good friends, and the family loved seeing them together.

After Jo's breakup with Larry, she and Michael tried to make another go of it, starting with Jo's moving into Michael's apartment uptown. Living together again was awkward at first, but these were old lovers with many happy, warm remembrances they hoped to recapture. Soon they were making love that was both passionate and unselfish, and, like the old days, they found plenty to laugh about, especially when they were making love and Michael introduced a new twist into his lovemaking. "Where'd you learn that one?" said Jo one night.

Even if he remembered, he wouldn't say. "Pretty good, eh?"

"Not bad, a little weird, but different," she commented.

"I got a million of 'em."

"Oh, boy!"

Years of separation had taken their toll on both of them, however. As the weeks turned into months, they saw less and less of each other, their lives drifting in separate directions.

Michael went on one business trip after another in search of a new vision for the company in an economy turned topsy-turvy by an unbelievable surge in technology. Although teaching was second nature to her, Jo seemed to be carrying a heavier work load each year at her school in lower Manhattan, and her classes were getting larger. When Michael was away, she visited her old friends in the Village and resumed her volunteer work on behalf of the neighborhood and world peace. Then one day she decided to set up her own residence again downtown.

"If that's what you want," said Michael, when Jo told him of her plans. "You need to do what you need to do." Secretly, he was crushed by her decision to move.

She seemed to feel his hurt, but he was right. She needed to do what she needed to do. "If you don't mind, I'd like to keep in touch with you," she said.

"I don't mind. You know where I live."

She threw her arms around him. "If you don't know it by now, I love you, Michael. I always will."

Michael wiped away a tear from her eye. "You have a strange way of showing it."

True to her word, Jo stayed in touch. From time to time they had dinner together and talked about their son John the airman, who lived with his wife Eloise and their two children in Virginia Beach. When the holidays came, Michael and Jo made a point of doing something together. Sometimes, doing something together meant going out with Casey and Jill Russell or buying some Christmas presents for the grandchildren.

Twice Jo ran into Larry Mazur. She was cordial but cool both times, resisting his efforts to renew their relationship. On one of those occasions, he apologized for his "bad behavior" in 1991, explaining that he must have been out of his mind with "despair over how the peace movement was going then." But she excused herself, pretending she had to meet Michael. Larry turned ashen with fear when he heard that.

Jo threw herself into her volunteer work with new vigor. This time around, she was determined to do something to stop a war from happening before it became a family issue with her. On the world stage, Jo kept a wary eye on the new President—George W. Bush, son of the President who led the nation during the Persian Gulf war—as conflicts in places like the Middle East rose and fell in intensity. With Saddam Hussein continuing in power, Iraq was always a problem. More troubling to Jo now was the rise in terrorism, which took a new turn with the explosion of Pan Am flight 103 over Lockerbee, Scotland, in December 1988 and with the truck bombing of the World Trade Center in 1993.

Anna was so happy to see Michael and Jo together.

What a dynamic couple John and Eloise Terranova made as they got out of their silver Lincoln Navigator. They came to the party with their son John, Jr., a five-year-old in constant search of adventure, and their daughter Rachel, a seven-year-old going on thirty, or so her parents thought.

John, a lieutenant colonel in the air force now, was not in uniform when he arrived at grandma's party, but he was a picture of confidence, the look of a man on the move with clearly defined goals. He had his mother's striking blue eyes; his hair was dark and, in his father's image, thinning prematurely, and there was a seriousness to his mouth that mirrored both parents. Even so, he enjoyed a good laugh on occasion, but he was not one to initiate it.

In his early years of service, John's duty to country often clashed with his mother's commitment to the peace movement, so he learned that subjects such as war and warplanes, combat missions, and bombs (smart and otherwise) were better off not discussed in her presence. It was different with his dad. John could discuss anything with him. Anything except his relationship with Eloise.

When John first learned his wife had cheated on him, he was devastated. He couldn't—didn't want to—believe it. After all, Eloise was an educated person from a rich Virginia family with a strong commitment to the Christian movement, and they—John and Eloise—had what he thought was a solid relationship. It was true that some things such as their imposing home came easily to them, gifts of her family, but John always thought he and his wife had their feet planted firmly on the ground and would always do what was best for their family.

It was on a recent mission he was carrying out abroad that John was told of his wife's infidelity. Coming from one of his wife's closest friends, the tell-all letter revealed to John an intimate meeting Eloise had with one of her college friends. "I'm sorry to have to be the one to tell you this," Margo Doolittle wrote in her letter, "but I thought it best to tell you for your sake and for the sake of the children." His calmness and coolness vanished, John wanted to take off on an unscheduled mission and crash his plane, himself, and Margo's letter into the ground. He didn't.

After much agonizing, he thought it best, for the sake of the children, to see if things could be repaired. He remembered how it was for him after his mother and father broke up. The hurt and pain in their faces! The fear and sadness he felt when he and mama walked into their new apartment in the Village! The strangeness when he first started seeing his dad again! He recalled those frightening, lonely nights in 1991 when he was getting ready to fly his first attack missions in the Persian Gulf war. He recalled writing his parents back then and reminding them of "the great times" the three of them shared doing "little things" together. John would do whatever he must to keep his family together. Initially, that meant not saying anything when he got back home. Maybe it was a one-time thing. Maybe it would all go away. Maybe it never happened.

The strain between them was evident, however. They chose their words carefully. They tried to say all the right things, often failing miserably. They focused on world events and avoided personal matters and personal contact. Finally, one night after the children had gone to bed, Eloise said, "Is everything okay, John?"

He searched for the right words. He couldn't find them. "Why did you do it?" he exploded.

Eloise saw the hurt in his face. She didn't, couldn't, deny it. She tried to explain. It was a chance meeting with an old college chum, Harper Rice. Harper, who was married with three kids and living in Chicago, was in town for a couple of days on his way to a pharmaceutical meeting. She was surprised at first when he called her, but she agreed to meet him. They met, had too much to drink, and things spun out of control.

"And who was watching the kids?" John wanted to know.

"Margo Doolittle."

John nodded.

"I'm so sorry, John," she finally said, tears flooding her eyes. "I was lonely. I know no one's to blame but me...you were away so often, for so long. I'd do anything if I could erase what I did. It meant nothing to me, nothing but pain and misery. Can you ever forgive me? Whatever you want to do...."

John put up his hand to stop her from continuing. "Let's give it another shot," he whispered. "For the children." Then he added, "If I ever see that son of a bitch around here, he's a dead man."

Their hands linked in family unison, John and Eloise and the two children made their way to greet the guest of honor.

All of her grandchildren and great-grandchildren were special to Anna, but her face lit up like a little girl's when she saw John coming toward her at the party. He was a frequent visitor to her West Side apartment when he was growing up, and she remembered with fondness that summer when she was his babysitter. "Is this little John?" she cried as she reached up with her two hands and kissed him. She saw something in his eyes. "You look so tired," she concluded. "You okay?"

"I'm fine, grandma. How are you? Happy birthday."

She kissed him again. "Where's your lovely wife?" she inquired.

"Right here."

"Remember me...Eloise?" she reminded grandma as she bent over to kiss her. "Happy birthday."

"I know who you are," said grandma Terranova. "She is very beautiful, John. Nice catch."

He smiled proudly. "I know."

CHAPTER 20

▼

By early afternoon, the party was in full swing. Anna sat on the terrace surveying the whole scene with so much love and pride, taking particular joy in watching the kids run around and play. Oh, how she wished Arturo were alive to see everyone together!

On the terrace with her were Aunt Loretta-Loretta, a widow for almost a year now, and her late brother Pietro's wife, Angelina Rubino, who came all the way down from Watertown with her unmarried daughter, Maria. Anna's other brother, Rafaello Rubino, was living in Arizona, but too frail to travel, so his grandson, Jason Rubino, who always wanted to visit the New York area, volunteered to come in his place. Uncle Ralphie's two former wives were both long gone.

One of the last to arrive was Ben's father, Abe Stern, a short, stooped gentleman who bowed politely whenever he was introduced to someone. Camille led him to a seat next to the guest of honor. Gradually, Abe joined in the laughter and shared stories about his early days in America following his arrival from Russia. Ben was delighted that for the first time in a long time his father was in such good spirits.

The conversations in and around the garden were lively, capsulizing what Americans—or at least New Yorkers—had on their minds on Sunday, September 9, 2001.

Although the football season was just getting started, baseball headed the list of discussion subjects among the diehard sports fans. "Can you believe it? Barry Bonds might beat Mark McGwire's three-year-old home run record," Casey Russell noted.

"How about those Mets?" observed Christopher Terranova. "*Now,* they're waking up. Hey, you never know." David Stern showed his Yankees pinstripes. "I can't get over that Roger Clemens," he said. "He's like the Energizer bunny. Just keeps going."

Ben Stern was interested in the outcome of the New York City mayoral race. "Who do you think will win?" he asked Jo. "It looks like Ferrer over Green," she replied, "but I think Bloomberg will take it all. Frankly, I don't like any of them, but I'm glad to see Giuliani go."

The subject was television at another group. "I think the 'Seinfeld' reruns are still the funniest show on the air," said Loretta Conway. Eloise agreed. Jill Russell liked "Will and Grace." Gloria, Tom Dempsey' wife, voted for "Everybody Loves Raymond," then announced to everyone that she was pregnant again, leading to screams that seemed to roll out to the entire neighborhood. Christopher and Patsy, who already knew, beamed.

The outburst was enough reason for two of the boys, Arthur and Thomas Christopher, to run into the house and play some games on grandpa Ben's computer. "Why do girls always scream when they talk about babies?" young Arthur wanted to know. "Yeah, boys never do," observed Thomas Christopher.

Michael Terranova was concerned about the state of the economy and the market. "The dot-coms are dot-gones. What do you make of the stock market?" he asked his nephew Jeffrey Stern. "Buy, buy, buy," Jeffrey suggested. "But I'm not sure we've hit bottom yet," he added.

"Where're you heading next?" Alex Conway asked John Terranova, whom he hadn't seen in a while. "Home—Virginia Beach—I hope," the airman replied. "I've had my fill of traveling, for a while."

Annie, Jeffrey's wife, raved about Chrysler's new PT Cruisers. "They're so stylish. What do you think?" she asked Christopher's son, Anthony. "Not my speed," he replied. "Literally. Not enough power for me."

On the fringe of the party, Tom Dempsey, the firefighter, and Jason Rubino, from Arizona, were drinking beer and having a quiet conversation. The younger Jason, himself a volunteer firefighter, was curious about fighting fires in a big city. "You'd be surprised by the number of nuisance fires we have to answer," said Tom. "Hey, you never know. I'm still waiting for the big one."

"Can we go into the pool, Aunt Camille?" John, Jr. begged.

"Oh, please, grandma, please," pleaded Little Ben.

"No, no pool today...not on great grandma Anna's birthday," said Camille.

"Too many shark attacks lately," her daughter Loretta chimed in.

"And don't forget the West Nile mosquitoes," Dottie Wood added.

Eight-year-old Rachel, always serious, was one of the few who didn't laugh. "What next?" she wondered out loud.

Throughout the day and into the evening, neighbors came and went, extending their best wishes to Anna and contributing to the flow of conversation. When friends and neighbors drifted away, the only ones left were family. Some of the children, secure in the presence of so many familiar faces, fell asleep in the warm night air.

Monday, September 10, was a travel day for some of the partygoers. John and Eloise and their two children headed back to Virginia after spending the night at Michael's place in the city. Angelina Rubino and her daughter Maria headed back home to upstate New York after an overnight stay with the Sterns. Aunt Loretta-Loretta planned to stay another night before going home to Long Island on Tuesday. From cousin Camille's home, Jason Rubino planned to do some sightseeing in the city over the next few days before returning to Arizona. Anna enjoyed seeing everyone and looked forward to spending another day with her sister. Except for a couple of the kids, who were repeatedly denied a swim in the pool, everyone agreed the party was a smashing success.

Early the next morning, Camille was lying in bed when she suddenly started kicking her legs furiously in her sleep. It was only a dream, but it seemed so real.

A child under her arm, Camille is trying to outrun them, but on every street in the city she encounters another hostile gang. In close pursuit, gang members bang their metal pipes on the sidewalk. Where to go? All Camille knows is that she has to get back home to New Jersey. Not a taxi or bus or train in sight. She can feel the pain and fatigue building up in her legs as she runs and runs. Behind her, flashing knives and pipes. Some of the gang members are getting awfully close. Nothing she can do but thrust out her legs backwards and kick and kick....

"Honey, honey, take it easy," said Ben. "It's alright. Take it easy."

Camille was soaked with sweat when she woke up. She was breathing hard, and her heart was beating like a piston, but she was relieved when she saw Ben. "I had a dream, a terrible dream," she explained. "I was being chased in the city."

"Again?"

"Yes, again. It was like I couldn't get away from these gangs, and they were gaining on me, and there was no one around to help me."

Ben reached out and held her hand. "It was just a dream. It's over now."

Camille shook her head. "Why can't I have nice dreams again?" she asked no one in particular. She looked at the clock on the night table. It was almost 6:30, and she remembered it was Tuesday, September 11, 2001. She decided to get up and make some breakfast.

Once again Ben tried to soothe her. "They say it's going to be a beautiful day."

Not far away that same morning, Loretta Conway decided to make Alex and Arthur waffles. "What's the occasion?" inquired her husband Alex, enraptured by the aroma and the sounds of soft rock spilling out of the radio. Close behind him, Arthur also picked up the scent. "Is it Sunday?" the boy inquired.

Loretta laughed, lifting the lid of the waffle maker and pulling out another batch. "It's a beautiful morning. Sit down and eat before they get cold," she said, as she looked out the kitchen window at the New York City skyline across the Hudson River. Loretta Conway always loved the sight, but this morning it was particularly beautiful.

Often, she thought about the people she knew who lived across the river. Uncle Michael and Aunt Jo. The Long Islanders: Uncle Christopher and Aunt Patsy, along with cousins Anthony and Gloria and her husband, Tom Dempsey. Then there were Jeffrey and Annie and Little Ben and, of course, David, who was always there when you needed him. Would he ever find himself? How she had grown to love her brothers, and, though they were only a river away, she missed them when she didn't see them for a few days.

Early that morning, Christopher Terranova bent over and kissed Patsy before leaving for the gas station. He had a lot of jobs on his work sheet for today. Mr. Moresco's Taurus needed a tuneup. There was "a strange scratching sound" like "a squirrel going up a drain pipe" in Judy Gnagy's Neon. It might take the better part of the day to find the cause of the electrical failure in Tim Kelly's pickup, and, of course, he hadn't finished the break job and tire rotation in Nancy Fung's Camry.

Christopher was going to call Anthony one more time but decided not to wake him. He had been out late again with the boys. As happy as he was about becoming a grandfather—and now the whole world was aware of the good news—Christopher was worried sick about Anthony and his brewskies. He knew he had to have a wake-up talk with his son. Today, no-fail.

Michael Terranova didn't do anything different when he got up that morning. He worked out for half an hour on the treadmill, showered, and made himself a bowl of cereal—a blend of Cheerios and Fiber One with half a banana. His sugar was a little high, and he had to watch those carbs, like the good doctor said. Boy, what he wouldn't do for a doughnut loaded with vanilla custard and laced with chocolate, but he settled for the cereal and a cup of coffee. He flicked on CNN, but his thoughts were elsewhere. *I wonder if everything is alright with John and Eloise. They seemed a little subdued, and later, here at the apartment, a bit anxious about heading back home. I'll have to talk with Jo and see what she thinks.*

Camille was still trying to shake off the dregs of her dream when she went into the kitchen. Jason Rubino was at the table spreading some more cream cheese on a bagel. "Can't get enough of these New York bagels, Mrs. S," he announced, licking his lips in mock tribute to his loaded sesame bagel. Camille wondered how he stayed so thin. "What're you doing up so early, Jason?"

"Meeting a friend from college in the city," he replied. "We're going to do some more sightseeing."

"Where're you going today?" She flicked on the "Today Show."

"Don't know yet," said Jason, polishing off his bagel and getting up from the table. "Maybe we'll explore downtown. Sorry, I've got to catch my bus."

"Be careful," said Camille, as he bolted past Ben in the hallway.

"You have a nice day, too," said Ben with a smile. He was heading for his morning walk.

It was almost nine o'clock when Anthony pulled into the parking spot next to his father's car. Christopher was finished with the Explorer and working on the Neon. Anthony had a wild, anxious look in his eyes when he walked into the bay where his father was working. "Dad, turn on the TV."

"We need to talk first, son."

"Dad, quick. I just heard it on my car radio," Anthony insisted. "You won't believe what just happened."

CHAPTER 21

▼

The morning sky was cloudless and hung like the Virgin Mother's mantle, pure and blue, over the city. It promised to be a gorgeous day, sunny and warm but not muggy, sure to make some forecaster's list of Top 10 best weather days of the year.

New Yorkers were stirring, tuning up for another day. People of all sizes, shapes, and backgrounds were getting ready to go to work or school in search of a good or better life for themselves and their families. Rich mingled with poor, although most were somewhere in between. There were morning people, cheerful and smiling, mixed with zombies on cruise control and cranks who needed time to warm up. All over the city, they bought their Starbucks coffee and bagels and headed for work, while thousands of glum-faced children lugged knapsacks back to school, their long summer days at the beach or in the hills a fading memory now. At designated areas, the last tourists of summer lined up for bus and boat trips around the city, checking their maps and formulating their strategy for the day.

Downtown in the heavily congested financial district, workers jostled with tourists, vendors, and cyclists for position on the sidewalks and streets. Jason Rubino couldn't believe the confusion and excitement in that part of the city. So many people in such a small space, and ahead loomed the two tallest structures in the city along with five satellite buildings, which together made up the World Trade Center.

According to the literature, the WTC was where 50,000 people went to work each weekday in 12 million square feet of office, hotel, and commercial space, and thousands more came to visit or shop. It was estimated that as many as

10,000 visitors rode the nonstop elevators to the top of the Twin Towers every day.

By 8:30 A.M. many of the city's workers were already at their desks. There were just too many things to do in too little time. Like so many other Americans, both David and Jeffrey Stern were finding lately that they had to work harder and longer with less and less help. With the economy in a downturn, companies were not adding to staff as they had in the past. In fact, they were starting to cut back. So, for David and Jeffrey there was good reason to report to work at the North and South Towers early that Tuesday morning.

The first plane—American Airlines Flight 11 out of Boston—slammed into the North Tower at 8:46 A.M. The Boeing 767, carrying 10,000 gallons of fuel and traveling at nearly 500 miles an hour, rammed into the upper part of the building, cutting a swath of fire and destruction from floors 94 through 98 and hurtling parts of the building, furniture, and bits of paper as well as a jet engine and airline seats into the streets below.

Coverage of the catastrophe was almost immediate in the media capital of the world. Camille was in the kitchen with mama and Aunt Loretta-Loretta when the news broke. "Oh, my God, oh, my God!" cried Camille, collapsing into a chair. "David is in that building."

"*Madonna mia,*" Anna Terranova wailed. Aunt Loretta-Loretta made the sign of the cross. The two widows, like human shields, threw their arms around Camille, who started sobbing uncontrollably. "I know, I know it, he's going to die."

"Shh, shh, *cara mia,*" said mama. "No, no. I know it in my heart."

"Listen to your mother," Aunt Loretta-Loretta pleaded.

"Those poor people, those poor people," Camille cried. Mama rocked Camille back and forth.

The front door slammed, and everyone jumped. Heavy footsteps could be heard in the hallway. It was Ben, back from his walk.

"I just heard. Mrs. Patel told me," he said as he rushed to Camille's side. With one eye on the TV, he tried to comfort his wife. He couldn't hide the fear and pain in his eyes, but he wanted to reach out and do something. "Don't worry, don't worry. I'll call David—and Jeffrey, too."

After her husband and son left for work, Loretta sat at the kitchen table eating the last waffle. When she heard the news bulletin on the radio, she jumped up and rushed out the door and down to the river where a group of neighbors began to cluster. In years past, crowds might have gathered there to watch a fireworks display, but today this small group was trying to get a firsthand look at the tragic spectacle that was unfolding across the Hudson. Loretta could see the smoke pouring out of the North Tower, and she stared in horror at the sight. "My brother's in there," she screamed and fell to her knees. Two women reached out to console her.

As they did, onlookers caught sight of another commercial jet flying low over the water down river. "You see that? You see that?" a young man cried.

"Where the hell is it going?" shouted another man as he watched the plane banking into the lower Manhattan area.

"My God!" said a woman just as a large section of the South Tower exploded, setting off a fireball and sending debris flying in all directions.

"Noooooooo!" Loretta protested. Neighbors tried to sit her down on a bench, but she broke away from them. "Let me go. I have to go," she insisted as she fought past outstretched arms and started back to the house. "I have to go to my mother's."

Like so many others that morning, Christopher at first thought that it was all a tragic accident. Why not? After all, how impossible was it for a jet airliner to crash into one of the world's tallest buildings in one of the most crowded skies? Only when the second plane—also a 767 out of Boston, United Airlines Flight 175—crashed into the South Tower at 9:02 A.M. and spewed destruction from floors 74 through 84 did Christopher and everyone else, including the news media, realize that this was no accident. Both planes had obviously been hijacked and smashed into the two buildings in an act of terrorism. Christopher wiped his grease-smeared hands on his pants and dialed Patsy. The sirens of fire trucks and ambulances wailed from both of their TV sets as they reviewed the catastrophic events taking place, live, in downtown Manhattan.

"Isn't this Tom's day off at the firehouse?" he asked.

"I think so," Patsy said, "but I don't know for sure. Have you heard anything from Camille about Jeffrey and David?"

"No, nothing."

They agreed that Christopher would call Gloria, and Patsy would contact Camille.

Christopher tried not to sound alarmed when he greeted his daughter, but he could tell she was crying when she answered the phone. "Are you alright, sweetie?"

"It's terrible, daddy," she cried. "I can't watch it anymore."

"You don't have to. Turn it off."

"I'm so worried about Tom," she sobbed. "He didn't have to go to work today, but he went in anyway. They need all the help they can get down there—and you know Tom—if someone needs help...."

"He'll be okay. They know what they're doing."

"I know, I know," she agreed. "I'm so scared."

"Hang in there, Gloria. Your mom and I will be right over."

"When he left this morning, it was different. I could see it in his eyes. It was like he was going far, far away, and I wasn't going to see him for while, or...."

"Mom and I will be there as soon as we can, sweetie. Just hold on."

Annie Stern came straight back to her apartment downtown after walking Little Ben to school, took two Tylenol, and, without removing her sneakers, threw herself on the bed. No radio. No television. Nothing. Nothing worse than a late-summer cold or a 24-hour flu, whatever it was. She decided to get some sleep until it was time to pick up her son. In the distance, sirens screamed, but, hey, this was the city.

Twice she thought she was dreaming that the phone was ringing. By the time she tried to answer the second set of rings, the caller was gone. Annie tried to fall back to sleep but couldn't. She decided to call her mom in Mississippi. "Did you just call me, mother?"

"No," she replied in a slow, gentle drawl. "Is everyone okay?"

"What do you mean?"

"I just saw it on the news. I know Jeffrey works in one of those buildings."

"Let me call you back, mother." When Annie hung up, she turned on the TV and saw big clouds of smoke and fire pouring out of the Twin Towers. A man and woman at an anchor desk were reviewing the morning's events. She dialed Jeffrey at his work number. No answer. She tried his cell phone. Dead silence. "Oh, my God!" she cried out, recalling the two phone calls she didn't answer. *Jeffrey was trying to call me.* Almost at the same time, another, more maternal fear overwhelmed her. *Little Ben! Dear Lord, please make sure he's safe.* She burst out the door, weepy eyes clouding her vision, and headed for her son's school.

CHAPTER 22

▼

Michael Terranova was about to attend a high-level meeting on ways to cut H. P. Ronald Publishing's 2002 budget when the first plane hit the North Tower. The meeting was canceled. Small groups formed around the coffee stations to talk about the crash, and anyone with a radio drew crowds of curious listeners from all over the company. When the second plane smashed into the South Tower, corridor talk focused on news reports of the hijacking of both jets and possibly other jets by bands of terrorists. This was a clear attack on U.S. soil, something Americans were not used to experiencing. To satisfy employees' hunger for ever more information, Human Resources set up a TV in the cafeteria. The last time it did that was when the verdict was announced at the O.J. Simpson murder trial in 1995.

Work was the last place New York employees wanted to be that day. This was a time to be home, holding loved ones close. After picking up bits of new information about the disaster, employees at H. P. Ronald went back to their offices and kept to themselves, mulling over what they had just heard and trying to call home and reassure everyone they were okay. The news worsened in a rapid succession of reports.

The Port Authority is shutting down all bridges and tunnels leading into and out of the city. President Bush announces that the country has suffered an "apparent terrorist attack." The FAA halts all flights throughout the country. A third hijacked plane—American Airlines Flight 77—crashes into the Pentagon. The White House is evacuated.

Michael noticed that his departmental employees were starting to leave the building. He wanted to do the same thing. "This was how Londoners must have felt when they came under attack by the German bombers during World War II," said one older employee heading out the door. Michael agreed. He could sense a vulnerability he had never observed before, along with a mounting fear and uncertainty about what would happen next, among the workers. All they wanted to do that day was be home with their families.

Michael tried reaching Jo at school on her cell phone, but he couldn't get through. He dialed Camille. No answer. He put in a call to Christopher. His answer machine went on. He left a brief message. He didn't want to call his son John yet and alarm him. Finally, briefcase in hand, Michael left work. But instead of going to his apartment uptown, he headed downtown. He had to make sure Jo was safe.

As Michael walked downtown, he could see the same vulnerability, fear, and uncertainty in the faces of people in the streets as he saw in the people at work. They stopped and gazed at the large billows of smoke pouring out of the upper floors of the Twin Towers. Sometimes, in a departure from their usual behavior, they exchanged a word or two with a stranger. They shook their heads in sympathy for those caught in the upper floors of the towers, then moved on toward their destinations, knowing that help was on the way. Against the screams of sirens, some New Yorkers were carrying on with their usual activities, walking their dogs, riding bikes, going to the store. This was life in a city of millions—multidimensional, unpredictable, rich with individuality. Life went on in the midst of catastrophe.

As if what had already transpired wasn't terrible enough, what took place next seemed unreal. This couldn't be happening, not now, at the dawn of a new century, not here, at the hub of this great city in the most powerful country in the world. Suddenly, Michael was no longer an observer of the enormous events unfolding downtown; he was a participant swept up into the action, an integral player in the drama. When he reached the area near Jo's school, he heard a deep, loud rumble and looked up at the towers a few blocks away. From the top down, the South Tower was collapsing, rolling down like a gigantic, black wave into the streets below. It was approximately 10:05 A.M., about an hour after the plane had hit that building.

People started running, slipping, falling, losing their shoes, squirming under cars to escape the tidal wave of building materials and the remnants of computers, desks, and humanity hurtling toward them. Some had just evacuated the buildings in and around the World Trade Center. Michael ran, too, and in his haste to prevent the black cloud from engulfing him dropped his briefcase and his glasses, which seemed like small matters. With all sorts of memos and computer printouts from the fallen tower swirling around him, he ducked into a hallway and crouched in the corner.

Over and over again, he prayed an old prayer Sister Regina taught him at Saint Paul the Apostle. *Angel of God, my guardian dear, to whom His love commits me here, ever this day be at my side, to light and guard, to rule and guide.*

Michael waited until the mantra numbed his brain. Then he got up, went to the front door, and looked outside. *This was how Pompei must have looked when Vesuvius erupted more than 2,000 years ago.* The street was littered with stinging ash and soot and all sorts of debris. A gray cloud blocked the sun, but it seemed to be clearing now. It was eerily quiet. If there were people out there, Michael could not see them. Nevertheless, he decided to make his move.

After tying a handkerchief around his face, he began walking toward Jo's school, which he figured was not far away because he saw it when he started running. There was the smell of fuel, burnt rubber, and sulphur in the air. He hoped the children would never see what he now saw on the streets. *Angel of God, my guardian dear....*

There it was, the school, finally. Michael hoped the big front door would be open. It was. When he entered, the hallway leading to the administrative offices and first-floor classrooms was empty and dark. Apparently, the building had lost its electricity. Covered in dust and soot, Michael looked like a Dickens ghost as he walked down the corridor. He saw a light flickering behind a glass door at the end of the hall and headed toward it. As he did, someone with a flashlight—a thin, wide-eyed woman with wispy and graying light brown hair—came out of a classroom and screamed when she saw him.

Michael had forgotten he was wearing the handkerchief. He yanked it off. "I'm sorry if I startled you. I was looking for someone."

"They're gone, they're all gone—I mean the children," explained Ms. Fiske, the principal, who had been checking out the classrooms. "All the children were moved out of the building when the first plane hit. They're safe now in a school uptown. Most of them have probably been picked up by their parents. It was awful," she continued. "Some of the children were in the school yard when the plane crashed into the building. They heard the explosion. They saw the ball of fire and the smoke, God knows what else. I thought it best that they be moved out of here—this building, this area—right away. Know what I mean?"

Michael nodded in agreement. He could see the anguish in her face. "I think it was a wise decision."

"Thank you," she said, tears welling in her eyes. "I hope so."

Michael hesitated. "Actually, I was looking for Jo…Josephine Terranova, I mean Trudell. I'm her husband, ex-husband."

"Oh, Josephine…follow me." She led him down the hall to the room with the flickering light. Inside, Jo and another teacher, Emma Whitman, were huddled next to a portable radio listening to the latest news. Three candles burned nearby. Jo turned. When she recognized Michael, she jumped up and fell into his arms. She started sobbing violently. "What are you doing here?"

"I could ask you the same question," he replied.

"You could have been killed."

"I wasn't. I'm here."

Jo kissed him tenderly. "That was such a great-looking suit."

"Still is," he said, smacking the dust off of his sleeves. "Just for the record, I tried to call you several times, but I couldn't get through."

"Me, too."

They were both startled when Emma started crying. "Oh, no! Oh, no! Now the North Tower is going down." They could hear the deep rumbling sound that signaled the collapse of Tower One. It was 10:28 A.M. As newscasters described the scene, the second tower fell in a gigantic, twisted heap, again sending crumpled building materials and other debris into the streets and further damaging nearby structures. By a twist of fate and its fortuitous location, the school escaped major damage except for some broken windows.

"My God, my God, those poor people," Jo sobbed.

"Rotten bastards!" Michael exploded. "They'll pay for what they did. Jeffrey, David…Jesus, my sister must be going nuts." They continued listening to the news.

A fourth hijacked 757—United Airlines Flight 93 out of Newark, N.J.—has crashed into Shanksville, Pa., a rural town 80 miles southeast of Pittsburgh. There is speculation that the plane was headed for the White House or the Capital or some other landmark…New York's primary elections, scheduled for today, have been canceled…At the urging of the mayor, thousands of New Yorkers are evacuating the area below Canal Street. Shaken and tattered, many New Yorkers are walking miles and crossing bridges into Queens and Brooklyn.

In the midst of it all, an unlikely hero was emerging, New York City mayor Rudolph Giuliani. Even as the buildings were falling, he was in the streets, his clothes and face smeared with soot, urging New Yorkers to stay calm and move away from the devastation. He showed a courageous and caring side New Yorkers had not seen before.

It was almost noon when Michael and Jo left the school and headed uptown to Michael's apartment. A layer of dust settled on the street like newly fallen snow. A man was picking up papers from the street and reading them. A few people were still wearing masks although the air had cleared. Michael and Jo looked toward the area where the two towers once stood. Clouds of gray and white smoke were billowing from fires burning in the mountain of twisted steel and concrete. There was a great hole in the sky where there was none before. Michael and Jo found it difficult to believe the great towers were gone—landmarks, beacons, symbols of national pride and power—each vanished in a matter of seconds. *Ripped just like that from this great city, our city, our beautiful city.*

"You have to help us now," said Jo, tears streaming down her face..

"I can't, not now," he said.

"We need you, Michael. You have so much to offer."

"Look what they've done to our city."

She loved the city, too. "There has to be a way to stop the destruction, and the terror."

"We can't let them get away with this."

"They kill, we kill. When does the cycle stop, Michael?"

"I don't know, Jo. But we can't let this go unanswered."

As Michael and Jo walked uptown, they saw a city on the move, and moving quickly. Emergency vehicles raced downtown. Sirens blared from all directions. Refugees of lower Manhattan quick-timed northward, occasionally turning for one more look at the smoking ruins that were their lives or their livelihood.

When Michael and Jo arrived at his apartment early that afternoon, Michael immediately tried to call Camille in New Jersey. Perhaps the phone lines would be working up here. He nodded to Jo, a signal the phone was ringing at the other end. Ben answered. When he found out who it was, he could be heard telling someone, "It's Michael, honey."

"Hi, Michael," Ben continued, his voice cracking. "No, nothing…we haven't heard from David or Jeffrey or Annie or anybody. What about Jo?"

"She's here with me in my place," Michael replied.

"That's good."

"How's Camille?"

"Well, you know," Ben tried to explain. "I was hoping…I thought they would have called by now. We haven't heard from Jason, either. Last we knew he was going to do some sightseeing, downtown. Jason's mother called twice from Arizona. And God help Tom Dempsey, wherever he is! Patsy called this morning to say that he volunteered to go to work today."

Michael tried to be encouraging. "They'll call, I'm sure. It's just…the city's a mess right now. Some phones are still knocked out…can't get in or out of the city. If there's anything we can do…."

"I know, Michael, I know. You take care of yourselves."

"Thanks…you, too." Next, Michael dialed his son's number.

CHAPTER 23

▼

In New Jersey, Camille and Ben Stern sat glued to the TV coverage of the terrible events, nervously waiting for a phone to ring. On Long Island, Christopher and Patsy were huddled with Gloria and her son, along with a few of Tom Dempsey's friends, quietly exchanging messages of comfort and hope. Out in Arizona, friends of Jason Rubino came calling on his family when news spread that he had been sightseeing in downtown New York City when the planes struck the World Trade Center. These were like wakes without corpses. Throughout the world, television reruns relentlessly reminded everyone of the day's events. Jets crashing into the upper floors of the two tallest structures in New York City, followed by great billows of fire and smoke. Both buildings collapsing into mounds of smoking rubble. People running for their lives. The Pentagon, center of America's military power, under another suicidal siege from above. More fire, more destruction, more death. The remains of a fourth hijacked airliner, repelled by a brave band of passengers, scattered in a Pennsylvania field. It would be hours, perhaps days or weeks, if ever, before anguished friends and relatives discovered what happened to their loved ones....

David Stern, a stock trader, got to work early that day in the North Tower. As usual, he checked his e-mail, and wondered. *Where the hell does all this junk come from? They must think I'm the king of porn or something.* Without opening them, he deleted the unwanted messages. There was also a note from his boss asking for updates on two clients. David tapped a brief reply and sent it on its way with a happy-smile face. Next, he wrote a "Good morning...miss you...call me" note to Ginny that he knew she wouldn't have the time to open until some time after lunch. He then attached a raunchy joke to two of his buddies from Mooney's Pub and was sending it off to them when the plane hit a few floors above him.

He heard the explosion and saw large and small pieces of something flying past his window, but, at first, everything on his desk remained still. It was only when he saw his friend Susan Hull in the doorway that the building swayed in one direction and back, and things started falling around him. "Jesus, what was that?" said Susan, holding onto the door frame. It was a question echoed by employees throughout the building. At first, David thought it was a bomb. The real answer was slow in coming: A plane had crashed into the building somewhere above the 94th floor.

David tried calling some friends upstairs at Cantor Fitzgerald and Marsh & McLennan. No answer. Instinctively, he picked up a couple of things that fell off his desk. His phone rang, and he answered it.

"Here we go again," said Jeffrey on the other end. Both were survivors of the 1993 truck bombing at the WTC towers that took the lives of six people. "Someone just told me what happened," said Jeffrey. "In case you didn't hear, a plane crashed into your building."

David fell back into his chair. "Holy shit!"

Even though he had no idea of the dimensions of the catastrophe, Jeffrey pleaded with his brother, "Get out of there. Now!"

"As soon as I take a leak."

"Now!" Jeffrey repeated.

The overbearing smell of jet fuel filled David's senses. "I hear you, brother. I hear you."

"Give me a call when you get out."

"Roger…love you, bro."

Equities investment manager Jeffrey Stern hung up the phone and shook his head. Sometimes it was difficult for him to believe David was his twin. *When the hell is he going to grow up, settle down, raise a family?* Ever since Jeffrey could remember he had been Big Brother to David. To tell the truth, there were times he had wished it were the other way around. Yet, Jeffrey couldn't complain—he had a great wife and son, a decent place to live, a nice job—and soon, if the early signs bear out, there would be a fourth addition to the family.

Jeffrey tried calling his wife Annie to let her know he was fine, but the phone merely kept ringing. He felt a blast of heat, as if someone had opened a furnace door nearby. He hung up without leaving a message and walked over to the window. Huge balls of orange flame and black and white smoke leaped out of the upper floors of the other tower, and there was a huge jagged hole where the facade of the building once was. He tried calling his wife again. No answer again. *Where the hell are you, Annie?* He slammed down the phone. Something told him to get going, now.

Walking outside his office, Jeffrey could see that his coworkers in the South Tower were nervous but under control. One woman was telling how she was knocked off her chair when the plane hit the other tower. Comforted by an elderly man from the mail room, another, younger woman was trembling and sobbing quietly. A small group—those who could take it—looked out a window at the horror taking place across the plaza. "Come on, folks, get away from the windows," the general manager tried to persuade the onlookers. It was a futile attempt.

For some employees, especially those who had worked in the towers during the 1993 truck bombings, there was only one thing to do: Get out of the building, now! Others weren't sure what to do. A message from the building staff said that the South Tower was safe and urged people to remain in the building rather than leave and run the risk of getting hit by falling debris from the other building. If conditions warrant, the building staff added, "you may wish to start an orderly evacuation."

"It's your call," the general manager told employees. Jeffrey knew what he was going to do. "I'm leaving," he announced, glancing over at his friend, Cary Baird.

"I'm out of here, too," said Cary, yanking his jacket off the back of his chair.

"Come on, Helen," Jeffrey encouraged his secretary. Cary turned to the young woman who was sobbing. "Let's go home, Mary."

"It's an individual decision," the general manager reminded employees.

To the elderly man from the mail room, Jeffrey said, "Had enough, Hank?" Hank nodded.

A few others joined the group on the local elevator heading for the sky lobby on the 78th floor. Others returned to their desks. The market was just opening, but most just wanted to call home.

In the North Tower, David was one of the last ones from his office to begin the descent. After looking for any stragglers in the conference rooms and toilets, he headed for the nearest stairwell. As he did so, a second plane smashed into the South Tower. There was no doubt now that America had come under awful attack at home from terrorists, but, in retrospect, many of those stuck in the twin towers did not know that truth or ponder its implications.

On the way to the stairwell, David saw an employee he knew well, Mrs. Brown from data processing, sitting in her office. He tried to convince her to walk down the stairs with him, but she didn't want to leave. A diabetic, she said she'd prefer to wait for the firefighters or police. "Come on, Mrs. B, you and me," said David with all the charm he could muster under the circumstances. She finally agreed. "Okay, okay, just let me get my purse."

Flashlight in hand—compliments of a fire marshal who had already left—David entered a dark stairwell littered with pieces of drywall that had fallen off the wall during the initial crash and the aftershock. Above, larger pieces of Sheetrock blocked access to the stairs, apparently trapping those who worked in the higher floors. Water from broken pipes ran down the stairs and mixed with drywall material to create a slippery slope in spots.

"I don't know if I can do this," trembled Mrs. Brown, holding onto the rail with both hands.

"We can do it, Mrs. B," David encouraged her. "Just keep moving, like you were going down the steps of your apartment building." He slipped and slid down a short flight of stairs. "Only not like that." He laughed.

Back in the South Tower, when Jeffrey and his colleagues reached the sky lobby on the 78th floor, they were again hearing that it was safer to stay in the building than to walk out into the streets. Another critical decision: Should they go back upstairs or continue going down and exit the building? It was not a question to be taken lightly. "I don't know what to do," said Cary, his eyes nervously following some people heading back up to their offices. "I know you have to go. Your brother's in the other building, and you want to know…. I got nobody. I got a ton of work, and the market's just opening."

"Put it on hold, Cary. I'll help you catch up tomorrow," said Jeffrey, a slight tremble in his voice. "Besides…I really need you."

Cary looked at his friend in disbelief. Was this Jeffrey? Mr. Confidence? The guy who always knows where he's going and how to get there? Our leader? "YOU NEED ME? Since when?"

"Since now. Hell, I've got reasons—my brother, my family, and…"

"Come on, let's get out of here."

Rather than wait for an open elevator in the crowded sky lobby, Jeffrey and his friends took the stairs. They were heading down the Northwest stairwell when the second plane crashed into the South Tower above them, between the 78th and 84th floors, just 16 minutes after the North Tower was struck. To those in the stairwell, it sounded as if a bomb had exploded. The building rocked in one direction, then back. Large and small pieces of drywall fell on the stairs, and the lights went out.

Jeffrey and his friends waited until their eyes adjusted, then continued downward, moving drywall out of their way and occasionally slipping on it. A powdery or smoky haze created an eerie, unreal effect as they continued to move downward. Floors 66, 65, 64. Starting to clear up. Floors 61, 60, 59. Conditions nearly normal.

On the 58th floor, Jeffrey and Cary tried to call home on their cell phones. Nothing. Dead air. A couple of floors below, they went into an empty office in search of a phone, while the others continued to descend. They found one, but the line was alive one second and dead the next. "Keep trying," said Jeffrey as he walked over to the window.

Looking across the plaza at the other tower, he saw some people waving towels or something in the jagged openings that once were windows or walls. He could see their faces. *Oh, my God!* Then—the unthinkable—a man jumped or fell from a ledge, hurtling himself gracefully and mercifully through space like the statue of an angel falling from the top of a great cathedral. Jeffrey turned away quickly, then turned back to see others staring down into the abyss, and another plummeted, and another.

As he watched, Jeffrey was overwhelmed by a sense of guilt and sadness that he was here and they were there and he was intruding into someone's last private moments. And then a terrible fear swept him. *Who were those people? Were they anyone I knew? Please, God, let none of them be David.* He felt sick, but now more than ever he knew he had to get out of the building. On the 28th floor, Jeffrey and Cary caught up with an older man who was limping badly; he was being helped by a young woman who was drenched in sweat but smiling. She didn't ask for any help, but the two younger men took hold of the limping man on each side and lifted him down the stairway, past two firefighters loaded with equipment on their way up the stairs, all the way to the plaza level, where they met more firefighters gearing up for the climb. After turning the injured man over to the emergency squad, Jeffrey and Cary were hustled by members of the emergency squad out of the building.

In the North Tower, David and Mrs. Brown continued downward, the stairs becoming more passable the lower they got. Streaks of light shot up to them from below. They later learned they were the lights from the flashlights of firefighters coming up the stairs.

At about the 42nd floor, David met the first of a long line of firefighters. Huffing and sweating, the men were loaded down with hoses and other equipment. "Need help?" one of them asked Mrs. Brown. "No thanks," she replied. "We're okay. You're the ones who need help. It's hell up there."

Further down, a loud roaring sound broke up the monotonous cadence of their footsteps. "What was that?" Mrs. Brown asked.

"Don't know," said David.

"Feels like we were hit again," she said, her eyes filling with tears. David put an arm around her shoulders. She started sobbing. "Why? Why is this happening? We're just people trying to make a living, for crying out loud." David tried to console her. "I should have never started working in this building," she moaned. "I should have worked on a lower floor. I should have...."

"Come on, Mrs. B. let's get out of here."

It wasn't until they reached the underground concourse that they found out what had happened: The South Tower had collapsed. David prayed his brother had followed his own advice and left the building before the plane hit.

After several minutes, they were led away from the towers into the streets and clouds of soot and dust.

Jeffrey and Cary were walking near old Trinity Church when the South Tower collapsed. Their plan, if that's what it could be called, was to cross the Brooklyn Bridge and go to where a friend of Cary's lived; once there, they would work out another plan to get home. Along the way, Jeffrey would try calling Annie again. When they heard the deep, rumbling sound, they turned around. Unbelievably, in a matter of seconds, the 110-story tower was gone, erased from the skyline.

At first, they just stood there, dazed. When the dust, soot, and debris from the fallen structure started rolling through the streets toward them, they ran, falling as they did, and, as the great wave engulfed them, they became separated. "Cary! Cary!" Jeffrey shouted, but he had disappeared, washed away into another street.

Battered, torn, and covered with soot, Jeffrey continued trudging toward the bridge, joining hundreds of others fleeing Manhattan. By the time he reached the bridge, the other tower had collapsed. Under the sacred arches of the bridge, the refugees moved silently across the span, overwhelmed with sadness and anguish, a terrible anger building within them. On the other side, Cary was waiting.

David was walking toward Ginny's uptown apartment when the North Tower fell. He was far enough away not to be submerged by the dust and debris pouring into the streets, but he ran anyway.

When he finally stopped to catch his breath, he turned around. Gone was the building where he and so many others had worked—people he knew as friends and colleagues, people he merely smiled at in the elevators, and people he didn't know at all. David sat down on a stoop and buried his head in his hands and wept.

Firefighter Tom Dempsey was returning from the triage center, where he had just brought a burn victim, when the South Tower collapsed. He was almost trampled by people rushing away from falling debris, but he managed to run into a nearby office building. Under a cloud of dust, he started making his way back to where his unit had been assembled when the North Tower came rumbling down.

He ran, again taking refuge inside a building, but he knew he had to get out of there. Not only because all buildings in the vicinity were probably unsafe but, for his own sake, he had better go. No, no. He had to return to where the Twin Towers had stood. He was a New York City firefighter and this was what he was waiting to do all his life. This was the big one. There had to be hundreds of people trapped under the shattered masonry and steel beams crying for his help. So many people, including so many of his buddies from the department, faces with names and families.

Back amidst the fiery and smoldering rubble, Tom and a group of other returning firefighters, police officers, and volunteers began the furious and largely futile task of digging and searching for anyone who might be trapped and alive. There were only a handful of survivors, including a few firefighters in their protective gear.

In the early afternoon, Tom sat down on a steel girder, exhausted after hours of digging, lifting, and searching. He was rubbing his eyes with a handkerchief Gloria always made ready for him when a sooty young man with a handful of water bottles approached Tom. "Like a drink?" asked the volunteer.

Tom looked up as he reached for a bottle of water. "Don't I know you?"

"Don't know. The name's Jason. Jason Rubino."

"Jason?" said Tom, surprised. "Tom, Tom Dempsey, in case you don't recognize me under all this dirt."

"Tom Dempsey. Holy shit." They hugged.

"What are you doing here, Jason?"

"Trying to help," the young man from Arizona explained. "I was coming into the city to do some sightseeing. I was just a few blocks away, on my way to meet a friend, when the first plane hit; then the second plane. I guess I saw more than I ever expected to see. It was incredible, horrible, and I was going to get out of there. But when the buildings collapsed, I thought the city could use my help, you know what I mean?" He began choking up.

"I know, I know. Thanks, Jason." Tom rose from the rubble. "Gotta get back."

"You guys are something."

"It's what we do," said Tom, walking away. "Be careful, Jason. Thanks for the water."

Camille and Ben didn't learn what happened to David and Jeffrey until the next day. It was early morning when David made contact. "I'm coming over," he said simply when Camille answered the phone.

"Oh, David!" she screamed. They both started crying.

"Please, mama...."

She tried to control herself. "Thank God! Thank God! You alright?"

"I'm alive."

"What about Jeffrey?" she asked, her voice reflecting a long night of worry.

"Don't know. I haven't been able to reach him, or Annie. I left word. How's dad?"

"He's good, worried, but he's good."

"And grandma?'

"Same thing."

"I hope Tom Dempsey wasn't down there," said David wearily.

"He was, but he's okay. He has to go back down there today."

"Christ, Gloria must be going out of her mind."

"Oh, David, I'm so thankful you're alive."

"I'll be over as soon as I can, mom."

Camille and Ben, along with Loretta, who dashed over to her parents' home as soon as she heard her brother was coming, didn't wait for David to ring the bell. When he got out of his car and started up the walkway that afternoon, they ran out to meet him. He was limping slightly and he had a mean scrape on the side of his cheek, but he looked like he was in reasonably good condition. One by one, they embraced him.

Camille was happy and grateful that one of her sons was alive, but, given the enormity of yesterday's tragic events and the uncertainty surrounding the fate of her other son, she still felt very sad. "Oh, what a terrible tragedy!" she cried, collapsing into his arms

"Thank God you're alive, son," said Ben. David had seen his father cry only once before, when grandma Stern died.

Loretta just sobbed and shook while tightly holding onto her brother.

Having been at the center of the catastrophe, Jason Rubino was moved to tears as he watched the whole scene from the guest room upstairs. He was getting ready for the trip back home to Arizona the following day, depending on flight schedules.

"Come on," said David, his eyes blood-red with emotion. "Let's go into the house. I'll tell you what I remember."

It was late in the afternoon, and David was at the point in his account when he had reached the concourse of the North Tower with Mrs. Brown. Suddenly, the doorbell rang, and Jason rushed to answer the door. Once again, emotions burst out into the open when the family saw Jeffrey and Annie, both obviously weary and mentally wrenched by the ordeal.

"In case you're wondering, a neighbor is watching Little Ben," Jeffrey announced when he saw his father.

"Come here, you two," said Ben as reached out to hug Jeffrey and Annie, his eyes flooded with tears again.

"Thank God you both are alright," cried Camille, exhausted but relieved. Grandma Terranova made the Sign of the Cross and kissed Jeffrey and Annie.

While the reunion with Jeffrey and David was a source of joy for the whole family, it had a special significance for the two young men. "The last time we spoke you were about to take a leak," Jeffrey reminded his brother, a slight smile creasing his face.

"I remember, Bro," said David. Then they hugged and wept.

CHAPTER 24

▼

They called it Ground Zero. For hundreds of families who had lost someone within the 16 acres where the Twin Towers had once stood, it was holy ground. At first, estimates of the casualties in New York City alone were being placed as high as 10,000. Later, however, the numbers were scaled back, eventually reaching 2,749 killed or missing/presumed dead at the World Trade Center, while 189 lost their lives at the Pentagon and 44 perished in Pennsylvania, bringing the total number of casualties to approximately 3,000, including those who died on the four hijacked planes.

Analysts were quick to make comparisons with the Japanese attack on Pearl Harbor, which finally drew America into World War II. Some 2,300 people lost their lives in the sneak attack of 1941.

Among those who died on September 11, 2001, were 343 firefighters and paramedics, 23 New York City police officers, and 37 Port Authority officers. One company alone, the bond trading firm of Cantor Fitzgerald, lost 658 employees who were working on four upper floors of the North Tower. It was estimated that perhaps as many as 25,000 people were led out of the World Trade Center to safety.

For nine months after the tragedy, Tom Dempsey attended one funeral after another for his firefighter friends, many of whose remains were found in the ruins of the collapsed towers. It was a shattering experience that became a way of life for Tom and his wife Gloria, who tried to keep their focus on the child who would be born to them in February.

David Stern postponed a vacation he had been planning with Ginny in order to attend funeral and memorial services for his friends in the financial field. Jeffrey was amazed at how much his brother had changed in such a short time. "I don't know how to explain it, Annie; you can see it, he's grown up," said Jeffrey, who also made the rounds of funerals with his wife. As difficult as these visits were, they were also helpful to the couple.

The release of grief made it a little easier for them to accept Annie's miscarriage a week after the September 11 tragedy. Annie especially, with her naturally compassionate nature, found life-restoring solace in helping others.

The terrorist attacks also took a heavy economic toll, causing consumer and business confidence to plummet and hastening recessions in the United States and Europe. New York City took a major hit. The damage to the city's economy was placed at between $80 billion and $100 billion. Tourism was expected to fall 25% during the first year after the attack, costing the city $5 billion. Retailers and restaurants in downtown Manhattan were particularly hard-hit in the months after September 11. Although David and Jeffrey managed to hold onto their jobs, hundreds of others were not as fortunate.

The impact could not be explained merely in economic or numerical terms. It could be seen in the faces of those searching for information about a missing person in the armory on Twenty-sixth Street and Lexington. It was visible in the faces of those taking to the streets to display snapshots of loved ones lost in the collapse of the Twin Towers. Then there were the homemade signs placed on lampposts and walls in or near high-traffic areas such as pizza parlors, subway stations, and hospitals. "Have you seen this person?" they cried out.

Suddenly, some 2,000 children lost a parent in the World Trade Center. Americans all over felt their grief. So many sad faces, joined in grief at candlelight vigils. In a reversal of an old bias toward big cities with their sin bins, people all over the country showered New York City with love and compassion for its tremendous loss. There were proud faces, too, united in a spontaneous outburst of flag waving, as well as fearful faces, worried about what lay ahead. *These things are not supposed to happen in this country. If aircraft are vulnerable, why not boats and bridges and buses and water purifying plants and nuclear power stations and....*

Published reports said that seven out of 10 Americans were experiencing some form of depression, and therapists reported that many of their patients were suffering from recurring nightmares, anxieties and fears, as a result of 9/11. To be fair, the tragic events of September 11 should not be blamed for every foul mood, but they might have stirred up the pot of anger that manifested itself in a short-tempered remark or impatient gesture.

With the anger, there was long-held frustration among some people that the ones who were behind those terrible deeds were still running around the world scot free, free to kill again. And, after an initial outpouring of compassion and closeness, rage on the country's roadways returned, bigger than ever.

Suddenly, it had become a more threatening, unsure world, and Gloria and Tom Dempsey, in their lowest moods, wondered whether they had done the right thing when they decided to have another child. That creeping doubt was not something they openly discussed with each other because, for a long time, they had wanted a brother or sister for Thomas Christopher, and now, through the miracle of science, they knew they were having a girl. They were thrilled by the expectation, and they tried to keep it alive in their minds as they traveled from funeral to funeral, paying their respects to the families of firefighters they knew, some more closely than others.

In the weeks after September 11, Tom didn't talk much about what he saw that September day, nor did Gloria press him to tell. But, behind brave fronts, they were both fearful every day he left for work and until he returned home. Slowly things were starting to return to normal, if there was such a thing, in the Dempsey household.

"Come on, Thomas," said Gloria to her ten-year-old son one October evening. "Pick up your things."

"Oh, mom, I'm still working on my model."

"What about your homework?"

"I'll do it, I'll do it."

"I wish your father were home," Gloria thought out loud.

Thomas started picking up pieces of his model. "Uncle John said this is just how the F-16 looks."

Gloria pulled back the curtains and looked out the front window. "He should have been here an hour ago."

"Uncle John says some day he'll take me for a plane ride."

Gloria kept staring out the window. "Where *is* he?"

Thomas offered one explanation. "Maybe there was a big fire." Too late. He couldn't yank back his words.

Gloria started sobbing. "Don't say that, Thomas. Please!"

"Sorry, mom."

The phone rang, and they both jumped. It was Tom. He was on his way home.

Christopher and Patsy Terranova had their work to keep them busy—he in the car repair shop, she in the hospital—but, like millions of Americans, they followed the news closely, wondering what would happen next. One of the earliest manifestations that the times had changed was the anthrax scare in which five people who received the toxic powder through the mail died. Coming as it did soon after the September 11 attacks, the poison mailings set off a new wave of terror that alarmed anyone with a mail box and threatened America's mail system.

News about heightened security measures at airports, bridges, ports, and tunnels also raised anxiety levels, as did frequent warnings of the government about other new terrorist attacks. At first, Americans didn't seem to mind the inconvenience caused by the extra security steps taken at airports and other mass-gathering places, but tolerance levels waned as time went on.

For Christopher and Patsy, Gloria was a primary personal concern. She was pregnant and, since September 11, a basket case, so both parents tried to stay in touch with her any way they could. As they did, they tended to overlook what was going on with Anthony. Until one sleety evening.

So many other times Anthony and his friends went to the diner after some drinks at the pub, and nothing happened. But there they were this night in Freddy Junior's Grand Am, continuing their heated discussion about the pros and cons of joining the Army, which they had started in the bar. Anthony was in the back seat, Freddy and Jimmy Raines in the front. Suddenly, turning a corner, the car slid on a slab of ice and slammed into a tree.

Freddy, who was driving, was killed instantly. Anthony was shaken up by the collision and suffered some cuts and bruises but was released after a long night in the emergency room; Jimmy Raines, who had a concussion and a broken wrist, was kept overnight. Anthony was quiet as his father drove him home from the hospital. "I can't believe he's gone," said Anthony, tears filling his usually cheerful dark eyes. "Me, too," said Christopher. "I liked Freddy."

Three weeks later, Anthony made up his mind what he was going to do, and he had to tell his father. Christopher could see that his son wanted to talk. "What's up?"

"I need to get away for a while, dad."

"What do you mean, Anthony?"

"I need some time for myself, away from here."

Christopher's thoughts took him back to an earlier time when he made up his mind to go to San Francisco. "Where will you go?"

"I know this might sound like deja vu to you, but….California."

"San Francisco?"

"Yes."

Christopher smiled. "You better tell your mom. She'll need time to get used to the idea."

CHAPTER 25

▼

If George W. Bush was looking for an issue that would empower his young administration after a controversial Presidential election that was decided by a narrow ruling of the U.S. Supreme Court, he found it in 9/11. The new President was quick to interpret the terrible events of that awful day.

"We're at war," he told a hurt and angry nation at the height of the crisis, vowing a wide, sustained effort "to eradicate the evil of terrorism." Almost immediately, the attacks were traced to the worldwide Al Qaeda terrorist network led by Osama bin Laden, a rich, Saudi exile linked to previous attacks against America. He had claimed he was waging a holy war on behalf of the Muslims against the infidel West and its supporters for Israel.

Nineteen men, all Middle Easterners, were part of the suicide squad that carried out the September 11 attacks. Using box cutters and plastic knives to avoid detection at inspection gates, the hijackers took over four planes bound for California. There were five terrorists aboard each jet except for United flight 93, which crashed in Pennsylvania; it had four hijackers.

Calling the fight against terrorism "the first war of the 21st Century" and "now the focus of my administration," President Bush vowed revenge by a wounded nation. Standing atop a pile of debris at Ground Zero, a bullhorn in one hand, the President declared, "I can hear you, the rest of the world hears you, and the people who knocked these buildings down will hear from all of us very soon." Exhausted rescue workers, including Tom Dempsey, greeted his remarks with loud cheers and chants of "U.S.A.! U.S.A.!"

Like millions of Americans, Ben Stern and his son-in-law, Alex Conway, kept a close watch on the events taking place after September 11. At first, they found much to support in the President's actions. They applauded his forceful stand against terrorism and his call for a homeland security office. They thought the President was right in denouncing acts of violence against Muslims and Arab-Americans in the United States following the 9/11 attacks by a group of Arab extremists. They hailed his change in foreign policy declaring that the U.S. was now targeting not only terrorists but also countries that "harbor or support" terrorists.

"About time," Ben declared.

"I agree," said Alex, the edge in his voice a little sharper than usual. "They play the game, they accept the blame."

The first country to come under attack for sheltering terrorists was Afghanistan. Al Qaeda camps there, which had been flourishing under the Taliban Islamic fundamentalist regime, were reported to have trained as many as 50,000 terrorists from some 50 countries. Ready to move on quick notice, bin Laden and his band, nevertheless, felt secure enough in Afghanistan to set up training camps and planning stations in mountainous regions of the country.

The first shots by the Allies under the Operation Enduring Freedom code name were fired on October 7, less than a month after the terrorist attacks in the U.S. The American and British bombing raids on that day were carried out by land-based bombers, carrier-based strike aircraft, and Tomahawk cruise missiles from warships. Three weeks of intense bombing took aim at Taliban air defense, communications and other targets as well as Al Qaeda camps. There followed lightning raids by Special Operations infantry forces, working with local tribal fighters and the CIA, on suspected Taliban and terrorist facilities.

Lieutenant commander John Terranova would have preferred to stay home in Virginia Beach and continue mending family fences than join the war on terrorism in, of all places, Afghanistan. But once again he was deployed to the war zone.

As he prepared to head overseas, John thought about what being home had meant to him. While there remained a wisp of distrust hanging in the air between him and Eloise, he was making progress toward overcoming the pain and hurt, and she was trying hard to get beyond the guilt and back to a life they once knew. The nights were the most difficult times, but the couple continued to make love, perhaps not as playfully or as freely as they did in the past, but just as ardently.

At the same time, John was getting to know his children Rachel and John Jr. better and come to appreciate their differences. Already, he learned, for example, that John Jr. was a serious-minded boy, perhaps a bit too serious, just as he had been, and for all her grown-up airs Rachel was really a sensitive, caring person longing to make a positive contribution in her life.

"You know what, El," said John one day, "we've got two terrific kids here. With a little guidance…I think we can help them."

"I know," said Eloise. "I'm glad you noticed. I need your help."

Then suddenly there he was, on a carrier in the Arabian Sea, flying sorties into the Tora Bora mountains and surrounding areas. For a time there, it looked like the Taliban, with reinforcement from Al Qaeda, would be able to withstand Allied air and land raids through the bitter Afghan winter. Then, abruptly in mid-December, the Taliban force in Kabul and other parts of the country started to collapse, and power passed to the local warlords favored by the Allies.

With a break in the fighting, John hopped a ride on a helicopter to spend Christmas with a couple of his buddies who were stationed at an air base in Pakistan. For the first time in a long time, John was feeling relaxed and at peace with the world, in the spirit of the season. He was enjoying a tall tale from one of the best storytellers in the Air Force when he noticed this beautiful black woman in uniform staring at him. He decided to see who she was.

A smile crept across his face. "Do we know each other, lieutenant?" he asked.

She looked at his name tag. "Terranova…any relation to the Terranovas of Manhattan, originally from Hell's Kitchen?"

"I just may be." He was smiling again.

"Any relation to Jo and Michael Terranova?"

"Would you believe mother and father? I'm John."

"Of course." She reached out to hug him, but didn't, deciding to shake his hand, instead. He returned the handshake, but wished he had hugged her. With her warm, radiant smile, she seemed friendly enough. "Nice to meet you," she continued. "I'm Tanya Allen, first daughter of Jill and Casey Russell."

"Tanya, my God! My father told me all about you."

"I hope it was good stuff."

"Actually, it wasn't too bad. Can I get you a drink?" he asked.

"No, I'm good." They decided to go outside so they could talk.

Tanya was flying light attack helicopters now and part of a growing group of U.S. servicewomen assigned to combat roles. That was a major change from the Persian Gulf war when women were not allowed in combat. She lived in the Washington, D.C. area with her husband Rob who was a lobbyist. They had no children, but were trying, as she explained.

Her openness surprised John, but at the same time it was refreshing. "That's a tough one when you're on the move so much," he said sympathetically.

"Yeah, I know, but we still have some time," Tanya agreed. "Hey, I just might take one of these nice Pakistani babies home with me."

"If you can swing it, why not?"

Feeling more relaxed now, John began talking about his own family, focusing first on his children. "I have two kids—Rachel, seven; John, five. I can't tell you how proud of them I am. I mean, here I am flying all over the place, and they are doing beautifully. Honest."

"I believe you. That says a lot about your wife...and you, of course."

They both laughed. "I know, but I worry about that sometimes," he went on. "Being away from home so much can take its toll on that other person in your life. Know what I mean?"

"I know exactly what you mean," she replied.

Time went by so quickly, and he didn't want to miss his ride back to the ship. It was time to go.

"Next time you come by," Tanya said, "I know a safe place we can get some good, local food."

"Deal," said John, enjoying her beautiful smile one last time. This time they hugged. "Merry Christmas."

On the way back to the ship, John thought about the meeting with Tanya and their conversation. He wished he hadn't said that business about being away from home so much.

Nine weeks after the bombing began, Taliban forces were routed by the U.S. and its Western allies, including Britain, France, Germany and other NATO nations, and soon after a transitional government was put in place in Afghanistan. Al Qaeda lost bases in that country, and some of its leaders were killed. Osama bin Laden and a few of his top lieutenants, along with Taliban leader Mullah Mohammad Omar, however, appeared to have evaded capture and fled.

"As long as those guys are alive we have a problem," said Alex.

For Ben, his sons were a constant reminder of the 9/11 terror. "I'm afraid you're right, Alex."

As the new year began, military strikes in Afghanistan abated while the U.S. turned its focus on helping the country get back on its feet and democratize its political process. Some Americans argued that, as a result of the change in strategy, the U.S. was letting up on the pressure to find terrorist leaders and supporters in Afghanistan; they felt that, to the contrary, the hunt for those leaders should continue, full-throttle, with strong military backing. Around the world, meanwhile, old and new threats loomed; nor were terrorist cells rolling over and playing dead.

President Bush now seemed to be broadening his target. Early in the year, he took aim at Iraq, Iran, and North Korea, calling them the "Axis of Evil" that was threatening the world with weapons of mass destruction. Later, in a speech at West Point, he also emphasized that the U.S. must be ready to launch "pre-emptive action" when necessary to defend freedom. "We must take the battle to the enemy, disrupt his plans, and confront the worst threats before they emerge," he told future military leaders.

Next, the President publicly began calling for a change in the Saddam Hussein regime in Iraq, which, he said, had failed to follow UN resolutions put in place after the Persian Gulf War to abandon all biochemical, biological, and nuclear weapons. Despite powerful voices calling for more patience, the Bush Administration said that time had run out for Iraq in meeting international demands and America stood ready to go to war there, with or without UN help—a position that met the disapproval of such powerful allies as France and Germany, as well as Russia.

A year after the 9/11 attacks, Americans continued to stand behind the President in the war on terrorism, but there was concern about a new war with Iraq. By targeting Iraq alongside of Al Qaeda, was the President confusing two different problems? Was the U.S. spreading itself too thinly at a time when terrorists were continuing their attacks around the world in places as far apart as Bali and Kenya?

"Now, he's going too far," said Alex Conway.

As much as he abhorred Sadam's policies, Ben Stern agreed.

2003

CHAPTER 26

▼

Fifteen minutes to go. Michael wondered why it felt like an eternity today. Exercising on the treadmill used to be such a walk in the park. Outside his bedroom window, the flakes were getting larger and more plentiful. Michael shook his head in disgust. *Damn! Just what we need—another snowstorm!*

Like so many other New Yorkers, he thought he had seen the last of the white stuff, and he could start formulating some warm-weather plans such as visiting John and Eloise and his grandchildren in Virginia. For a long time, he had been worried about his son and daughter-in-law. He sensed a growing tension and distance between them, and Jo shared his feelings.

The last time Michael saw his son—just before Christmas 2002—they didn't talk much, nor did John volunteer information about his home life or recent tour of duty in the Arabian Sea. The young man was in the area to visit grandma Terranova in New Jersey after learning she had become ill with complications from diabetes and a newly diagnosed condition, heart failure.

Before returning home, John had one other place to visit: Ground Zero, the site of the 9/11 terrorist attacks in downtown New York City. For Michael, who accompanied him, the visit was long overdue. He had not been back to the area since that terrible day.

What they saw left a durable impression. Stubs of granite and rusting steel columns were all that remained of the Twin Towers and surrounding structures in a 16-acre area cleared and made ready, with amazing efficiency, for the next step, the formulation of a rebuilding and memorial plan. Among the visitors who came to the site that day, one could sense a profound sadness and respect for the more than 2,700 souls who died here and whose spirits lingered over the scattered ruins. It was obvious that a proud and mindful city and nation were resolved to keep the memories of those reluctant heroes alive.

On the way home, Michael could see that John was visibly moved by what he saw. He would save the more personal, delicate talk he had planned with his son for another day.

Now here it was, March 2003. Another war with Iraq—the second since 1991—was imminent amidst persistent fears of new terrorist attacks. Once again, John had received his orders for deployment to the Persian Gulf. As proud as Michael was of John's courage and commitment to country, he wondered how many times his son could, and should, be placed in harm's way. It seemed that the price of John's safe return rose sharply with each mission.

Michael looked at his watch. Realizing he had to get going if he was to be on time for his early morning meeting with company CEO Sam Nelson, he shut down the treadmill. After he showered and dressed, he headed for work. The snow was accumulating fast. Michael wondered why his boss wanted to see him now.

When he entered Sam Nelson's office, Michael was not surprised to see the thirty-five-year-old executive-wonder from Canada who made it to the top of his company in record time, playing with a Slinky. He was always doing things like that. It was his way of letting off steam or working through a problem, he would explain to anyone curious enough to ask. Youthful and outgoing, Sam had an easygoing, friendly management style that charmed many clients and won him support from his colleagues on the way up the executive ladder. It also belied a tough, competitive core with a brilliant knack for numbers.

"Hey, Michael, come on in."

"Morning, Sam."

"Great weather, eh?"

"Gorgeous." They both laughed.

"Listen, I wanted to ask you something," said Sam, switching gears. "Been looking at the numbers for the first quarter. So far, so good. I really think we have a shot at making our plan this year." Then, pumping a victorious fist into the air, he added, "This is the year we climb back, baby, big-time. Agree?"

Michael paused slightly, trying to work past his puzzlement. *So what's the problem? Why did you call this meeting?* Then, he said, "If that's what you wanted to ask me, I agree."

"There's something else," Sam continued, tossing the Slinky on the desk. "Now, don't take this wrong, and don't feel there's any pressure on you. But you know how this company is always talking about 'succession' and bringing along the future leaders of the firm, and with the cutbacks and everything. By the way, would you like some coffee?"

Michael shook his head, anticipating the worst.

"Well," Sam continued, "a few of the board members and I were talking, and we were wondering whether you've made any plans for your future."

The sudden inquisition stunned Michael, but he had learned over the years not to show his emotions. He wasn't sure he was doing a good job of it now. "Do you mean, Have I thought about retiring?"

"Not really…well, yes, that's part of it."

"Tell you the truth, Sam, no. I haven't. I love my job, I love what I'm doing, and I do a damn good job doing it."

"Oh, absolutely, Michael, absolutely. Like I said, no one's pressuring you to do anything. Hell, we go back a long way, you and me—what, five or six years? It's just…all we want is a heads-up in the event you're planning anything. Know what I mean?"

"You'll be the first to know, Sam."

Later in his office, Michael tried to figure out what had just happened. *Was Sam trying to tell me something, or did he want me to tell him something? Was he showing me the door? Is this how it all ends?* Just because he was sixty-six, Michael wasn't ready to retire. Still plenty of life—and smarts—in the old workhorse. Michael had to talk with someone, someone he could trust. He reached for his Rolodex, flipped through it, and dialed Casey Russell's work number. Casey answered the phone after one ring. Michael was terse. "Lunch?"

That same morning, Christopher sat down at his cluttered desk at work, snapped on the radio, and poured a cup of high-test coffee from his thermos. He didn't even bother taking off his leather jacket. *Too damn cold!* Taking two sips, he began reviewing the work log for the day. A full schedule loomed, and Newsradio 88 was predicting four to seven inches. *My luck!* With the tow calls, dead batteries, and assorted other emergencies, snow only complicated things at Christopher's auto repair shop. He took a gulp of coffee and started organizing the jobs for the day. The door slammed in the rear of the shop. *Thank God, Gerry Koslowski is here!*

Christopher had hired Gerry soon after his son moved to San Francisco, and with the passage of time he had come to rely heavily on his new mechanic. A recent immigrant from Poland, Gerry proved he had the technical knowledge to handle a broad range of vehicles, especially SUVs, which was one reason Christopher had come to depend on him. Another was that in spite of the fact that he lived in Garfield, New Jersey, Gerry was at the Long Island repair shop on time every workday, come rain, shine, or snow. Most of all, the young man knew what he was doing, and he was ambitious. As he told Christopher on several occasions, he hoped to open his own place some day.

"Good morning, Mr. Terranova," said Gerry as he tramped the snow off his boots.

"Morning, Gerry. How're the roads?"

The young mechanic was just learning the English language, but he knew what he wanted to say. "They stink."

"Figured. Have some coffee. First job today is the silver Mountaineer. Check the brakes. If there's no major problem, Mr. Cooper will pick it up at ten o'clock. Okay?"

"Sure, boss."

Christopher liked Gerry. He felt he was "a clean-cut guy with a lot on the ball, and ambitious, too," and if there was any way he could help him realize his dreams, he would. At the same time, Christopher felt a deep longing for his son to come home and assume his place as heir to the family business. At one time, he had no doubt that Anthony wanted to take over the repair shop. But since his son went to California, he wasn't sure anymore.

What's more, Christopher was looking for ways to move on with his own life. Over more than 25 years of sobriety, he took nothing for granted. Knowing that the tumult of addiction was, in his case, only a drink away, he led a very structured life that had left little room for anything except his family, his work, and his Sunday morning 12-Step meetings. Now, at age sixty-four, however, he was thinking more and more about life after the Terranova DeLuxe Auto Repair business. With strong encouragement from his wife Patsy, he started talking about what he would like to do in retirement.

"Maybe I'll find a nice little job somewhere," he said one night.

Patsy winced. "Oh, come on, Christopher. Think fun and games. Think travel. Think community service. Think...anything but work."

"How about watching TV?"

"Bigger. Think bigger."

"What about watching sunsets?"

"Now you're talking."

"Well, there *is* something," he continued.

"What?"

"I always wanted to live by the sea and paint."

She smiled. "Well, you're halfway there. We live by the sea."

And so the retirement conversations went. They usually petered out when both Christopher and Patsy realized that there were a few major obstacles to fulfilling their dreams.

Was Anthony ever coming back home to take his place by his father's side, or should Christopher turn over the business to someone else? It had been more than a year now since Anthony had left New York City for San Francisco. Recent conversations with him indicated that he was settling down out there. He had found a place to live and work, and there was this "nice girl from Alaska" he met. He was even beginning to take on a California accent.

Then there were Gloria and Tom Dempsey. Would they ever feel that sense of security and peace they once knew? A bundle of jangling nerves since September 11, she was very protective of the newest member of the family, Patricia, and hovered over her twelve-year-old son Thomas Christopher like a hawk.

As for her husband Tom, he was wrapped up in his job, working longer and later shifts at a time when his family appeared to need him the most, and whatever social activities he engaged in were tied to his friends from the firehouse.

Lending a hand with the new baby as much as they could, Christopher and Patsy could see that Gloria and Tom were still hurting deeply from the events of the past. They wondered whether they would ever be able to overcome the dark, terrifying shadow of 9/11. In their hearts, Christopher and Patsy knew their daughter and son-in-law needed them.

CHAPTER 27

▼

The voice, first distant, grew louder. "Camille, Camille, wake up."

Camille, her heart pounding, opened her eyes and wiped the beads of sweat off her brow with a tissue. The pain in her chest slowly subsided when she saw Ben. "It was that dream again, the one where I'm being chased in the city."

"I figured. Try to relax, honey," he said.

"I was terrified," she continued.

"Take deep breaths."

"Only, this time I'm holding two children, instead of one," she went on.

"Were their names Jeffrey and David?"

Camille turned quickly toward Ben, jarred by the inference. "Probably. I suppose parents never stop worrying about their kids."

"What are you worried about? Everyone's doing fine," Ben assured her.

As far as she was concerned, the jury was still out on that.

After 9/11, both Jeffrey and David Stern took a hard look at their lives and changed jobs and career paths. Jeffrey was now selling insurance; David was in emergency medical care.

Jeffrey and Annie bought a townhouse in Yonkers, while David moved into an apartment on the Upper East Side of Manhattan. Nor was Loretta Conway standing pat. She went back to work—three days a week with a law firm in Hackensack, New Jersey—and she and Alex were starting to look at houses closer to where her parents lived.

"Maybe you should stop watching the late news," Ben added.

"What do you mean?"

"I mean, what do you expect, with all that's going on?" he explained. "I'm no psychiatrist, but just look around. So much terror, so much uncertainty; now they're talking war again. It's no wonder you have such bad dreams."

"You think?"

"I think."

"Sorry I woke you, Ben."

Camille put on her robe and slippers and headed toward the kitchen. On the way, she decided to stop by and see how mama was doing. She was surprised to find both lamps turned on when she entered her mother's room.

Anna was in bed. Her head, which lay claim to more dark hair than women half her age, was resting against a couple of pillows. She had on glasses she let slide to the tip of her pointed nose and was trying to read something. Ever since Aunt Loretta-Loretta died late last year, Anna's health had been declining. Today, she looked paler than usual, but her skin was luminescent.

Camille didn't try to hide her worry. "Mom, what are you doing? It's very early. Why aren't you sleeping?"

"I try to read Anthony's letter," Anna explained.

"Dr. Spiegel says you need to rest, you know that."

"Some words I don't understand. Please, you read."

Camille hesitated for a moment, recalling Dr. Spiegel's private conversation about her mother's heart failure complicated by diabetes. She finally took the letter, sat down on the sofa, and began reading aloud:

Dear Grandma,

I hear you haven't been feeling well lately, but I hope, and pray, this letter finds you in much better health. I would like very much to call you next week—if it's okay with you.

Can you believe it? It's been more than a year now since I came out here to California. Boy, do I miss talking with you! Even though we don't always speak the same language, I think you understand me better than, well, a lot of people.

Anna reached for a glass of water next to the bed, then changed her mind. "Such a good boy, that Anthony. Such good kids, all my grandchildren," she said. Camille nodded, then read on.

San Francisco is a beautiful place. Recently, I moved into a small, but clean apartment near the bay, which I share with a guy from Chicago, Tommy Dwyer. As I mentioned to you the last time we spoke, I have a pretty good job servicing cars in a used car dealership. It's a start.

Oh, I also made some new friends, including a girl from Alaska, of all places. Her name is June Cadwell. She works in a bakery.

She always smells like doughnuts. I think you would like her.

Anna smiled, recalling someone who also smelled like a bakery—a German woman who worked in the Gottfried Bakery on Eleventh Avenue. "What was her name?" Camille shook her head, as if to say she didn't know, and continued reading.

Yesterday, I went on another peace march. I can't say I'm as dedicated to the movement as some of the people out here. This is all new to me. After all, I was just a guy from Long Island minding my own business until a few months ago. But I'm learning. There's got to be a better way. As you know, war brings too much pain and suffering in so many different ways, sometimes in ways we don't see or understand.

Anna nodded, as if she understood. Camille pulled a tissue out of her pocket and wiped away a tear, then began reading again.

We need to stop thinking of terror or violence or war as a solution. Maybe someday war will become as foolish as sticking your hand in the fire.

Muttering something under her breath, Anna reached for the glass of water again. This time she slowly brought the glass to her lips and took a sip. Camille noticed that her hand was trembling. "Did you say something, mama?" she asked.

Anna nodded. "I say, 'someday' will come, you see."

Camille wasn't so sure about that, given the state of current world affairs. She continued reading.

After my friend Freddy Junior died, I knew I just couldn't go on doing what I had been doing. I had to change. So I came out here, to start fresh, to find something, maybe to find out why I'm alive and Freddy is not. I don't have the answer, but I'm working on it. About six months ago, I started going to meetings, and I haven't had a drink since.

There are no secrets in a close family. Camille reached for another tissue before reading the rest of the letter.

I lie awake here sometimes thinking of everyone back East. Do you know what I miss a lot, next to my family, of course, and you, grandma, and Uncle Ben and Aunt Camille, and all my relatives and friends? It's your focaccia.

Can you send me your secret recipe? I'm sure June, the baker, will help me make it.

Love you. Always,

Anthony

Camille folded the letter carefully and gave it back to her mother.

"You have recipe, you write, please," said Anna. "He is good boy, that Anthony, so young, so wise. So are all my kids."

Camille nodded. "Do you want some breakfast?"

"Sure, I like pancakes," said Anna, half in jest.

"Mom!"

"Alright, piece of toast, and some tea."

"Okay, now try to rest."

Anna lay her head back against the pillows. "I love you so much, Camille, but you worry too much for such a young woman."

In the kitchen, Camille walked to the glass doors leading to the terrace and looked up at the sky. It was blanketed from end to end with huge puffs of gray and white, and a few flakes were falling. They were predicting more snow on top of the dirty, white mounds that had accumulated over one of the snowiest winters in years.

It didn't seem like anyone or anything would be outside on a March morning like this. She wondered whether Mr. Bentley, the most faithful runner in town, was having second thoughts about venturing out today. So, when a cardinal swooped out of the gray and white puffs and landed on her bare, long-limbed maple, Camille's spirits rose, and she felt hopeful. *Hang on, spring's not far behind!* She went to get some bird seed. When she returned, the beautiful creature in the old maple tree was gone.

Camille didn't bother to turn on the television. There would be time enough later to find out what terrible things had happened during the night. She put some jam on a piece of whole wheat toast, poured boiled water into a tea cup, and shook her head. Such a meager breakfast. She decided to make mama pancakes, after all.

Gripping the tray with both hands, Camille entered her mother's room. The two lamps were still on, though morning had filtered through the lace curtains on the big bay window. She placed the tray on the table, next to the picture of Anna and Arturo on their wedding day and walked toward the bed.

Anna was lying in an odd position, Anthony's letter crunched in one hand, the other arm extended over the side of the bed. Mama's eyes were closed. Apparently she had finally fallen asleep. That was good. Camille would not wake her. She took the letter from her mother's hand to make her more comfortable. Camille couldn't tell you why she did what she did next. Perhaps she was looking for some reassurance all was well. She put her hand over her mother's heart.

When Ben heard Camille's scream, he knew what had happened. The dreaded expectation that had been lurking in the shadows of his mind for years had finally surfaced. The matriarch was dead. Ben jumped up out of bed and rushed to Camille's side.

CHAPTER 28

▼

The sun had melted some of the snow, but much of the white substance stubbornly clung to the grounds of old Calvary cemetery in Queens. Now, an overcast sky was moving in quickly, promising new snowfall.

The mourners were quietly clustered around the grave site waiting for the priest to arrive. Finally, he could be spotted hurrying down the road, a tall, gangling figure with Bible in hand, who apparently had just left another interment. As it turned out, he was not a priest at all. He was Deacon Elliott from a local Queens parish who did not know the family. Some of the older mourners remembered when a priest who was a friend of the family, usually from the deceased person's parish, led the burial rite.

"In the name of the Father, Son, and Holy Spirit," the deacon began after introducing himself and apologizing for his tardiness. He went on to pray for the repose of the soul of the deceased (he was careful to continually refer to "Anna" by name) and to remind the mourners they all will be reunited with their loved ones in the next life—a familiar reassurance that seemed to gather strength with the passing of time.

Camille heard what he was saying, but her mind drifted back to the early fifties. She was young and waiting for her first great love, Harry Slovich, to come home from the war so that they could resume their lives. When Harry returned, he was a changed man, crushed by what he had seen in Korea and by the death there of his friend Maxie Myers.

Those were painful days for Camille, too. Lost in a world of sorrow and guilt, Harry grew more distant and eventually ended their relationship. Camille was facing a deep, unfamiliar abyss of despair. *If it weren't for you, mama! You were always there when I needed you. Remember the soup, mama. When Harry and I broke up, I didn't want to eat anymore, ever, but you kept making things, all sorts of delicious things, to get me to eat, but I refused. Finally, one day, you put this soup in front of me and said, "Eat, or I put the bowl on your head." We had a good laugh over that one. I ate the soup. Then Ben started calling. At first, I didn't want to meet him, but you kept encouraging me. "Have some coffee together, talk, laugh," you urged me. "Meet Ben, for Pete sake. He is just a friend." Who became my husband.*

Camille felt Ben's comforting arm around her shoulder. Nearby, Loretta and Alex stood quietly, while David, Jeffrey, and Annie glanced over at Camille, poised to lend a hand. These were difficult times of change for the twins, and now grandma was gone. Fortunately for Jeffrey, there was his wife Annie, loyal, compassionate, and optimistic as ever. For David, there was no one right now. His relationship with Ginny ended after he decided to change careers.

Deacon Elliott flipped pages and began reading a familiar psalm:

> *The Lord is my shepherd; I shall not want.*
> *In verdant pastures he gives me repose;*
> *Beside restful waters he leads me;*
> *He refreshes my soul....*

Camille drifted back in time to when she first heard the psalm, at Christina's funeral. She could not hold back the tears.

The deacon's words slipped past Michael like snowflakes, which began to fall. He was somewhere else, too. Michael was eight years old and sitting with mama on a sofa covered by a white sheet in the front room. The air raid siren had just sounded, and all the lights were out. It was such a treat for them to sit for a moment in the front room, even if they were sheathed in darkness. Mama was happy about the family's recent move to Fiftieth Street. She even laughed when Michael asked her what she was going to do with the contents of the remaining moving boxes. "Maybe I throw everything out window." Michael was glad to hear his mother laugh, as brief as it was. She had a lot on her mind. This was the day Christina first took sick. Strange, the things that come to mind.

Michael reached out and held hands with Jo on one side and his daughter-in-law on the other side. Eloise was shaking, and not only because of the chill in the air, in Michael's view. For some time now, he sensed all was not well between Eloise and John, and he suspected his son's frequent military assignments overseas might be partly responsible. Whatever was going on, he wished his son were here, but once again John had been deployed to the Persian Gulf in anticipation of a new war with Iraq.

Christopher stood in the back of the group, Patsy by his side. In his memory, he was seven or eight again, and mama was getting ready to take him to the cemetery with her. "Why do we always have to go to the cemetery, mama?" he asked one day.

"Because…out of respect. We show we not forget your sister," she answered.

"But I hate cemeteries, mama," he recalled saying.

"Oh, is not so bad, the cemetery," she told him. "Plenty of rocks to read there." By rocks, she meant tombstones, and when Christopher went to the cemetery that day and thereafter, that's exactly what he did—read the names, dates, and sayings on tombstones.

Life takes strange turns, Christopher was thinking now as the deacon sprinkled holy water over his mother's casket. Years after he told his mother he hated cemeteries, Christopher was found stretched, face down, across Christina's grave. Right here! Of course, he was dead drunk at the time, and, except for what Patsy had told him later in the hospital, he had little, or no, recollection of that event. Over the years he came to understand that what he had done that December day was somehow linked to the mystery of his twin sister's death and why she died and he was alive.

As the deacon led the group in The Lord's Prayer, Anthony stood near his parents. It was difficult to believe that grandma Terranova, his old friend, was gone. It seemed like only yesterday when they were talking on the phone.

From a long-ago memory, Anthony could still hear grandma's voice—tough, loving, strange in its blend of tongues, but eloquent in its simplicity. He remembered her words when he was hell-bent on running off with Tammy Justice, a girl he had met on vacation. He was 18, she was 24. "Do not be rushing so much," said grandma. "If she love you, she wait. You still young man with so much fish to fry." As it turned out, Tammy eventually turned her attention to someone else, and Anthony fried more than his share of fish.

One by one, the mourners placed flowers, as their final goodbyes, on the coffin and returned to their cars. Anthony looked back and tapped the top pocket of his black blazer. It was still there. He would treasure grandma's recipe for *focaccia barese* forever. Camille had given it to him when he arrived from San Francisco with June. His aunt never told him grandma was holding his letter when she died.

In a couple of days, Anthony would be returning to California, but not without talking with his parents. He knew what he had to say might hurt their feelings—and he was sorry for that—but he had thought long and hard about establishing roots in San Francisco with his friend June Cadwell. If that meant losing his chance to take over the family business, well, so be it. He looked back at the grave site of his friend one more time.

CHAPTER 29

▼

The following weekend, Michael left his apartment and started walking downtown, no particular destination in mind. After talking with Jo on the phone for almost an hour, he had to get out. The conversation was getting too intense for him. Too many threatening issues that needed to be resolved, and, after mama's death, Michael was not ready to face them.

Were John and Eloise splitting up? Eloise had always considered her in-laws approachable, more so than her own parents, and after the funeral she confided to Michael and Jo that she and John were having trouble communicating with each other. "Oh, we were doing fine there for a while, but then, I don't know. I think he's seeing someone," she finally sobbed, "and if he is, I deserve it." Michael wondered what Eloise meant by that. Was John really having an affair or was that only a suspicion based on some guilt feelings Eloise had?

Then there was that meeting with company CEO Sam Nelson. All of a sudden, Sam is peppering Michael with questions about his retirement plans. Was he pressing him to retire? Was Michael ready to retire? What would he do if he did retire?

On top of everything else, there was the gathering storm in Iraq. Every day, news reports flooded the media that a coalition led by the U.S. was about to attack that country. Most of all, he was apprehensive for his son. *How many times can he go into war and come back alive? What about all those young men and women waiting for the call to battle and, perhaps, to injury or even death?*

Michael was also conflicted about whether the U.S. should be over there in the first place. Like so many other Americans, he wanted Saddam removed from power, but he wondered whether a preemptive strike was the way to accomplish it, and could the U.S. build a stable government in Iraq if, and when, it were successful in overthrowing Saddam. He told Jo as much, and she just listened.

"We're forming a new group," she finally said. "We want to find peaceful solutions to conflict, but we want to be more open to a wider variety of views. Some of us will be marching against the war tomorrow." Michael was listening now. "If you'd like to join us, or discuss it more, call me," she added.

Next week was the Saint Patrick's Day Parade, the prelude to spring in the New York City area, but the remains of a stubborn winter were in the air. Pulling up the collar of his leather jacket, Michael continued walking until he found himself back in his old neighborhood after a long absence.

At the corner of Fifty-fourth and Ninth, a rough-bearded man in a checkered flannel jacket reached out and grabbed Michael by the shoulder as he started crossing the street against the light and in the path of a sanitation truck. Michael made a gesture of gratitude. "Ass hole!" he could hear the rough-bearded man muttering as he crossed the street ahead of him. Michael was almost sure he was not the target of that comment. He smiled. *Welcome back to Hell's Kitchen.*

Since he could remember, Michael had harbored a love-hate relationship with the neighborhood of his youth. He admired it for its toughness, its spirit, and its big heart, especially in times of trouble. He was not proud of its periodic descents into gang rule, violence, and bigotry. While they were living on the West Side, the Terranovas had more than their share of personal adversity, but they also shared many happy times there. The family plummeted into deep despair when Christina died, but it was also uplifted by the generosity and compassion of so many neighbors and strangers during that difficult time. Yes, papa lost his business there after accepting some bad checks, but he had a good, long run, managing to build the store into a successful neighborhood enterprise with many trusted customers before selling out. Camille found and lost and found the love of her life in Hell's Kitchen. There, Christopher discovered his sobriety with the help of family and neighborhood friends like Patsy Espinosa.

Over the years, Michael had heard that the West Side was changing, and this was a good time to see for himself what was going on. At first glance, he noticed that the streets and sidewalks were not paved with designer stones, but there were clear signs of renewal. Trees lined the streets where only lampposts and fire hydrants had stood in his youth. Some of the old tenements had put on a new face, and others were in the midst of refurbishing.

Within the bustling neighborhood, a variety of ethnic cuisines reflected a widening diversity of tastes and people in an area of the city previously dominated by a few population groups. Professional and artistic strivers in upscale townhouses

and apartments were now rubbing elbows with working-class folk in rent-stabi-
lized walk-ups. Nearby, an expanded theater district and a revitalized Forty-second Street added luster and jobs to the surroundings.

Gone were the factories, slaughterhouses, and vacant lots filled with garbage
Michael remembered. Swept away or dislodged, too, were the more notorious
gangs that had helped give the neighborhood its rough-and-tumble reputation.

Gentrification, city watchers called it. Some residents now preferred to refer to
the neighborhood between Thirty-fourth and Fifty-ninth Streets west of Eight
Avenue in Manhattan by another name—"Clinton," after former mayor and
governor DeWitt Clinton, rather than "Hell's Kitchen." Michael would always
remember it as the place where the Terranovas came together as a family during
the height of war.

Michael walked by the spot where papa's store had stood. It was a parking lot
now. Further down the avenue, a high-rise had replaced Dottie Wood's old
apartment building. The public library where he met Jo and the local church
where they were married were still there, but gone were the old mom-and-pop
delis, saloons, hardware stores, and candy stores, replaced by a wider variety of
more upscale stores, shops, and restaurants that made up the neighborhood's new
pulse.

On Fiftieth Street, Michael stopped in front of the building where he had
lived. It hadn't changed much on the outside except for the black wrought iron
gate and the forest-green door with the digitally coded lock. He wondered what
the apartments were going for now. He had heard that West Side real estate was
going through the roof.

As he looked up at the third-floor windows, a flood of memories poured down
over him. There was Christina, before she took ill, sitting on the floor counting
the pennies and nickels she had been saving for a trip to Coney Island. Camille is
complaining that Christopher drank the last drop of milk, while Christopher is
crying that Camille "hogs" the bathroom. Michael is playing deejay while Camille and her friends dance barefooted in the front room. It's Sunday afternoon,
and papa is relaxing with a glass of Burgundy and a Helmar's cigarette. Mama is
there, as always, laughing, cooking, sewing, making peace, cheating in cards, and
loving every minute of it.

Oh, mama! Oh, papa! They came so far. They started a new life in a strange,
new land in search of its treasures—life, liberty, and a measure of happiness. For
them, those treasures translated into someone with whom they could share life, a
loving family, economic security, good health, and peace. They found most of

them. *Oh, mama! Oh, papa! Where do people who once were so important in our lives go?*

"Michael? Michael Terranova?" he heard someone whispering.

"For God's sake, is that you, Harry?" said Michael when he noticed that the whisperer was Harry Slovich, walking three dogs.

"Yeah."

After they shook hands, Michael reached out and embraced Harry. One of the dogs, a small, white terrier, barked.

"He's very protective," Harry explained. "Sit!" All three dogs obeyed.

"How're you doing?" asked Michael.

"Hanging in there," Harry replied. "I'm retired from the Sanitation Department now. As you can see, I'm doing a little dog-sitting."

"Well, you always loved to work with animals."

"Yeah." Then after a slight pause, Harry added solemnly, "Sorry to hear about your mom. She was a first-class lady."

"Thanks, Harry."

"I was going to go to the funeral, but I got sick, asthma."

"That's okay, Harry."

Harry looked at the building, then at Michael. "What're you doing 'round here? Planning to move back?"

"No, can't afford it." Michael laughed. "Actually, I was just visiting the neighborhood. Lots of changes."

"Yeah," Harry agreed. "It's not the same place. All the people we knew are either old or dead, know what I mean?"

Michael nodded. "But the neighborhood's looking better, don't you think, Harry?"

"I suppose. Now they're talking about building a stadium on the West Side, and God knows what else."

"That'll do wonders for traffic," said Michael, a sly smile across his face.

"And for our lungs. But they say it'll bring in more money, and jobs. Who knows, some of the old-timers will start moving back." Harry laughed for the first time, his blue eyes sparkling—something Michael had not seen in years. They walked down to the corner together.

"If you have some time, why don't you come up to my place for a cup of coffee or a beer or something?" asked Harry, when they got to Tenth Avenue.

"I'd love it, Harry, but I can't. Got some work to do. If you don't mind, I'll take a rain check."

"Sure, Michael, anytime." They shook hands and embraced each other. Once again, the terrier barked.

As they started moving in opposite directions, Harry stopped and turned. A long-simmering thought had apparently reached the surface. He said, "You know, that was the biggest mistake I ever made, not marrying your sister. What a beautiful woman! I must have been nuts."

"It was the war, Harry."

"Yeah, I know. I know that now. Pretty shitty business, war is. So many ways it can mess you up without killing you."

Michael hugged him again.

At the corner, they waved good-bye to each other and went their ways, just as the sun broke through. Michael hailed a cab headed uptown. He had seen enough. Perhaps it had something to do with the changes that were gradually reshaping the old neighborhood, together with the more visible, dramatic trans-formations taking place at other points around the city, including Ground Zero. Perhaps it was seeing Harry, a spirit wounded by war, lost love, and trampled dreams who was carrying on in spite of everything. Maybe it was a feeling that we cannot live in the past, stuck in remembrances of what used to be; we have to keep going forward and changing and making new memories.

Michael felt renewed. Ready for the future. Nothing was impossible. Yes, there were important, new issues in his life, but they all would be resolved in time, one way or the other. As for the war that was looming, he could no longer sit on the sidelines and watch it unfold, from a safe distance, on a TV screen. His family knew, firsthand, the terrible, pervasive cost of war. Michael took out his cell phone and dialed Jo's line.

Four days later, Operation Iraqi Freedom began. The "shock and awe" of the military assault during the first days seemed to confirm a feeling in the land that this would be a quick war, just like the Persian Gulf War of 1991. Nor was the toll in human, economic, military, political, psychological, and emotional terms expected to be high. Based on long experience, the Terranovas had their fears and their suspicions, as well as their hopes.

Acknowledgments

This is a fictional story about a family and war, but it could not have been told without making reference to some actual historical figures, places, and events. Fortunately, library and bookstore shelves are amply stocked with excellent books and chronicles about war, military life, and our times, which were most helpful in my search.

I am especially grateful for *The Wars of America,* by Robert Leckie (Castle Books); *World War II Day by Day* (Dorling Kindersley Ltd., London); *This Kind of War, The Classic Korean War History,* by T. R. Fehrenbach (Brassey's, Washington, D.C.); *The Vietnam War,* by Bernard C. Nalty (Barnes & Noble Books); *The Vietnam War Day by Day* (Barnes & Noble Books); *The 20th Century, An Illustrated History of Our Lives and Times* (JG Press, Inc.); *A Nation Challenged* (*The New York Times*); *New York September 11,* by Magnum Photographers (powerHouse Books); and *After September 11, New York and the World,* by the Journalists of Reuters (Prentice Hall).

When it came to more recent events such as the 9/11 attacks and their aftermath, the news media provided detailed accounts from many different perspectives and did a wonderful job of capturing the spirit of those heart-wrenching days. Two media sources deserve special praise: *The New York Times,* for its stunningly graphic descriptions of what happened in the Twin Towers, as related by many eyewitnesses, and PBS, for its informative and compelling series of documentaries on the 9/11 attacks. My gratitude and respect to all of the fine journalists.

Much of what I've written was also inspired by personal experiences, for which I relied, to a cautious extent, on my own recollections. I also drew on the remembrances of many others, including family members, who were there. Sadly, a few of them have passed on since they told their stories to me.

The list of storytellers is long, but I'm particularly indebted to Mary and George Simmons, Angelina and Edward Lennon, and Josephine and Mark Prasinos for sharing their wartime and neighborhood memories.

To Paul Lennon, Gerard Lennon, and Vincent Baudone, among others, thank you for providing valuable insight into what it was like to be in downtown Manhattan on September 11, 2001.

I'm also grateful to Kathleen and William Waytowich and to Anthony Vecchione for their suggestions and support, and *grazie tante* to Nancy Jillard, a gifted copy editor.

All in all, this was a labor of love that took more than three years to complete. Being a journalist for more than 35 years was reason to try and get it right. But there were other reasons. As the son of immigrants, a native New Yorker who grew up in Hell's Kitchen, and a member of a war family, I also had a personal stake in the story.

Finally, no one was more helpful to me in this undertaking than my wife Mary. For her unwavering encouragement and patience, quiet words of advice, helpful answers to my endless questions, and numerous readings, my eternal gratitude. And she's still the prettiest girl on the West Side!

0-595-33888-7